All Paths
Lead to Paris

ALSO BY SABRINA FEDEL

All Roads Lead to Rome

All Paths Lead to Paris

SABRINA FEDEL

Delacorte
Romance

Delacorte Romance
An imprint of Random House Children's Books
A division of Penguin Random House LLC
1745 Broadway, New York, NY 10019
penguinrandomhouse.com
GetUnderlined.com

Delacorte Romance and the colophon are trademarks of
Penguin Random House LLC.

Editor: Wendy Loggia
Cover Designer: Casey Moses
Interior Designer: Megan Shortt
Production Editor: Colleen Fellingham
Managing Editor: Tamar Schwartz
Production Manager: Tracy Heydweiller

Library of Congress Cataloging-in-Publication Data is available upon request.
ISBN 978-0-593-90027-7 (pbk.) — ISBN 978-0-593-90028-4 (ebook)

The text of this book is set in 11.75-point Adobe Garamond Pro.

Manufactured in the United States of America
1st Printing

The authorized representative in the EU for product safety and compliance is
Penguin Random House Ireland, Morrison Chambers, 32 Nassau Street,
Dublin D02 YH68, Ireland, https://eu-contact.penguin.ie.

For all of us who struggle to understand
the language the Universe speaks
and
For Flossey

One

Remy grabs my hand and tows me through the crowd to the marks. The black-and-white Christian Dior step-and-repeat backdrop will pop against the emerald of my dress and his midnight-blue suit. My black Doc Martens and Hermès foulard keep the green alive.

"Smile," he reminds me.

I look at him before I do. A tiny rebellion in a long day. Then I turn to the cameras as they whir and flash with the precision of an orchestra, and I smile. Radiant. I let the word cascade to every part of me like a waterfall. It's a mantra our manager, Lille, taught me, and it works every time. At least, it always has. Today it feels off, as if I'm only going through the motions. One more day spent trying to be what everyone expects me to be. But maybe that's just the cramps I'm having as the ibuprofen wears off.

When we step away from the photos, a flock of reporters from *Teen Vogue* and *Seventeen* surround us.

A blond reporter jabs a thumb-sized microphone to my lips. "Aurélie, how are you enjoying Paris Fashion Week?" I search my brain for her name. Sarah, I think. She's from the States. Remy squeezes my hand over this delay.

"It's magical, as it always is." The same thing I say every time I'm asked, said in a different way. I'm about to add how fresh this season's show is when it hits me that my tampon has sprung a leak.

"You're stanning Dior today, but you smell like Chanel," she says.

"Well, no one will ever be as classic in perfume as Chanel. But I love the new Dior line. It's unironically sophisticated and yet still really playful for autumn."

"But the rest of your outfit is . . . ?"

I recite my accessories, including the short charcoal trench by Givenchy I thrifted. I don't mention the vintage rose-gold necklace I'm wearing that belonged to my dad's mom. The one she gave me before she forgot who I was.

"No head-to-toe Prada for you, then?" Sarah asks with a laugh. She's referencing my first Fashion Week three years ago, when I was fourteen and made that mistake, although it was Valentino.

I rub my gran's necklace between my fingers before I return her laugh as if what she said is funny. "Not until I have some yachts in the water, Sarah." She has a Southern accent, so I'm betting she chose the Prada dig because of the country song about a girl wishing she could turn her ex's lies and her memories of him into dimes to afford the iconic brand. It's a risk, but the fashion world is always high-stakes. The reporter laughs in truce and turns to Remy to ask him what he thinks about being here with the world's favorite teen fashion influencer, now that we're officially "out" as a couple, and whose clothes he's wearing and whether I chose them. I scratch my pinkie nail against his palm to tell him to hurry up, but he just squeezes my hand in reply. My other hand searches my coat pocket. The extra tampons I set aside must be sitting on my dresser, where I'd meant to grab them.

Another reporter is waiting, and we go through the same routine, like I'm an athlete in a postgame interview. At least this one doesn't backhand-serve me. She asks Remy a slew of questions about us as she tries to drag romantic details from him while he fidgets his fingers in mine as if he's playing chords. This reporter asks in French, so I don't have to translate for him.

When we finish the interview, Remy gazes over my head at a group of people across from us. "There's that lady from *Rolling Stone*," he says. He steps forward and tugs me along.

I stop, and our arms pull out like taffy until he turns. "Remy, I have to go to a pharmacy."

"Now?" His dark hair shifts and settles like he's in a shampoo commercial. I raise my eyebrows at him, and he raises his back in confusion. A mention in *Rolling Stone* would be huge for him, with his second EP dropping next month.

"You go ahead. I'll find you after."

"What could you possibly need so badly right now?" His green eyes remind me of fresh mint in summer.

"Don't worry about it," I say, even though each passing minute is adding to my certainty that I'm teetering on the verge of disaster. "I'll be back before it's over."

Remy droops his head to one side. "Aurie."

"I will," I say with more conviction than I know is fair. "You should do this on your own anyway, so the focus is on you. You'll smash it." I smile my confidence at him.

"What if I need a translator?" His fingers are still interlaced with mine.

I laugh. "It's music talk. They could ask you questions in Navajo and you'd understand."

He bites his bottom lip as he returns my laugh. "D'accord," he says, and pulls me in. We make la bise, kissing each other's cheeks, since there are cameras poised to capture everything we do. He tells me to be careful, even though I won't be in any danger, because he's so used to looking out for me.

Then he strides off. Heads turn to follow him the way the Greeks must have watched Apollo walk by. They don't know how his mamie yells at him to take out the trash, shaking a wooden spoon when he doesn't get off the sofa the first time she asks. Or that he'll duck rather than take one of her stinging swats. I think she usually misses on purpose, though. She loves Remy the way everyone loves him. Without guardrails.

I scan the crowd for someone who could help, but there isn't anyone I know well enough to ask. Rays of late-afternoon sunlight stream down from the great glass dome of the Grand Palais as I weave through the pulsing throng of models and celebrity fashionistas. People grab me for a quick la bise as I pass, or call and wave to me, so close and yet impossibly divided by the swarm. The hall rings with thousands of voices competing to be heard. Photographers jump in front of me. "Smile!" they command, as if I'm a sea lion performing tricks at the zoo. When I finally emerge through the gauntlet of security, the noise inside fades, replaced by the constant hum of traffic. My phone says the nearest pharmacy is only a few blocks away, so I run down the steps to the bustling avenue. The map points me away from the river and the chilly wind.

When I reach Avenue Montaigne, the map says the shop is around the corner and five stores down. I turn and see a crowd of people right in front of the pharmacy. It's a School Strike for Climate, with signs on recycled cardboard. An oil and gas company logo crowns the building. Twenty kids or so, all around my age, are milling about and trying to engage every passerby, even the cars going along the street.

"Pardon," I say as I dodge between them.

"Were you at Fashion Week?" a tall girl asks. I nod. I wish I were better at lying, because I definitely should have lied based on the scowl she throws me.

"I hope you're proud of yourself," she says. "Your consumerism is destroying the only planet we have!" She's ginger-haired and pretty and somehow reminds me of a powerful show horse.

"Reine's right. It's people like you who are the problem!" another girl says.

"Sorry," I say, and keep moving as the Reine girl calls me a name. Some of them boo me.

I try to sidestep a guy obstructing the door. He's tall, too, and he matches my step to block my way. He's so close, I have to tilt my head up to see his face.

"Look," I say, "I'm not trying to disrupt your protest—in fact, go for it—but I need to get to the pharmacy."

He shakes wavy auburn hair from his eyes, which are strikingly blue. "You don't look like you support School Strike." He has on a plain blue T-shirt and a canvas jacket that makes me think he hikes a lot. He belongs in a Patagonia catalog.

"And you don't look like someone who would keep a girl from getting into a pharmacy when she's desperate."

He scans my face. "Your mascara isn't running," he says with a short laugh.

I harden my jaw, staring him down. Lille calls it "the model chill," and she's trained me in it relentlessly. His smile droops away. He steps aside and pulls the door open in mock gallantry that doesn't deserve a thank-you. I sweep past him. The pharmacy is small, and I spot what I need almost immediately. There's a middle-aged man behind the counter, but he's used to looking away discreetly as people get their creams and other unmentionables to bring to him so they can be rung up. There are no secrets from pharmacists and mail carriers. Still, I wish he were a lady pharmacist.

I place the package on the counter, along with a small packet of panty liners and some ibuprofen. My morning dose has definitely worn off. The boy who opened the door is outside, but he sees my stash, and then he catches me seeing him see. Behind him, Reine watches him. I turn my head.

"Did you have any trouble coming in?" the man asks, nodding at the protestors as he rings me up.

"Not too much."

"Idiots," he says. "Mon Dieu."

"Don't you believe in climate change?"

He looks up. "D'accord, but do you know how many buildings in Paris are the headquarters of polluting megacorporations? And they have to choose this one! Right in front of *my* door?" He stamps the tip of his finger on the counter and presses his lips together.

I nod agreeably. Now I need to find the nearest public bathroom. I'm pretty sure I passed a small bistro just after I turned the corner.

The door opens and the boy walks in, the noise of the street spilling in with him for just a moment until it swings closed again. The man shakes his head. "This one is the ringleader," he says quietly, as if he's sharing a secret. The pharmacist's eyes are the color of a Grecian bay as he holds my gaze. He could be playing the gray-haired lead in a rom-com for older women instead of running a pharmacy. "I should call the cops," he adds.

"I think this young lady could use the restroom," the boy says. He stands framed by the light of the door like an action movie hero.

My face burns.

"We don't have a public bathroom," the pharmacist protests. Every Parisian knows regular stores don't have them. Only restaurants and bars or big department stores do. This kid really is too much. No wonder the guy is angry.

"It's not a problem," I say.

"If you make her go to the bistro, she's going to have to buy something to use the bathroom." He must be a do-gooder about everything, not just the environment.

The pharmacist shrugs. They're watching each other like gunslingers from the Wild West.

"Honestly, it's fine." I just want to get out of here before these two start a fistfight. Or worse, break into a conversation about my girl problems. "Could I have a small bag, please?"

"Let her use ours, Dad."

Dad? I bite my lip to keep from smiling as I study the current flowing between them.

The pharmacist stares at his son and lets out a heavy breath. The boy steps closer. His eyes reflect the blue of his father's. "Bon, Kylian, show her the way. At least then you won't be in front of the door scaring away my customers. She's the first one I've had in an hour!"

"It's okay, I can go to the bistro," I say. This is the most awkward moment I've had since middle school. And then a paparazzo walks in. His camera is already raised and focused. I swipe my packages from the counter into my coat pocket. I really hope they aren't in the shots.

Kylian's dad throws his arm up. "What are you doing? This is a pharmacy, not a tourist attraction!"

The photographer smiles, tilting his face for a moment

around the large, professional-grade lens. He's around Lille's age, in his late thirties. "Definitely not, but Aurélie McGinley *is* a tourist attraction, especially during Fashion Week!"

Father and son look curiously at me. This is a disaster. Lille is absolutely going to yell at me for not calling her instead of coming out on my own. I just want some ibuprofen, a shower, and my bed. In that order. And some food would be nice. I haven't had anything since breakfast. I fight the stinging in my eyes.

"Allons-y," Kylian says. It sounds like *allonzee* and it means "Let's go." He slips his hand around my wrist and pulls me through a little security gate in the counter and then a door to the back of the store as the camera sends flashes bouncing around the walls like a northern lights show. Kylian shuts the door behind us.

My eyes need a moment to adjust to the darkness. He lets go of my wrist. "Bathroom is there," Kylian says, pointing to the end of a short hall. "And the exit is the one beside it if you don't want to go out the way you came in."

"Thanks."

He ticks his head toward the front of the store. "What should I tell your friend?"

I hesitate. There is no easy way out of this. No matter what he tells the guy, the tabloid will just make up whatever story goes with the photos. Remy's going to be so mad at me. And I may send Lille into a full meltdown. I should have been more careful. That paparazzo must have followed me from the show.

"Just give me a head start and then tell him I went back to the Palais. Tell him I had a wardrobe malfunction and bought blister covers?"

Kylian smiles. It's the kind of smile that makes you feel like someone is watching over you. He nods, and I head for the bathroom.

"Hey," he says.

My hand is on the doorknob, and I turn.

"I'm sorry I was a jerk outside."

"Me too," I say, and catch his laugh as I close the door.

Two

When I come out of the bathroom, the hallway is empty. Voices trickle in from the storefront, but I can't make out what they're saying, or even whose voices they are. I'd like to say thank you to Kylian and his dad, but I can't take a chance on the paparazzo making any more out of this than he already will. I slip out the back door instead.

I'm in an alley. A few doors up, servers from the bistro are taking a break. I turn in the other direction. When I emerge from the alley, I'm on a side boulevard to the one with the pharmacy storefront. The quickest way back to the show would be past it, but the paparazzo is probably waiting for me. I take a right instead.

After a block, I glance behind to make sure no one is following me. I can usually spot them, but anyone following me now has blended into the rush hour crowd. It's best to act nonchalant, as if I've got nothing to hide, just like a normal girl. Sometimes I wish I were a normal girl.

My phone starts buzzing. It's my dad, hoping for a video chat. Seriously. On the Friday of Fashion Week. He doesn't get that every Fashion Week for me is the equivalent of tax season for a tax attorney, which he is. I press decline and message that I'll try to call tomorrow. I turn down Avenue Gabriel and skirt the park. I should cross the Champs-Élysées, but I walk instead to the fountain in front of the Théâtre Marigny. Most Parisians are either part of Fashion Week or are scurrying home from work right now to avoid the tourists who flood the city to be part of the industry's crowning jewel of each design season. Water cascades from the top and middle of the fountain's sculpture, like tiers of a wedding cake held up by a central pillar. Four idyllic, chubby-faced children who represent the seasons stand between the upper and lower streams, each facing outward expectantly.

I can relate to them, suspended there in the in-between, waiting to be called to their destiny. I kind of envy them. At least they know which expectations to follow. I close my eyes. The garden smells of roses and lavender. My breath slows.

I slip my lucky American penny from my wallet. I know it's not actually lucky, but my dad gave it to me the day he put me on a plane because my mom wanted to come home to France after their divorce. I was nine and they made me choose between them and their continents. Not that it was really a choice. My dad worked ten-hour days, six days a week. "Remember," he said, "this is also your home." I finger the penny, the raised Lincoln Memorial so familiar to my touch, and I think for a moment about throwing it into the fountain and making a wish. Just one quick wish, to tell me what to do, which direction to turn.

"Aurélie!" someone shouts. A camera is waiting for me to find it. I slide the penny into my wallet and obediently turn my face toward the sound of my name and smile long enough for the paparazzo to get her shot. Maybe I won't look as worn out as I feel. I turn and head to the Grand Palais.

I flash my entrance badge to the few security guards still manning the doors and they nod me through. The building is almost empty except for some cleanup crews starting their work, and a couple of small groups of fashionistas clinging to the excitement of the day. Just like with a sporting arena after a match, the crowd has suddenly disappeared. Remy leans against a wall on the other side of the hall. Lille sits on a bench beside him, her nose aimed at her phone. Remy waves to me as he says something to Lille, and she looks up and stands.

"Sorry," I say as I reach them. Lille gives me la bise.

Remy has his hands in his pockets.

"Where have you been, darling?" Lille asks. She has on a crisply tailored yellow suit with a high-necked blouse and matching pumps, the kind of outfit that would make your first guess be "lawyer." She actually is a lawyer, though I don't think she's practiced outside of talent management for years. "Litigation is mostly paperwork," she says. "I prefer the people side of things. Much more interesting." Still, there isn't a single important detail she's missed in any contract Remy or I have signed since she's managed us. Even my mother can't find fault with Lille's contract skills.

"We don't have much time for costume changes," Lille says

without waiting for an answer. She turns toward the exit. "I'm parked just outside."

I'll break the bad news about the pharmacy in the car, where there won't be any cameras waiting to catch their upset faces for the gossip mill.

As always, she's managed to double park without getting a ticket. I'm almost convinced she has the gardiens de la paix, otherwise known as the traffic cops, on her payroll. Remy opens the back door of Lille's sleek black Audi for me, the new one she bought with the commissions she's earned on our ever-increasing popularity, and we slip in like she's our hired driver. I guess she kind of is.

"So," she says as she pulls into traffic, "Aurie first and then you, Remy?"

Remy answers with a slight shrug, but Lille catches it in the mirror. I live in the suburb of Auteuil, in the 16th arrondissement, but Remy lives in Le Haut Marais, in the 3rd Arrondissement. We'll be closer to the party once we get to Remy's.

"So, where were you?" Lille asks.

"I had to go to a pharmacy."

"Oh," she says. "You should have called me."

"What does that even mean?" Remy says. "People kept asking me where you went, but I didn't know if I was supposed to say."

"Seriously, Remy?" Lille and I say in unison. She's glancing at him in the mirror with the same look I have, but then she turns to the front and slams on her brakes to avoid plowing into a scooter. She's a great manager but a terrible driver.

Riding with Lille is like being shotgun in a bumper car. The really bad ones they have at decrepit amusement parks.

It's not like Remy to be so clueless. He's always looking out for me. But from the way he darts his gaze to the sidewalk, I think we've hurt his feelings.

"Girl stuff, Remy," I say. "I had to go for girl stuff."

He turns to me, and it takes a full second for it to register. Then his oval face becomes even longer as he forms an O with his mouth. He looks like an embarrassed seventeen-year-old instead of his usual seventeen-going-on-twenty-two, and it's kind of adorable.

"Anyway, about that," I say, "there was a bit of an incident at the pharmacy."

Lille examines me from the rearview mirror.

"What do you mean 'an incident'?" they say, one right after the other. I've prickled their bat senses again.

I launch into an explanation of the fiasco, leaving out the unnecessary but memorable details of that Kylian kid's Grecian-blue eyes and the way he makes you feel like you matter for something other than your celebrity.

Remy brushes his hair back as if he's a forty-year-old businessman who just watched a deal fall through. Lille is deep in thought, so deep she keeps stopping just shy of the car in front with more than her usual alarming closeness as we inch through traffic.

"What do you mean, he grabbed your wrist?" she says. "Was he being aggressive? We could have him charged with assault."

I shake my head. "No, he was trying to be protective, I

think. He seemed to feel bad about blocking my way to the pharmacy once he realized why I needed to be there."

"He should feel bad for being rude to you," Remy says. "You're sure the papo got the shot?"

"I don't see how he could have missed it."

"So, we're going to have a series of shots in the tabloids of you being grabbed by this kid around the wrist and following him to the back of this store, where you both disappeared?" Lille calculates it all out in her head like an accountant adding up numbers.

I nod. "I'm pretty sure." They both probably know this is my chickenhearted way of saying absolutely.

"How long were you back there together?" Remy asks. He's leaning against the door so he's facing me.

"Less than forty-five seconds or so," I say hopefully.

"Long enough for a goodbye kiss," Lille says in her usual worst-case-scenario fashion. "And then he went out front?"

"Yes, while I was in the bathroom. I didn't see him again. He'd already told me how to leave the back way if I wanted. I figured it was the best option in the moment. But now I'm worried it was a mistake."

The silence stretches out between us.

"And you don't know what he said or did once he went into the shop again? Or who the shooter was? What tabloids he sells to? If he followed you?" Lille must have been good in depositions when she was a litigator.

I shake my head. "I'm pretty sure he didn't follow me again. I watched for him."

Remy lets out a "Hoo" as he runs his hands over his legs.

"Look, I don't know anything about the kid except that his name is Kylian, his dad owns the pharmacy, and he's big into fighting climate change."

"That seems like a lot for somebody you just met," Remy says.

I sigh dramatically to let him know he's being totally unhelpful.

"You should have texted me," Lille says. "I'd have brought you supplies."

"You were across town, and it happened quickly. You know how it escalates the first day or two."

In the mirror, I watch her reluctantly shrug in agreement.

"Look, I'm sorry. I didn't plan for any of this to happen. I've never seen the kid before in my life." I meet and greet a lot of people, but he's not someone you would forget you had met.

"Aurie, we just told the world we're together," Remy says, as if I don't get the gravity of it looking like I'm cheating on him.

"I know, I'm sorry."

"Well, if you thought we were under a microscope before, you'd better prepare for a dissection," Lille says. She loves to use the royal "we" when she talks about Remy, or me, or us to the extent there is an us.

I drop my head to my hands and take a breath to combat the feeling that someone is squeezing me from the inside. Normal girls can just go to the store and buy tampons.

Lille pulls into a parking space in front of my house. The houses here aren't laid out in neat little boxes like they are in the States. Instead, they're interspersed between apartment buildings on streets with weird angles. Ours is a renovated "period house," which is the Paris real estate agent's way of saying it's at least a hundred years old. But you wouldn't know it. The house has been completely modernized except for the floorboards and stairs. Even the beautiful windows and old French doors are mostly gone, replaced by sleek glass.

"Do you guys want to wait inside?" I ask.

"No," they both say before I've even finished the sentence. They don't like coming to my house because my mother—also a lawyer but the kind of lawyer who works for the European Commission's representative office in Paris—will be ready with an impromptu interrogation on my career and my relationship with Remy, while my stepdad, Armel, will stare at them with the same look he must have when he watches his college students take an exam. Then, to top off the fun, my little sisters and brother will suddenly imitate the monkeys at the zoo just before feeding time as they jump on the sofa and cartwheel from the kitchen.

I take a deep breath. Remy puts his hand on my arm as I open the car door. "Please hurry." The look on his face is kind of funny. There's always the risk my mom will come out and insist they come in.

I bite my lip and nod.

When I step onto the front stoop, there's a hideous screeching coming from inside that must be Camille fighting with Thierry. I rest my hand on the doorknob for a second before I turn it. All I really want is my bed, but first I have to get past my family and through an after-party most people would do anything to be invited to.

Three

As soon as they hear the door open, my siblings are in flight to get my attention. Thierry runs to me with a stuffed bear clutched in his hands while Camille chases after him howling like a *Dawn of the Dead* actress as she tries to grab his beautiful blond hair. He'll be three in June, and she's just turning four. He bounds up into my arms quicker than a cat can scale a tree.

Camille grabs me around my waist and lifts her legs off the ground so that I sway from their weight. "It's my bear!" she yells.

Delphine, who turned five last October, looks up from the table where she's perched across from our mom. They could be the same statue, except one has been shrunk down to child size. They're both hunched over an assignment. Delphine is probably working on her spelling homework, while my mother has brought work home from the office.

"It's *my* bear," Delphine says.

This makes Camille shriek so loudly I instinctively pull my

head away. I stumble backward and brace myself against the wall to stay upright under the weight of two out of les trois petits, while my mom launches into a negotiation over the bear. Armel peeks out from the kitchen and I send him a pleading look. He looks around the room vaguely, as if he doesn't see it.

I call them the trois petits, or TPs for short, because they're my siblings, but they're also separate from me. If their acronym happens to have another connotation in English, that's not my fault, blame the Romans. Or the Gauls or the Franks or any of the other Celtic groups who helped to create French. Armel is their dad. I'm first family for my mother. They're second. I'm older, they're younger. They're the new, improved version of our family. We're one, and we're not one, all at the same time. My mother has very different expectations of them, but maybe that's just because they're still so little. Or maybe it's because she's still with their dad. Or maybe because they aren't half American.

Remy calls them the untouchables because every time he's with them, they crawl all over him and he ends up sick afterward. Last time it was the stomach flu and he cursed me for a week. I seem to have developed an immunity to their onslaught of not-quite-deadly communicable diseases.

My mom convinces Thierry and Camille to go stand by her while they negotiate rights to the bear, and I head to my room.

"Aurie," my mom says, stopping me in my tracks, "could you please help Delphine for me?"

I turn so she can see my face. "I can't, Maman, I have the Dior after-party tonight. We're already running late."

Armel comes to the kitchen doorway and scratches his beard. "Surely you have a few minutes?"

I shove down the urge to scream like Camille. "You guys do get that this is Friday of Paris Fashion Week? And that I just attended the Dior show because they paid me to be in the dress I'm wearing right now?"

Armel shoots a look at my mom and goes back into the kitchen. Since I paid for the family's vacation to Italy last summer with the money I make as an influencer, it's hard for them to be as critical of my fashion vlogging career as they used to be. Plus, I have enough in my savings to pay for most of my college. Even Armel can't argue with that. But they still don't understand how going to a party can be a job.

"I need help with my cédille," Delphine says, unfazed by my needs. Her softly curled hair is losing the blond she was born with, already turning toward a chestnut brown. All the TPs were born blond. I'm the only one with our mom's dark hair.

"Cédille, ssssss," I hiss to her. The cedilla is the little squiggly tail that sometimes hangs off the letter *C* in French. It makes the letter sound like an *S*. My mom has always spoken both English and French to me, especially when we lived in the States with my dad, but my first couple of years of school here were a nightmare with all the accented syllables and words that smash three and four vowels together at once. I still make mistakes sometimes when I write in French.

Delphine giggles. "But why isn't it used with an *E* or *I*?" She rubs a purple crayon against her cheek.

"Because a *C* in front of those letters already makes an *S* sound," my mom and I say together. We look at each other and smile. Then she chucks her chin up to tell me I can go change.

I run to my room and switch into automaton mode before she changes her mind, five minutes allotted for a shower, which feels heavenly. I already have my outfits for the week hung up in order of use, so I grab the party dress reserved for tonight, a beautiful blue silk bodycon with a stained glass effect over the heart. Beneath it are matching shoes. I slip the dress I wore today onto the same hanger I take tonight's dress from and drop the Doc Martens underneath. Usually I'm not this organized, but during Fashion Week I don't have a choice. I touch up my hair and grab a makeup case for the car.

"It may not be a school night, but I still want you home at a reasonable time," my mom calls as her gaze follows my dash for the door. I don't answer because I need to outrun Thierry and Camille if I'm going to escape without a drama fit for Netflix. Sometimes I wonder what happens once I leave, but not enough to ask. I don't need any more guilt trips from my mom and Armel than I already get.

I slip into the car as Remy watches the walkway to the house, clearly still afraid my mom or Armel will pop out to slow us down.

"Go," I tell Lille as the door shuts, and she hits the gas pedal like we've got Russian assassins on our trail. The neighbors must really wonder about me.

Lille and Remy look at me, Lille from the rearview mirror.

"It was fine," I say. They purse their lips, totally not believing me. But it was much less of a battle than it usually is.

I hand Remy my phone and he takes it without question. He already knows what to do.

"Ready," I say, and he nods when he taps the record button. I do my vlog in English with captions in French and an English translation below.

"Hi, guys, it's Aurélie here on my way to the Dior afterparty, which is going to be epic! But as you can see, I still don't have my face on, so I thought I'd give you a quick peek at how I'm rolling tonight." Remy pans to my open makeup case. I take out the products I'm using one by one and show them to the camera, explaining why I'm choosing each and showing them how I wear it. I'm not that big on makeup, but for this type of function I go more dramatic than I normally would. "I love this eyeliner," I say, wiggling it for the camera, "because it's somewhere between a smoky blue and black, so it's perfect for a party. And this is how I pull it out, a little thicker at the edges." Lille manages to glide to a stop rather than have me impale myself with eyeliner, which makes me wonder if she could be a better driver if she chose to be. "And thanks to our driver for letting me get that on safely," I say as Remy laughs. If Lille understood what I was saying she would shoot me daggers. Then I line my lips with a pretty pink pencil before filling them in with a cream blush that's way too sparkly for anything but lips.

I get an endless supply of makeup from several companies I promote. But I don't do exclusives or let designers pick what

I wear. I only agreed to the Dior dress today because it was a one-off and they paid me three times what they would for a single social media post, which made my dad complain that the college fund he has set up for me is a complete waste of money if I can make thirty thousand dollars a day. But that's only one or two days out of the year, and it doesn't include Lille's cut.

Remy doesn't understand half of what I say in my vlogs, and Lille doesn't understand any of it until she reads the French captions. She's one of those Parisiennes who can't stand to admit that English is more useful in the world than French, the kind who refuses to learn English so they can glare with contempt at American tourists who can't speak the language of the country they're visiting for a week. But when we go to New York, she's mad that the only places where French is spoken are some of the fancier French bakeries and restaurants.

I'm almost finished when Lille gets a phone call, which Bluetooth lets everyone know before she has a chance to hit decline. I don't want to edit this vlog, though, so I laugh and tell the camera there's no time for calls when the Dior after-party is waiting. Remy picks up on my brush-off and keeps filming.

"Oh, and in case any of you were wondering," I add, "my cameraman tonight is Remy!" He turns the camera on himself and says bonjour, a dimple in his smile. Then he swivels back to me.

"Well, we're just pulling up to Remy's place so he can do a quick change for the party. I'll see you all there in my next video!" I give my signature goodbye wave, an odd little twist of my hand I came up with when I was a silly fourteen-year-old, but my fans like it and now it's a habit.

"Clear," Remy says, and I slump into my seat.

"That was a good one," he says.

I smile. "You don't even know most of what I was saying." He's trying to learn English so he can reach the US and UK music markets, but when I tried to tutor him, it went about as well as when he tried to tutor me in math. Remy had me so confused we ended back at Aristotle. And I couldn't keep a straight face at his accent when he tried to speak English, which made him make fun of my French accent. We never got past pronouns because we were laughing so hard. Lille was really mad at us.

Remy ticks his head to the left. "I can always tell when you're on—there's something about the way you work the camera that's just different. I don't need to know everything you're saying."

He hands me my phone as Lille pulls the car up in front of Remy's grandmother's pâtisserie in Le Haut Marais. It's named after her, La Petite Marie, or "The Little Marie." She also has a shop in St. Germain, but this is the original one she's owned since 1984. Remy has lived with her in an apartment above the shop since his famous musician parents died in a plane crash when he was twelve. He's saving up to buy her a big apartment in St. Germain, but I think she's too attached to this neighborhood to ever leave it. Plus, even though their flat here is small and very old, it's absolutely gorgeous, just like the pâtisserie. The shop and their apartment, which seem so intertwined, are the best places in all of Paris to me.

"Ten minutes," Remy says.

"Don't forget the sage tie," I say. He nods.

When Remy is gone, Lille turns to face me.

"What?" I already know what she's going to start on me about, though.

"The clock is ticking." She sounds like a mafioso.

"I know." I look out the window.

"You promised," she says, and then she pauses and restarts. "*We* promised your mother that you'd start math tutoring. You're never going to get into the kind of college your parents are expecting if you don't start tutoring soon. I think I've found a graduate student at the American University of Paris who could teach you."

"I don't need it to be in English," I say, more annoyed at my math disability and my parents' expectations than Lille. "I am fluent in French, even if I have an American accent." I hate when I sound petulant.

Lille holds her hands up in surrender. "I just need to make sure she'll sign the nondisclosure agreement."

"Next week," I say. "I can't deal with it right now." Just thinking about it makes me feel like my brain is scrunching up and shrinking in my head.

"You have to pass Le Bac," Lille says, as if this is information I don't already possess. Or maybe that possesses me.

Le Baccalauréat, not affectionately known as Le Bac, is the French version of the Scholastic Aptitude Test, except a lot longer and harder and everyone needs to pass it to graduate high school. It used to have different tracks based on what people were going to major in at university, but then they decided to change it, which just so happened to coincide with a worldwide pandemic. Now it's based on the core curriculum you chose in high school. I've already taken the first part, last summer. But the hardest part is still to come in June. Especially since my core curriculum includes la spécialité mathématiques, or specialty math. I'm lucky, though, because the specialty portion is supposed to be in the spring now, but this year it's been postponed. So I don't have to face reality until summer.

"I shouldn't even be worrying about this," I say. "What kid with a math disability has to take advanced math?" I need more ibuprofen, but it's too soon.

Lille raises her eyebrows in agreement. "Unfortunately, your mother decided that making you fight through your disability would build character."

"Well, it hasn't." It has, however, built complete confidence that I am scholastically hopeless outside of history and literature, have a ridiculous level of math anxiety, and I need to consume chocolate whenever I do my homework.

"You still need to pass it, Aurie."

"Yes, Lille. I know." What she really means is that I not only need to pass Le Bac, I have to get honors to satisfy my parents. Even Armel expects me to get into Université PSL, or Paris Sciences et Lettres University, the best school in the capital of France. My dad, however, has much more realistic expectations. He made me apply to Harvard because he really wants me to come "home." Whatever that is. None of them seem to have any idea that the likelihood of me passing the math portion of Le Bac, let alone getting into a top-tier school, is statistically as probable as the next Fashion Week being held in Boise, Idaho.

I should be deciding now if I'm going to school here or in the States. But going home, as my dad calls it, feels a lot like abandoning my mom, even if she does have a replacement family. At least my dad hasn't done that to me. I miss the States and my American family, but I'd miss Paris and my family here if I left. No matter which continent I choose, I'll be letting one of my parents down. But if I don't get into a great school, I'll be letting them both down. My chest quivers like butterflies have set up an encampment in it.

Lille watches as I exhale. "Can I give you some advice?"

She asks it like it's a question, but it's not. I press my lips together and wait.

"You have to stop hiding from the hard things."

"I'm not hiding from my disability." Even I don't believe me.

"I'm not just talking about that," Lille says sort of quietly, her eyebrows raised at me, and this time I have no idea what she means. I've never seen Lille's soft side before, and it scares me a little.

Remy pops the door open and jumps in. He hands me a bakery box. "Mamie sent you these."

I open the box to find three of my favorite pastries. "Bless her! I'm so hungry!" I shove a chocolate marquise into my mouth at full throttle and catch Remy looking at me like he's watching a starving bear eat.

"What? I haven't eaten since breakfast," I garble through the chocolate mousse.

"Aurie, did you intentionally not wear a necklace tonight?"

I throw a chocolate-covered hand to my throat and feel for the necklace I had on earlier today.

"Oh my God," I say, not even remembering to speak French. "My gran's necklace! Where is it?" I look at Remy like he might tell me it was just hidden by my dress or something, although I know this can't be true. I look around in a panic.

Remy knows which necklace I mean. "It's okay. We'll find it." He grabs my sticky hand.

"It could be anywhere! I've been all over Paris!"

"When do you remember having it last?" Lille asks.

I think for a moment. "At the Palais, when we were being interviewed by that reporter from *Teen Vogue*."

"It probably fell off at your house when you were changing," Remy says.

I nod. "That's right, you didn't notice it missing before."

Lille shakes her head. "I don't think you were wearing a necklace when I picked you up at the Palais." I catch her gaze in the mirror for just a moment before she slams to a traffic stop. Lille is good with details. She's probably right. I must have lost it before she picked us up.

"I have to find it!"

"We aren't going to be able to find it tonight," Remy says. "Tomorrow I'll help you. We can check at the Grand Palais and that pharmacy you went to, first thing in the morning."

I start to cry. "What if it fell off in the street? Or someone didn't turn it into lost and found at the show, but kept it?"

"No messing the makeup!" Lille commands with the voice of a drill instructor. "Don't cry until we fail to find it. It isn't a tragedy until then!"

I really want to believe her, but I don't think I could handle losing that necklace. I take a deep breath and dab my tears away so I don't have to redo my makeup. Then I wipe my hands and neck with some wet paper towels Mamie sent along with the messy pastries. Lille pulls into the valet area for the party.

Remy puts his fingers to my chin and brings my gaze up to his. "I promise," he says. "As soon as the Palais opens tomorrow, I'll help you find it."

I nod and blink back tears as a valet opens the car door. I need to focus on work, so I do my best to force a smile. I slip my hand into Remy's and follow him out to the waiting cameras and crowd.

Four

For once, I wish Paris traffic had kept us in the car longer. I need more time to wrap my head around losing my gran's necklace. I'm not ready to put on a brave face. This day has mostly been a disaster. I can't wait to go home and look for my necklace and go to bed. Cameras click and flash all around us while people lining the VIP carpet scream our names to get us to turn toward them, just for a moment, so they can get a good picture to sell to a tabloid or share on social media. Giant bodyguards search the crowd for problems as they gesture for us to keep walking. Girls cry just because they're so close to us, and outstretched hands reach to touch us as if we're museum exhibits or talismans.

Remy pulls me in close as the crowd pushes against the ropes lining the carpet. He leans down to whisper in my ear. "Please smile like you mean it, Aur. People are really going to think something is wrong between us."

He squeezes my hand as I catch his gaze. I do love him, even if it's not the way the public thinks. That was Lille's idea. She decided we needed to boost our profiles by pretending we're a couple. "People love romance," she said. "It will help both of you. Besides, you practically live in each other's pockets anyway. Everyone already believes it. You'd just be going along with their fantasy."

I'm not sure how she talked us into it, except that once Lille makes up her mind about something you'd have an easier time stopping a plane from landing while standing on the runway than you would telling her no. I think she really just wanted an excuse to have her two highest-profile clients going to all the same events. But she wasn't making up the rumors about us. It's been established underground chatter that Remy and I were secretly a couple for at least a year.

When Lille first started managing me, she'd only been managing Remy for a year or so. She threw us together so Remy could help me navigate the negative side of celebrity, and we just clicked into fast friends. We both needed someone who would have our backs, someone we could trust, someone who knows what it's like to live under a spotlight. Now people believe we're a couple. Between those photos from the pharmacy everyone will see by tomorrow morning and me fighting tears tonight, there are going to be way too many questions.

Radiant, I tell myself and let the feeling cascade through me. I lean my temple against Remy's arm, and I smile as if I'm the luckiest girl in the world. After all, I am on the arm of Remy St. Julien. Even as his best friend, that's pretty amazing.

A young girl about twelve stretches her arm over the ropes and catches my hand, so I give hers a squeeze. I just hope this will all be enough to counteract tomorrow's tabloids.

Inside, the party is raging. It's even louder in here than it was outside, but at least no one is shouting our names. Giant fountains of champagne flow on tables set out in a diamond pattern, while roses and delphiniums seem to float just above us, tiny lights flickering through them. Swaths of white silk cascade from the ceiling, and an alternative band has the dance floor packed. Celebrities and models flit around the room, trying to lift themselves just one step up on the celebrity ladder. Lille finds us, having entered through the not-so-VIP entrance, and asks us how it went. I'm too busy posting content to hear what Remy tells her, beyond "Aurie really pulled it together."

Remy and I do some meet and greets and then catch up with other influencers and celebrities we know while Lille photographs us, and then we take a selfie in front of a chocolate fountain sculpted in the brand logo of a giant CD. Remy tells me to post it. "What do you guys think of Remy's look tonight?" I ask in the caption. "Guess who picked his outfit? Oh, and how cute is he with that five-o'clock shadow?" Then I post a bunch of emoji, like the smiley face cat with hearts for eyes, and pick the hashtags, including #Remaurie, our celebrity mash-up name. Lille thought it should be #Aurem, but our fans picked it, not us. Besides, Aurem sounds like an eighties band, not a couple. Before I even close the app, there are hearts and shares rolling on the analytic tags as if it's one of those slot machine memes with the cherries and lemons.

Lille gives me a nod, but my eyes shift to the buffet. "You should do a video of just the two of you," she says.

"Aurie needs something to eat first," Remy says.

I nod. "And some water, before I completely shrivel up."

We're just settled at a table when Remy gets introduced to someone who has written songs with Ed Sheeran and wants to maybe collaborate with him on some songwriting. Remy gives his plate one yearning look and the two of them go off together.

"I have to be home by eleven-thirty," I tell Lille as I shovel some fancy little cheese appetizers into my mouth.

"School night schedule even on a weekend," we say in unison and smile. Sometimes, Lille is more like a teenage co-conspirator than an agent. But in the end, she always enforces my mom's rules because she has to if she wants to keep managing me. My mom put that in our contract.

Some influencers stop by and chat, which brings my dinner to a standstill. When they go, I'm about to take another bite of a pretty delectable but now ice-cold potato creation when a security guard approaches us.

"Mademoiselle McGinley?" he asks. He's not much older than I am.

Lille jumps into action. "What's this about?"

She says it quietly but with enough authority to scare a prison warden.

"There's a gentleman at the entrance. He says he needs to speak with mademoiselle."

"A gentleman? Who wants to speak to me?"

The guy nods. "I told him we couldn't confirm that you were here, and we can't possibly bother the guests, but he insists, mademoiselle, that you will want to see him."

"What's this person's name?" Lille asks. "How old is he? Does he look dangerous?" Last year, she had to get a restraining order against a forty-year-old guy who followed me for over a month, insisting I was the love of his life. My mom made Armel get a security system for the house, and Remy had his security team tail me until we were sure the guy had given up. Remy and I usually don't need security, only at his concerts or if one of us gets a specific threat, which is rare, until it dies down. Mostly we just have people stopping us for photos and autographs.

The guard shakes his head. "He's just a kid, madame. But a very insistent one."

"Does he have impossibly blue eyes?" I ask.

"Oui, mademoiselle."

I look at Lille as panic rolls through me. Could that Kylian kid be stalking me? He could have seen my post about the party.

"Is it him?" Lille asks.

"I think so?"

Lille's face scrunches into a unibrow. "He must have figured out what his story is worth."

She stares into space as she strategizes every move this guy might be contemplating.

"You can't be seen with him," she whispers, with so much ferocity I shrink a little.

"What should I do?"

"He's not leaving unless I call the police," the security guard says, "and I thought you would want this to be more discreet."

Can this day get any worse? Leave it to me to run into a sociopath at a random pharmacy when I was supposed to be at one of the biggest designer shows of Paris Fashion Week. If it's even him. Maybe it's some other weirdo. It's not like there's a shortage of them on my social media feeds.

"Is there a private room where we could meet him?" Lille asks.

"Certainly," the guard says.

"And make sure no paparazzi see him enter," she adds.

He tells us where to find the room while he goes to escort my unwanted guest to us.

We slip upstairs to a small conference space without windows. Brown leather chairs line the walls with a coffee table in the middle instead of a big table and chairs. "Whatever he wants," Lille says, "it's best to find out now, and quietly. Maybe we can buy him off."

"You think he wants to blackmail me?" The amazing potato concoction I loved turns to a lump in my stomach. I guess it's a good thing I didn't get very much of it. Although blackmail might be better than stalking. I think.

"Why else would he track you down here and threaten to make a scene?" She's pacing. "He must have figured out what those photos could do to you and Remy."

Lille is right. This is bad. Her pacing might be helping her to calm down, but it's got the opposite effect on me.

"Don't cry," Lille says. "It will just make him think he's got leverage over you. You look ashen. Let me do the talking."

I exhale and pinch my cheeks. "Okay." I cannot believe I did this to Remy. Or myself. I will never forget feminine hygiene products again.

"Steady," Lille whispers as the door opens.

Kylian walks in with the security guard, his eyes searching the small space until he meets my gaze.

"I've checked him for weapons," the guard says. "Do you want me to stay?"

Lille contemplates Kylian a moment. "Could you wait outside? This shouldn't take long." She could teach a course on how to be a girl boss. She is so going to say she deserves a bonus tomorrow. And honestly, she probably does. I've really screwed up.

"Hey," Kylian says, his hands nervously brushing his jeans.

"Why are you here?" I ask. I don't move toward him, and he stays by the door.

He reaches into his jacket pocket.

"What are you doing?" Lille says, and she jumps in front of me like a bodyguard. At this rate, she'll ask for a raise, too.

Kylian pulls his hand from his pocket and shows his palm. "Relax, madame. I just came to give a necklace back to Aurélie. At least, I think it's hers. I found it in the bathroom at my dad's pharmacy." He reaches into his pocket and pulls out my gran's necklace.

I'm so relieved I gasp. "Thank you so much!" I step forward and he hands it to me. The clasp is broken, but it's still attached and otherwise just fine. I feel like crying. My grandma trusted me with a family heirloom, and I almost let her down.

I'm so grateful that I go to hug him. He looks a little alarmed and I stop myself just in time, instead moving past him and back toward Lille to cover up how weird I almost was.

"This, this is so great," I say and turn around. "Really, I can't tell you how much this necklace means to me."

"It's nothing," he says. He smiles that smile from the pharmacy, the one that makes me forget there's a major Fashion Show party downstairs, and for just a moment it feels like I can breathe.

Five

"Sorry I had to insist on seeing you," Kylian says. "I had no idea how to find you otherwise. All the DMs on your socials are closed. And I didn't think you'd want me tweeting it at you or something." He pushes his auburn hair from his eyes.

"I have to keep them closed or it's just a creep festival. Most legit people who want to contact me get in touch with my manager." I gesture toward Lille and introduce them.

"Sorry," he says. "It didn't occur to me that you'd have a manager." He looks a little embarrassed at not understanding how my life works.

"I thought you might ask my dad tomorrow," he adds, "but if you didn't, I wasn't sure how to find you. I knew your name because of the photographer, so when I was checking for socials, I saw a video of you arriving here with Remy St. Julien. Anyway, I figured I should take the chance while I had it. It seems like an old necklace that maybe has sentimental value."

"It was my gran's, so it means, well, it means more than I can say. Thank you."

"You're welcome." He smiles and turns to leave, but Lille gives me a look as if I should stop him. I have no idea why, though, so I shake my head at her.

"The papo," she mouths at me.

Right. I nod. "Hey, Kylian?"

He's already at the door, so he swivels. "Yes?"

I wet my lips. I don't like interrogating the kid. "This was really great of you. Can we pay for a cab home for you?"

"No thanks, I have my bike." He gestures with his thumb like his bicycle is just beyond his shoulder.

"Oh, right," I say, and he starts to leave again.

"Kylian," Lille jumps in, "let us at least get you something to eat."

Kylian looks at her and then at me. "It's okay, really—"

Lille cuts him off. "It's the least we can do! Have a seat there, with Aurie. I'll be right back." She practically pushes him into me. I gesture awkwardly to the chair nearest where I'm standing and sit down. The look on his face lets me know he's wondering what we're up to.

He doesn't seem like a stalker or someone looking for a way to take advantage of the situation. My luck has been all over the place today, so I decide to shoot from the blue line, as my hockey-loving, Boston-raised dad would say.

"Lille and I were wondering what happened with that paparazzi guy after I left your dad's place. Did you talk to him?" I don't mention the nondisclosure agreement she'll want him to sign.

Kylian laughs. "Oh, yeah, he had a million questions about you."

"Oh."

He shakes his head. "Don't worry, I didn't tell him anything. I mean, how could I since we'd just met? But he sure was fishing."

"Well, what did he ask? And what did you say?" He has a little scar on the left side of his chin.

"He asked how long I'd known you," Kylian says.

I nod to tell him to go on.

"I told him thirty seconds, maybe a minute, that he had the wrong idea about us knowing each other at all, and that I didn't even know who you were, just how badly he wanted your picture. Oh, and the bit about you buying blister covers."

My eyebrows crease while I consider this.

"I mean, it's the truth, except for the blister covers, which was your request. Was I supposed to say something different?"

I'm not sure how to explain it diplomatically. "It's just that he's never going to believe it with the way you took my hand. Did he give you his name or the outlets he works for?"

"He gave me a card as my dad was shoving him out of the shop, but I threw it away."

"Do you remember his name?" I bite my lip.

He thinks about this. "Pierre something?"

Lille comes in with a heaping plate of food and hands it to Kylian, along with a glass of Italian soda. The room suddenly smells warm and cheesy, with undertones of rosemary and parsley, like an expensive perfume made from food.

"Thanks," he says, and then swigs half the glass of soda. The dish has sautéed shrimp and some of those crispy potatoes in Parmesan I didn't really get to enjoy when Kylian arrived, a zucchini galette, and some beignets for dessert.

"You didn't bring me anything?" I sound kind of pathetic, but I'm too hungry to care.

"You've had enough to eat tonight," Lille says.

Kylian chokes on his mouthful and then swallows. "I'm sorry, but do you think she's overweight?" He points at me, an incredulous look on his face that's pretty adorable.

"It's just because she's used to seeing me next to models who are eight inches taller than me and weigh the same, with arms the size of hockey sticks."

Lille looks a tiny bit remorseful.

Kylian glances from Lille to me. "Is she starving you?" He offers me his plate, genuine concern on his face.

I laugh and shake my head. "She is a tyrant, but I promise I get enough to eat. Today's just been a whirlwind where I didn't have a chance to grab something."

He relaxes a little. "At least have the shrimp. I'm vegetarian. It's better for the planet." Then he seems to think this might be rude as he adds, "Or, I mean, take anything you want, honestly."

I don't think he realizes how sweetly funny he is.

"If you aren't going to eat them anyway," I say, and pluck one from the plate. Then I fill Lille in on the situation with the papo.

She starts pacing again, while muttering "This is bad" over and over, which cures my appetite pretty quickly.

Kylian watches her, a half smile playing on his lips. "I'm not sure I understand what's going on."

"Remy and I have just told the whole world we're dating, and by tomorrow morning that photographer is going to lay out a photo story in which it looks like you and I know each other really, really well and disappeared together into the back of your dad's shop."

"We were back there for about thirty seconds," Kylian says.

"Not the point," Lille snaps. "Do you have a girlfriend?" She stops and shrugs. "Or boyfriend?"

His gaze darts over to me. "No, no, I don't have a girlfriend. Why?"

Lille shakes her head. "It probably wouldn't help anyway. You're handsome, though. Have you ever thought about modeling?"

Kylian grimaces like you couldn't pay him to do that.

"Lille," I say, "could you focus, please?"

"Oui, oui, you're right." She instantly frowns again. "Call me if you change your mind, though," she adds absentmindedly.

Kylian gives me an amused smile. "I think you are blowing this way out of proportion."

Lille and I look at each other. He has no idea.

"The tabloids are going to paint it that you and I know, and like, each other and that I'm cheating on Remy."

"That's ridiculous. I mean, seriously," Kylian says. "The statistical probability of us meeting like that is not that high. It would be easy to blow up any theory that says otherwise."

Lille stops pacing and stares at him. I know that look. The monster truck that is her brain has just revved its engine and Kylian is about to get run over.

"What do you mean by that?" she asks.

Kylian shrugs and then launches into an erudite explanation of the probability of us randomly meeting and him grabbing my arm based on the number of pharmacies in any neighborhood radius to which I could have walked, the time of day and day of the week, the obstruction of the little counter gate, and a bunch of other data points that start to make my head scrunch up.

Lille listens, enraptured, while I think about how good the galette on his plate looks.

When he's finished, she pulls a chair up across from him and leans forward, the way cheetahs gaze on prey right before they strike.

"You're exceptional at math, aren't you?"

Oh boy.

Kylian looks confused by the sudden change of topic, but he answers with a nod. "It's my best subject."

She rolls her gaze to me slowly, like those big roller machines that flatten asphalt. I shake my head no. My phone buzzes. It's Remy, texting to ask where we are. I reply to tell him how to find the conference room.

Lille rapid-fires questions at Kylian. Where does he go to school? What year is he in? What are his grades? His plans for the future? Has he ever tutored anyone? Committed a felony? Used street drugs? Been suspended from school?

Kylian answers each question a little haltingly, as if he isn't sure why he's being asked or whether he should even go along with this bizarre interrogation. He's in his last year at one of the prestigious high schools, and he's on track to go to school for advanced sciences, probably at PSL or any other school he chooses in the world. It's enough to satisfy Lille as she peppers him with her interview demands. She whips out a business card and hands it to him.

"Don't throw this card away," she says. "Be at my office, Saturday, ten a.m. sharp."

"You forgot his favorite sorbet flavor," I say. Lille ignores me.

Kylian's gaze travels from Lille to me, his eyebrows scrunched tight. "Why?"

"To tutor Aurie in math for Le Bac. We'll pay double the going rate. You'll have to sign an NDA, though."

"A what?"

"A nondisclosure agreement. It's standard, nothing to worry about." She waves her hand the way a princess would dismiss a servant.

"I'm sorry," he says, and stands up. He pushes his hair from his eyes. In this light, they seem like the ocean at night. "I'm not looking for a job." He drops the card on the table.

Lille stands so she can meet his gaze better. "Look," she says, "you got Aurie into this mess. It's the least you can do."

Kylian glances at me. I get up, too.

"I'm sorry about her," I say. "She's had way too much espresso today."

Kylian nods and skirts around Lille to the door.

"Hey, Kylian," I say, and he pauses. "I'm really sorry."

"It's cool," he says, turning back. "I've had weirder encounters before." He doesn't seem to believe this any more than I do.

"No. I mean, you're going to be hounded for the next couple of weeks solid. At least. Every paparazzo in the city will be following you. Just keep your head down and it will blow over. But for the next couple of weeks, don't expect much peace."

His face creases while Lille shoves another one of her cards into his hand, and then he's gone.

"Alors, that didn't go well," she says.

"Lille, I mean this with all the love in the world, but sometimes you could tone down the tiger part of your personality."

She presses her lips together a moment. "I could try to talk to him on Monday. Find him through that pharmacy."

I sit down and shake my head. "Just let it go. I don't think we need a nondisclosure from that kid. If he had wanted any part of this circus, he'd have taken you up on your offer." I reach over and pick another shrimp off his plate. It's glazed in a delightful lemon cream sauce.

Remy appears in the doorway, a heaping plate of food in his hands, which he holds out to me. He sweeps his gaze between us.

"What did I miss?" he says.

I cough as I choke on the cold shrimp, not sure where to even start.

Six

Lille spends the next week doing damage control, which is all my fault. Okay, a little of it is that Kylian kid's fault for grabbing my arm instead of just pointing out the way to the back for me, but most of it is my fault. I should have remembered my tampons. I should have checked whether I had some before it became an emergency. I should have asked Lille to bring them to me, although she would never have brought the right ones no matter how explicit I was with directions. I should have noticed a papo was following me. I should have walked out the front door of the pharmacy and gone to the bistro and paid for a drink so I could use its bathroom, shooter in tow or not. But, just like models, fashion vloggers aren't supposed to have real girl problems.

Besides, the real problem is me. Of course I would forget the one thing I really needed to bring. My disability is technically just about math, but it exacerbates everything. My organization, my anxiety, my ability to strategize or be on time. I shut down long before my teachers expect me to. It's a physical sensation, but I don't really have words for it, beyond saying it feels like my brain is shrinking up like those plastic Shrinky Dinks drawings that kids bake in an oven to make charms and other toys.

It's not a headache. It's a sensation. And it happens every time I'm in math class. Or I need to make any other calculation in front of people. Or I need to figure out some math equation, and I have no idea where to start. I once gave a cabdriver in Boston a fifty-dollar tip for the worst cab ride of my life, as he made Lille seem like a professional driver and wouldn't put the air-conditioning on though it was 95 degrees out. It wasn't until he and his enormous smile drove off that I realized how much I'd overpaid him.

I'm just as mad at myself now as I was then. More now, because this time Remy and Mamie have been hurt by it. Remy and I spend the whole weekend making sure we're seen together instead of Remy getting time to work on his music or both of us helping Mamie in the pastry shop.

On top of that, I haven't told my mom or Armel the truth about Remy and me, so they think we're dating for real. My mom would never go for this publicity stunt, and she'd be furious at Lille for dreaming it up. So when my mom sees the tabloids, which she always checks to see what's being said about me, it's even more awkward to explain why it appears that I'm getting super-cozy with "the very adorable boy" from the pharmacy. The pictures make us look like total lovebirds. I almost have trouble believing we just met. This papo should be in

Hollywood making blockbusters. The photos are credited to a Pierre Naillon, but even Lille's never heard of him.

The whole fiasco has made Remy and me the paparazzi's number one priority until some bigger celebrity gets their attention. "Be glad we're in the City of Light," Lille keeps saying. "Someone much bigger is going to do something even more ludicrous any day now. If we're lucky, that American singer with the new boyfriend every month will be in town soon." This really isn't the pick-me-up she thinks it is. But until said bigger and more rash celebrity eclipses my mess-up, I've made a huge disaster. Every new edition of the tabloids is filled with photos of us, paired with questioning text about why Remy is looking at me the way he is, or why I'm turned away from him, or how sad Remy looks. Instead of the usual shots of us walking on the street, there are pictures of us through the window of Mamie's pâtisserie, inside Lille's car, and coming out of Lille's office building as photographers stalk us everywhere we go. Even France's tough anti-paparazzi laws can't shield us from this.

"We could sue them," Lille says with a frown of doubt as we sit in her office on Friday after school and strategize more damage control.

I shake my head. "They'll just come after us harder, in some other way."

She raises her eyebrows.

"I keep expecting them to pop up at the next urinal when I'm in a public bathroom," Remy says. He fidgets with a guitar pick, his fingers turning it over and over in a barely perceptible rhythm.

Lille scrolls through her phone at the latest stories. She's particularly upset by one that says I looked "disheveled" yesterday.

"A fashion influencer cannot look disheveled, Aurie." She says this without her usual commanding tone, and a compassionate Lille is somehow worse than an angry Lille.

"She didn't look disheveled," Remy says. He smiles at me. "She looked adorable."

He's kind of right, at least about the disheveled part. I wouldn't call how I looked a mess, exactly. It just wasn't my usual neatly put-together style. I went for a shabby chic look because I've been spending so much time on damage control that I didn't have time to properly plan my outfits. So, of course, the world that critiques the people who critique fashion would call me out.

"I really am sorry," I say. Remy shakes his head like it's not my fault.

"There's no point in crying over what's done," Lille says. She's back to pacing, though.

"I've been thinking," Remy says. He leaves the rest of the sentence hanging, like a leash.

Lille and I turn to face him and wait.

Remy squirms in his seat and clears his throat. "I think Aurie should have a security detail."

My mouth drops open. Lille stops pacing.

"Some of the comments by people who've decided she's cheating on me are a little extreme," he says. "Especially from the guys who follow me who think they're super-alpha."

Lille nods thoughtfully. I start to form words to say it can't be that bad, but I've seen some of those comments myself. Remy blocks anything really bad that he sees, but there are lots of bullies in cyberspace. Most of them are just that, cowards who stay behind a curtain. But there is always an element that's more to worry about for any celebrity.

Lille's phone lights up with a text and she stands over her desk and reads it without picking it up. She darts her gaze to us.

"*How do I make this stop?* it says. It must be him. Do you think it's him?"

"Kylian?" I ask.

She nods. "Who else would send such a cryptic message to me?"

"Maybe some papo who wants you to think he's Kylian," I say.

Remy laughs. "You stream way too much American TV."

"Says the guy who wants to put Secret Service on me."

He holds up his hands in surrender, but he's smiling.

"Well, we can't be too careful," Lille says. She texts the number back, speaking the words to herself as she types *Who is this and what do you want to stop?*

It's Kylian. How do I make these paparazzi go away?

When Lille shows us the message, Remy and I smile. "I did try to warn him," I say.

Remy sighs. "The innocence of the young." I nod dramatically.

"You two are a regular vaudeville show," Lille says. "This is good, though," she adds as she takes her circuit to the window and back to her desk. The bright yellow rug reveals the wear of her heels. "It means he'll agree to tutor you." Her office is large, with bookcases behind her desk and two black leather chairs in front of it. Remy and I are perched behind those on a red leather sofa. Opposite the window is a small conference table with six chairs.

I shake my head at Remy to ask *What kind of plan is that?*

To Lille, I just say, "Why would we even want him to do that? I'd have to see him regularly and the tabs would get wind of us spending time together and it would give them even more reason to think I'm cheating on Remy." I look over at Remy with doe eyes and say in a soap opera voice, "Which I would never do, my beloved."

Remy picks up my joke. "I trust you implicitly, keeper of my heart."

Lille crosses her arms. "Are you two finished?"

Remy and I chuckle and then nod in unison.

"If we get this Kylian on board to tutor you, then we control what the tabs can say. We tell them that, yes, you and Kylian met for the first time at the pharmacy, where you went to see if you wanted to hire him as a tutor—which is perfect because it's partially true. Then we get him to sign the NDA."

"That's good," Remy says.

Lille levels her cheetah-on-prey look at him. "This is why you pay me fifteen percent. And if we can keep this thing in check, Aurie won't need a security detail."

They seem to think we've found a solution, but I shake my head. "No. I'm sorry. I am not telling the whole world I have a math disability."

"Lots of people get tutored without having a disability," Lille says.

"No, it will get out. There will be relentless questions about why I need a tutor and why him, and it will come out and then I'll have to talk about my dyscalculia, and I'll go from being Aurie McGinley, fashion influencer, to Aurie the dumb-at-math girl. Nope. No way."

Lille narrows her eyes at me. She hates it when I'm difficult, as she calls it. I call it not agreeing with everything she says. "Lots of celebrities talk about their disabilities and mental health now. It's considered chic—heroic, even—not something to hide."

"That's people with dyslexia. Beautiful people with dyslexia. Keira Knightley, Salma Hayek, Tom Holland. No one runs around telling the world they have dyscalculia. No one's ever even heard of it. They'd think it was something contagious, like Covid. Or some vampire condition."

"It does make me think of Count Dracula," Remy says.

"See?" I practically yell at Lille.

"You could be the first, then," she says. "A trailblazer. It's a great marketing idea."

I jump out of my seat. "My disability isn't a publicity angle, Lille. Not every little detail of my life is a 'marketing thing.' I don't want people to know." I fight tears.

"Hey," Remy says, shifting in his seat to catch my gaze, "why is this bothering you so much?"

"It just is." I go to the window so that I don't have to look at them. Lille's office is in a building not far from the Eiffel

Tower. The street below is busy. There's nothing in sight that would particularly make you think you were in Paris. Trees in the center of the boulevard are just beginning to bud. Cabs and cars and delivery trucks fight their way along the avenue in little bursts of progress, while pedestrians jostle each other on the crowded sidewalks. I knew I couldn't do what the other kids could long before any teacher or psychologist or test told me what it was. Learning math was like the traffic below, it came in jerks and spurts and then complete standstills. And no matter how hard I tried to understand, it was like being in a world where everyone else spoke a different language. Another exclusion I know a lot about.

Even with accommodations at school, it takes me twice as long, at least, as anyone else to do the homework. I never fill out forms correctly, and I can't do anything that requires reverse thinking, like sewing or carpentry. I volunteered to help Habitat for Humanity the last time I was in Boston, and they literally took me off sawing duty because I couldn't cut any of the pieces of wood to fit together, no matter how many times I measured them. I constantly invent compensations, like I can only find percentages by using ten percent and then guesstimating the rest. I need Remy or my mom to figure out what time I should leave for events, and I'm still always ten minutes late. Not five, not eight, not thirteen, but ten. Apparently it's some magic lateness number for dyscalculiacs. Or whatever we're called. Even I don't know. But everyone knows what you mean when you say dyslexic.

"Please, Aurie?" Remy asks. God, I love his voice, even when

I don't want to hear what he's saying. It's like sinking into an oversized chair while you gaze through a panoramic window at the Alps in winter.

I shake my head, but I don't turn around. "I can't. I'm sorry."

"Well," Lille says, "do you have a better plan? Because I don't." She plops down in her chair, and it squeaks as if it's also annoyed with me.

"You know," Remy says very quietly, like he's picking out the notes of a love song, "you're going to have to get a tutor at some point. Then the tabs are going to be asking those questions, whether it's about this Kylian kid or someone else."

I make an angry face at him, but he can't see it because I still have my back to them.

"But the tabloids won't think I'm cheating on Remy if it's someone older. Why can't we get someone else? A nice old lady? Kids in France don't even tutor other kids. That's a US thing. I'm surprised you thought of it." I press my hand to the window and let its coolness flow into me.

"Well, you are American," Lille says, as if she's listing another disability. "And we could get someone else, but that doesn't make the Kylian problem go away. It will eventually die out if you don't see him again, but there won't be any way for us to control when or how that is. Or make everyone believe you weren't cheating on Remy already."

"You'll never convince everyone anyway," Remy says. "Some people believe Earth is flat." I glance at him. He's stretched his head back and looks at the ceiling as if he wishes this could all be lifted off his shoulders.

"We just need to convince enough people to keep Aurie's reputation bankable," Lille says. "It's what's best for all of us." Us. Why is it that the one time I belong in a group it's one where I'm dragging everyone else down?

They're waiting me out. I know it, and they know I know it. The longer I stand at the window, the more my anger starts to feel like tears coming. Tsunami-type tears.

You kind of owe me.

Remy doesn't actually say these words. He doesn't even think them, knowing Remy. But my guilty conscience says them to me loud enough.

Remy comes over and stands beside me. "I know you're scared. But not facing it isn't going to help you pass Le Bac."

I wait for Lille to chime in, but she must be using all her restraint to let Remy work his Remy magic on me.

I turn and let him fold me into a hug. When I have heels on, the crown of my head rests under his chin. Today I'm wearing custom-embroidered Chuck Taylor high-tops, so my ear rests just against his softly pulsing heart, muffled only by the worn cotton of an old Springsteen concert T-shirt I bought him on our last trip to New York.

I'm so used to Remy being close that he feels like home to me. We've been squeezed in together at concerts and fashion shows, fallen asleep on each other on trains and planes, and danced around one another in the kitchen of the pâtisserie. I always give him a good luck hug before he goes onstage. Cling to him on the Vespa. We've been there for each other since we met, which is good because it's made this whole fake dating thing so much easier for us. But now I've messed it all up and I owe him the fix.

I pull away. "Okay. You win."

"It's not about winning," Remy says, catching my fingers with his, but I can tell by the contented look on Lille's face that she thinks it *is* about winning. It doesn't matter, though. It has to be done.

Lille picks up her phone and sends Kylian a text, and then shows it to Remy and me. *There is a solution. Can you come to my office?*

I'm not sure what will happen next. In fact, there's only one thing I am sure of: The feeling I've had lately that my life is off-kilter has been a whole lot more than just a feeling.

Seven

"There are going to be a hundred shots of him walking into this building," Remy says as we wait, perched once more on the sofa. The three of us look at each other and then look away, a family of prairie dogs watching for the vultures to start circling.

"Well," Lille says, "the chances of us successfully sneaking him in are low, and this way it will add an air of transparency about the whole thing."

"But if he doesn't go along," I say, "then it will look like we tried to buy him off and failed." Remy grabs my hand to distract me from biting my lip. When I was little, I'd do that until it bled, and now I have a small scar.

Lille gets up from her chair and starts pacing. She crosses her arms, which is her most worried pacing. "It's a risk we have to take. If he doesn't go along, then I'll think of something."

"Please don't let it be telling the tabloids that I was desperately buying tampons and he took pity on me."

Lille shrugs. "If worse comes to worst. It's not such a big deal. Sometimes you are such an American." Lille thinks America is one big evangelical commune. When she comments on my Americanness, it's never a compliment.

She stops and stares into space. Her eyes shine, which only happens when she's hatching a plan. She's like a werewolf at the beginning of the transformation, and Remy and I glance at each other. "We could really shame the tabloids, then," she says. "Picking on a girl in that situation, when women's rights are in the news. The moment is right to take our power back!"

"Cue the evil music and sinister laughter," Remy says.

"Bwahaha."

Lille juts out her chin and turns her head away. We've hurt her feelings a little. But Lille never pouts for long, so Remy and I smirk at each other.

"I almost forgot," she says without turning to look at us. "Tom Ford."

"For Remy or for me?"

She turns back to us. "They want Remy in one of their suits next weekend at that charity gala you two are attending."

"That's a yes," I say.

Remy looks at me. "You think I'd look good in Tom Ford?"

"Ridiculously so," I say. He smiles to himself, and I have to turn away from the cuteness overload, but not before I catch Lille narrowing her eyes at us more than usual.

"He's here," Lille says from the window. She's already told building security to send him up.

Lille's secretary knocks on the door a few minutes later and opens it for Kylian. His glance immediately takes in the room and us. Remy and I stand and say hello, and then Lille gestures to the table and chairs. He's wearing jeans, an old green *Star Wars* T-shirt, and black hiking boots.

We sit down and Lille offers Kylian a Perrier or Orangina from her mini-fridge. He tells her no thank you.

"I'll have a Perrier," Remy says, which makes Lille press her lips together for asking instead of helping himself, but she hands him one anyway.

"Let's get down to business," Lille says. It's one of her favorite sayings even though she always complains that I'm too American.

We spend the next half hour discussing the paparazzi problem and explaining to Kylian that the dose he's gotten over the past few days is just the beginning with them. Lille wants to make sure he understands the gravity of the harm they can do before she offers him the solution to all his problems.

"I'm not interested in celebrity," Kylian says. "In fact, I think the whole culture is harmful to people and the planet."

I glance at Lille. Surely she can see what a wild card this guy is? She's chewing on her lip, but she doesn't seem ready to give up.

"Still," he says, "if I can turn it around so that, instead of being Aurélie McGinley's latest love interest, I'm just someone she knows who is fighting for the climate, I'd consider this. The only reason I want attention is to refocus it on the planet."

Remy raises his eyebrows to ask if this guy is for real.

"You act like I have a Taylor Swift line of ex-boyfriends," I say. "I've never even had one." Then I look at Remy and Lille because I'm not sure if this plan includes telling Kylian the truth about Remy and me. "Before Remy, I mean."

Kylian frowns. "I just don't see how this could work."

"Well, if you start from a negative attitude, it won't," Lille says. She's not trying to sound judgmental; she's just a sports car stuck in seventh gear.

"Look," Kylian says in English as he leans toward me, his accent British, "I didn't even know who you were when you showed up at my dad's place. I'm not trying to be mean. But I don't get any of this, and I don't particularly want to. I couldn't care less if you're famous. Or about fashion."

Imagine a world like that, where celebrity didn't matter. But a world without fashion? I'm not sure what else Aurie McGinley is any good at doing.

Lille zeroes her gaze in on him. "Tu parles anglais?"

She doesn't know what he said, but she recognizes English when she hears it. Kylian's English was perfect.

"Oui," Kylian says.

"Fluent?" she asks.

"More or less."

Lille jumps up to pace. This is only going to get weirder.

"Where did you learn to speak English so well?" I ask.

Kylian's face turns more serious. If that's possible. "We lived in London when I was little."

"You!" Lille says, turning and pointing at Kylian. "You will tutor Aurie in math and Remy in English!"

Remy and Kylian groan at the same time.

I bite my lip. It's so ridiculous it's kind of funny.

"Why would I do that?" Kylian asks. "I don't even want to tutor her."

"Thanks," I say.

"Excusez-moi," he says as he gestures his hands apart. "It's nothing personal. I just have other things to do with my time." He wears a pink string bracelet on his left wrist. The kind that supports breast cancer research.

"Like save the planet," Remy says.

Kylian and I both shoot him a look, and he shrugs in surrender. Kylian stands up. "I have other places to be. These paparazzi can't follow me around forever. They'll get bored at some point."

"Well," Lille says, "we'll pay you triple the going rate, and you can donate it to your favorite environmental charity. It's a win for everyone."

Kylian hesitates and then pushes back his auburn hair. His jawline trails down to soft lips set in his round face. "Why would you do that?"

"Because, if you are tutoring both Remy and Aurie, it's even more aboveboard than if you are only tutoring Aurie. The tabloids will have nothing to work with. And Remy needs to learn English if he's ever going to make it in the international music scene."

Kylian nods, but it's more *I get it now* than *I'll do it.*

"This is a ridiculous idea," Remy says.

"We finally agree on something," Kylian answers.

I wish Kylian and his friends had been doing their school

strike anywhere but in front of his dad's pharmacy that day. I wish I'd walked to a different pharmacy. I wish I'd never met him and none of this was happening. But it is. And it's mostly my fault.

"Look," I say in English, "if you help us out here, I'll try to find ways to help you with your environmental stuff."

He gazes at me a moment before he answers in English. "Why is this so important to you? I want the media out of my life, but all you're getting is them not running a story about you that isn't even true. Why do you care so much what people think of you? Especially people you don't know?"

Remy and Lille watch us, trying to figure out what he's saying. It's hard to form the words I need because the blue of his eyes makes me think of faraway places where none of this would matter.

"Every business, every goal, has a currency. For some, it's euros or dollars. For others it's practice. Or investing time in school strikes. For my goals, and for Remy's, it's public approval."

He holds my gaze. I want to flinch, but I have the feeling that if I do, he'll walk. Time spreads out like tissue paper stuck together, as if each second is unwilling to let go of the last.

He shifts his gaze to Lille and returns to French. "D'accord, I'll do it. Triple the going rate."

I let out a breath as Lille breaks into a big smile. I wish I had her confidence that this is going to be the solution to all our problems. But something tells me it's just the beginning of them.

Eight

fter Kylian leaves, Lille bounces up and down like
Camille when she walks into a toy store.

"You were brilliant," she says.

She has no way of knowing if I was brilliant or if Kylian
just caved because he decided it was worth it for the money,
but she got what she wants and that always makes Lille happy.
Somehow I'm not feeling very brilliant right now.

"It's getting late," Remy says. "We should go."

I glance at Lille, expecting her to give us orders for where
we are to be seen, but instead she smiles at us.

"Oui, it's movie night, non?"

Remy and I exchange the same quizzical look.

"Yes, it is," he says.

"Well, you two run along and have fun," she says, as if this
is a perfectly normal Lille thing to say. Remy nods at the door.
We should get out of here before she changes her mind or says
something even stranger. Our twice-monthly movie night is the

best part of our friendship, but Lille considers it unproductive since it's not about making money, and I don't want her to ruin this one. It's the stress-free zone I've been looking forward to all week.

At the elevators, Remy gazes over my head as if he's checking to make sure she isn't going to chase us down and insist we spend the night in some trendy restaurant after all.

He smiles his mischievous smile. "That's as happy as I've seen Lille since she was first dating that Italian soccer player."

"The one who broke her heart or the one who turned out to be married?"

Remy scrunches his face. "Weren't they the same guy?"

I laugh. "No. I think she caught on to the married one before she got too carried away."

"Oh, then I mean the one who broke her heart." The elevator doors open, and we step in. Lille was ridiculously happy then, at least until the guy decided she was too assertively French to bring home to his Italian mother. Lille's disastrous love life is the one thing she's terrible at controlling, mostly because she always goes for the flashy type.

The elevator reaches the first floor, and the doors open. "Ready?" Remy asks.

I nod and he grabs my hand. We cross the lobby, say good night to the security guard, and plunge onto the street. A group of about ten paparazzi pounce on us.

"Remaurie, why was the pharmacy boy here?"

"Aurie, are you breaking up with Remy for the pharmacy boy?"

"Remy, your rival left here very unhappy! What did you do to him?"

"Are you two breaking up?"

The questions come at us all at once, as if in surround sound.

"Sorry," Remy tells them, "Aurie and I have plans tonight, and they don't include interviews. I'll just say that there's no story on the pharmacy boy and save the rest for our spokesperson." He says it with so much boyish charm it would be hard to feel like you'd been brushed off. I look up at him, and it's easy to smile like we're in love. Movie night is the one reprieve we get from homework and our jobs. Although music isn't really a job for Remy, just the part of trying to be famous enough that people find his songs. He opens the door of a waiting taxi for me while cameras click like ice popping and cracking.

In the cab we keep the show going, just in case the driver would talk, but we're both so happy to have a night off that it doesn't even feel like a show.

"What are we watching?" he asks, holding up my hand that rests in his as if it were contract.

I smile and raise my eyebrows and he mock-groans.

"Please?"

Remy laughs. "Okay, Aur. We'll finish that Korean rom-com series."

"Thank you," I say. "I've been dying to see the end."

He nods and I raise my shoulders like a self-hug and grin at him. He tugs me closer. He looks out the window at the cars and people going by and smiles.

When we get to his apartment, it's quiet. Some old friends of Mamie's are in town and took her out for the evening. She's left us money to get dinner, as if we can't afford to buy it ourselves, and a plate of lovely macarons.

"What should we eat?" Remy asks as I unzip my school backpack. He holds up the forty euros Mamie left and smiles like we just won a jackpot. "Pizza? Jambon-beurre? Steak frites?" He pops a pistachio macaron into his mouth.

"Ooh, let's get pizza from that place a few streets over. We could have stopped if Mamie had texted us." He holds out a raspberry macaron and feeds me like I'm a puppy as I rummage through my book bag.

"You know she hates using her phone. Why are you frowning?"

I stop and look up. "I forgot to bring a change of clothes. Now I'll be in this uptight dress all night." I groan. I swear I always forget the things I most want to remember.

"Wait," he says, and goes to his room. He comes right back and hands me his a-ha *Hunting High and Low* world tour T-shirt and a pair of navy-blue sweatpants. I bought the shirt for him in a thrift shop in London. "Take On Me" tops his all-time best music videos list. Now I never go into a thrift store or on a trip without finding him a vintage concert tee. I don't know if it's my favorite shirt of his because it's his favorite or because he looks so totally Remy in it.

"I can't wear this," I say, fingering the worn blue cotton.

"Just don't get pizza grease on it," he says, a small smile on his lips. "And I outgrew those sweatpants like three years ago, so they shouldn't be too big if you tighten the drawstring and let them scrunch at the ankles."

I look at him to be sure he's truly okay with me wearing his favorite shirt. "I promise not to stain it."

"You'd better not," he says. "Now why are you frowning?"

"I can't go out like this."

Remy contemplates me. I don't have to tell him that I'm tired and just want to crawl into comfortable clothes. Or that there's no way I can be seen wearing anything of his. "We'll order in," he says.

"They don't deliver, remember? Let's just go now and I'll change when we get back." I give him a dramatic sigh.

"We could get delivery from somewhere else. Or I could go myself?"

I shake my head. "I really want that pizza. And the last thing we need is for you to be seen without me, even if it does seem like you're picking up food for us."

Remy puts a hand on his head and exhales. "You're right." He places the order online and we go to pick it up. There's a lone paparazzo stalking us as we leave the bakery, and people take photos of us as we walk. It's good that I didn't risk wearing his old sweatpants and a shirt he's been photographed in a million times. Most people from Le Haut Marais don't bother us since they're used to seeing us around, but it's a very touristy area. There's no way we wouldn't be photographed in the three blocks it takes us to get to the restaurant. I would have been labeled disheveled and who knows what else. Probably something that would have sent my mom into a full freak-out. Instead I smile, as if walking around in a dress and heels is exactly how I wanted my night to go.

A trio of girls stops suddenly before us, their faces lit up.

"Oh my God, I can't believe it!" they say, one after the other. They grab their phones and beg for pictures.

They ask me what brand I'm wearing.

"Emporio Armani," I say, and they squeal and chatter about how they'd love to wear a dress like mine.

Remy and I step out of the flow of pedestrian traffic and into the recesses of a building with a Greek Revival doorway. Probably it was once a chapel, but now it's apartments. The bright blue door reflects the dusk of evening. The girls crowd into us and take selfies, and then each wants a full picture with us. I hope the papo catches this, as it will be good press. They giggle and talk over each other, desperately trying to get Remy's attention. For just a moment I see Remy through their eyes. It's almost hard to mesh the boy I know with the celebrity version of him, weighted down by the legacy of his mom and dad. The Remy that goes onstage or meets fans is so confident and easy, as if he's made a promise to never let his parents down, but the real Remy carries his ghosts everywhere, always worried about whether Mamie and I are safe. Always afraid to let people in because he knows how much it would hurt if he suddenly lost them. Remy didn't even get to find out from someone he loved that his parents had been killed. The paparazzi announced it before the police had even told Mamie. He heard about it at school from some older kids.

When Lille first threw us together, she warned me that he could be standoffish, even prickly. He was at first, but I was so clueless about being famous that I think he felt too sorry for me to remember to keep his distance. Besides, there's something about taking trains at night that brings people together as they rumble through the dark, exhausted.

A small crowd gathers for more pictures, and one guy asks Remy to sign his shirt because he doesn't have any paper with him. It takes us longer than my stomach would like to get to the restaurant, which is crowded. Even though it's still spring, the sidewalk tables are all full. There's Italian music spilling out of the place, and servers carry trays of wine and pasta dishes. Some people take our photos as we pick up our order, and then we escape to the street. The crowds have thinned a bit on our way back, and we manage to get to the apartment while the pizza is still hot. Remy picks up his clothes from the sofa and hands them to me. "Come on," he says. "There are still a gazillion episodes of this show left. Go change and I'll get the plates and drinks."

"That pizza smells so good!" I say before I run to the bathroom.

I yank off my sheath dress and slip into his clothes. They're soft and safe. Most of the time, this life of celebrity feels big and adventurous and exciting, but it can also be overwhelming and even frightening when people get too close, or push too hard to be near you, or want too much to know every detail of your existence. At his show in Oslo, I was nearly crushed when I got swept into the crowd as people pushed to get closer to the stage. Someone elbowed me while pushing me against someone else and the wind was knocked out of me. When Remy saw I was hurt, he stopped the show until security had the situation under control, but I ended up pretty bruised. Another thing I never told my mom about. It was Remy's first big gig, and I had to miss school for the afternoon to get there in time. I'd had to beg her to let me go at all. Somehow, though, whenever it all feels like too much, Remy makes it less suffocating. Like that night, he had them take me backstage while he finished. He insisted we go to the hospital and stayed with me until they declared it was just some bad bruising on my ribs and back. And then he took Lille and me for ice cream, down this little snow-covered street that was all lit up in twinkling lights that looked just like a fairy tale. He turned what was one of the scariest moments of my life into a beautiful memory.

"I'm starving," I say as I walk into the living room. Remy grabs his phone and takes a picture.

"You can't post that!"

He laughs. "Duh. This one's for me."

"I don't even look good." My gaze falls to his sagging sweats and oversized tee. I run my hand through my hair even though it's too late.

Remy smiles. "That's the point. Besides, musician grunge on Miss Perfectly Tailored still looks pretty cute."

I laugh, and we settle in on the sofa for our margherita pizza and rom-com. We spend the first episode eating, but by episode two we're bantering over the lovestruck characters. Even the side characters struggle through relationships in these series, but somehow you know they'll all be okay in the end. I wish real life were like that, instead of people dying in plane crashes or getting divorced. But these shows are also weirdly deep, always delving into some loneliness or heartbreak. Remy never makes fun of me when I cry at the sad parts.

"Ah, come on, how does he not know she likes him?" Remy asks, throwing his hand up.

"Boys are clueless," I say, and hit him with a pillow, which makes him push me, which makes me snuggle up closer to him, which makes him shake his head in surrender. Maybe this is why I love movie night so much. Remy and I can be totally goofy and there's no one to see it, no one to critique us. Even when Mamie watches with us, she just says we're "too much."

Remy suddenly dumps me off him and pauses the rom-com. "I almost forgot. I have a song I want you to hear."

He jumps up and goes to his room to retrieve his songbook and his dad's acoustic guitar. He flips his notebook to the page he wants and hands it to me. "Remember that song I wanted to write about the concert at Oslo? But I got stuck? Well, I think I finished it."

I read over the lyrics while he picks the song out.

"Why aren't you saying anything?" he asks. He stops playing, his hand suspended over the strings.

It's like he's written me a love song.

Remember that snowy night in Oslo
When you missed school
Just to be there with me
I was trying to be so cool

Your mom was mad already
And if she ever knew
The way I let you down
She'd say she told you, too

My first big gig
You smiling by my side
Remember that night in Oslo
Do you forgive me for that ride?

The whole place it was shaking
That Gibson burned my hand
And all I saw was crowd
All I saw was band

My first big gig in Oslo
You smiling by my side
Remember that night in Oslo
Forgive me for that ride

The hospital, the X-rays
The purple round your ribs
Remember that night in Oslo
We ate ice cream just like kids

My first big gig in Oslo
You resting by my side
The night train took us home
You slept but girl I cried

My first big gig in Oslo
Please forgive me for that ride
Forgive me forgive me for that ride

Remy sets his guitar down. "You don't like it? I know some of the English might be wrong."

"No, the English is fine. This is beautiful. Really beautiful. But me getting hurt wasn't your fault."

"I shouldn't have let it happen."

"Remy, you didn't let it happen. Sometimes bad things are just out of our control."

He bites his lip. He knows that. I shouldn't have said it. Not that way.

"This is beautiful. Thank you," I say. "It sounds like a love song." I glance up to see how he reacts, because I'm really not sure if he's trying to tell me something.

"Well, everyone thinks we're together," he says, but he doesn't look at me. "They expect a romantic song."

"Right, of course they do."

He pauses a moment. "I mean, you are my best friend."

We both nod.

"So, you don't think I need to change anything?"

I look it over again. "I mean we would say 'she'd say she told you so,' but then it doesn't rhyme, so I think it's okay this way."

Remy flattens his whole face. "So, you like it?"

I smile. "I love it."

He grins and picks up the remote control and starts our

74

rom-com again. I snuggle down into him. Because we're best friends and this is how we are.

"Oh, I love this background song," I say.

Remy pulls my phone off the coffee table and finds it for me to add to my K-pop list. "I should write you a K-pop song," he says as he scrolls. He pinches his eyebrows together, his lips slightly apart.

"Ooh, would you?"

Remy scoffs. "You think I can do anything, don't you?"

"When it comes to music, I know you can."

Remy gets a half smile on his face. I don't think he believes he can, but he knows I believe he can.

"This Yoon Seon-Ho guy is so good," I say when he angles my phone to show me the song is downloaded.

"You're such a sucker for a love story." He pets my head like I'm a stray dog he brought in. I kind of am. I don't know what I'd do if I didn't have Remy in my life. Then he gives me his indulgent smile, the one that tells me I'm too overboard but in the same way a cute puppy would be, and his lips are somehow prettier tonight than I ever noticed before. I jump up and go get the plate of macarons and we share the cookies like popcorn, in bits and pieces, crumbs all over the plate.

By episode four I've mostly forgotten about his beautiful lips. We're sprawled on the sofa with my head against his chest, as if we're on a train rolling home from some gig or fashion show. Before much longer, he's waking me up.

"Come on, sleepyhead," he says, shaking me. I open my

eyes and try to remember where I am. "Hmm," I say as it hits me. I hug him like a pillow.

"Aur, your mom's going to be really mad at me, come on." He's right. I wish she could just like him.

I yawn and sit up. Remy's paused the show right where I dozed off. I know I slept for a while, so he's just been sitting here, letting me sleep and holding the place for next time.

"We were so close to the end," I say.

"Gives us something to look forward to," he replies, though he only watches rom-coms to make me happy. We tried to watch horror movies together, but I jumped and gasped so much he said he couldn't take them seriously. He stands and extends his hand to pull me up. The April night is still too cold for his Vespa, so he grabs the keys to Mamie's little old Peugeot, which looks like a bright orange-yellow SUV someone squashed at both ends. Le Haut Marais is still bustling, at least the bars and restaurants are, but we head out the back door to the alley and slip into the car quietly enough.

When Remy drops me off, I turn before I get out of the car. "Text me when you get home safe."

He nods.

I blow him an air-kiss and hop out. He waits to pull away until he's sure I'm inside. I go upstairs and call good night to my mom as I pass her room.

"You're late again," she calls back, and turns out her light. I wish she could understand how Remy looks out for me.

I brush my teeth and wash my face before I go to my room and slip off my bra and Remy's sweatpants. I keep his a-ha

T-shirt on. I yawn and crawl into bed, sliding a big, stuffed polar bear named Ernie from my childhood to the other side to make room. Then I wait for Remy's text, sitting up so I don't fall asleep. When it finally comes, I send him a good-night gif of a teddy bear hugging a heart-shaped pillow as it falls over and a string of *Z*s float into the air above it. Remy marks it with a heart. Tomorrow the pressure will start all over, and there's sure to be some new incident considering the last two weeks, but tonight I'm just going to drift to sleep still wrapped up in the peace and happiness of movie night with the best best friend anyone's ever had.

Nine

We decide the correct place to have tutoring sessions is Mamie's pâtisserie because it will seem more transparent than any of our homes and less public than a library. Even my mother was happy when I told her Lille had finally convinced me to work with a tutor. She was uneasy that Kylian wouldn't know enough to help me since he's my age, so she made him send her a screenshot of his class list and last marks, and her only response was to raise her eyebrows and say "Bon." The kid is enough of a math genius for my mom. Great.

Kylian's response to my lawyer mother acting more protective than my lawyer manager was to text me to say *This is a lot of work for a job I never applied for and don't want.*

My response to that was to do an internet search for an article about how good teachers build confidence in their students through positive relationships, which of course I sent to him.

Sarcastic message received, he replied.

Seriously, though, of all the people in Paris who could have tutored me, why does he think I'm any more thrilled about it being him than he is? He's the last person I would choose, considering the embarrassment of our first meeting, the public scrutiny we'll be under, and the way he's distracting just by existing. It's hard enough for me to retain math vocabulary and processes without having those Grecian-blue eyes watch the wheels in my head clunk around like they belong on a monster truck. And he already doesn't like me. Usually with tutors, that comes after we've had a couple of sessions.

Lille put out a pretty brilliant press release, though. She made it sound like Remy and Kylian will just be a couple of dudes chilling together to improve Remy's English and that he'll be helping me because I'm in advanced math, like I'm some sort of prodigy.

Of course, people in my school know I barely hang on in specialty math, but I don't think anyone would tell the tabloids. I keep friendly with everyone, and I even have a few real friends. But I can't socialize much outside of school. It takes a lot of time to create content, and I'm only allowed to keep my vlog if my grades are high. Math is the only grade my mom will give me any slack about, and I have to keep that above an 8, which basically means I need to keep a B– average or above.

Remy isn't any happier than I am about being tutored by Kylian. "This is your fault," he says as we wait in the pâtisserie on Saturday for our first sessions. His dark hair is pulled back

in a sloppy mun, and he's wearing a vintage Soundgarden concert T-shirt I bought him the first Christmas we knew each
other. Even going grunge, though, he's more gorgeous than any
model I've ever seen.

"I am sorry about the pharmacy." I squeeze in beside him
and take a selfie for our social media. Remy slaps on a fake
smile and then watches as I post the picture.

"Not about that," he says, throwing his hands apart help-
lessly, "but if you hadn't made me laugh so much when you
tutored me, it could still be just us."

I get up and slip behind the counter. Claudette, the university student who works the front of the store on Saturdays, pretends she doesn't see me pull out a four-inch lemon tart from
the pretty glass case. I slide it onto a plate and grab two forks.

"Sharesies?" I ask in English as I set it down in front of
Remy. It's what I always say when we split a pastry.

Remy sets his jaw.

I pull in my lips and raise my eyebrows to plead with him.

He smiles and takes his fork from me. I mouth, "Merci."

We have a system. We each start at nine o'clock and move
counterclockwise until we reach the middle. Then we split the
very, very middle as evenly as we can, except Remy gives me
the most meringue. I have no idea why, but this seems very
funny to us every single time.

Remy has almost forgiven me, I think, when Kylian walks
into the shop and drops his backpack at our feet.

Remy glares at me instead of looking at Kylian.

I look up for the both of us. "Salut!"

"Bonjour," Kylian says.

The table is small and only has three chairs. I scooch around to the chair beside Remy, and Kylian takes the seat I just left.

"Can I get you something?" I ask. "This is the best pâtisserie in Paris."

"No," Kylian says, which is probably good since I'm kind of trapped against the wall. "But thanks."

I nod.

He looks from Remy to me and then to Remy. "So, who's going first?"

"Remy," I say at the same time that Remy says, "Aurie."

Kylian lets out a big sigh and looks toward the front windows. "Uh-oh."

I follow his gaze. There's a papo outside. It's the guy from the pharmacy, Pierre Naillon. He doesn't have his camera up. He's just taking in the scene before him, camera dangling from his neck. Remy and I exchange gazes. He leans in to me.

"You go first. I'll help Mamie." He brushes hair from my face and kisses my cheek as he slides his thumb along my other cheek. It's just for the papo, but it leaves the unfamiliar trace of a tingle on my skin. Remy has a bit of his dad's rock-and-roll showmanship. Kylian looks away as if his breakfast is trying to come up.

"I guess it's me, then."

Kylian nods and reaches into his backpack for some books. I've already brought graph paper and regular paper and a pencil and a giant eraser and a ruler and my school calculator.

He looks over my supplies. "You carry too much gear on camping trips, don't you?"

I shrug. "I've only been camping once. When I was eight. My uncle made us all go to Maine, and my only memory is that the beach was a thousand degrees hot and the water was just above freezing and I got bitten by every mosquito in the state."

He raises his eyebrows. "It seems like there may be a tiny bit of exaggeration in there, but I get the point. You don't camp."

"Remy says my idea of camping is any hotel that doesn't leave chocolates on your pillow."

Kylian frowns. This information has definitely lowered me even further in his estimation. Assuming that was possible.

"Okay, so let's start. I brought some practice Le Bac questions for you to do a mock test to see where you are."

I can already feel my brain scrunching up, and his cold attitude isn't helping the panic growing inside me. He slides the paper in front of me and every inch of my body wants to run out of the pâtisserie. Oh, which reminds me, I have a papo watching this fiasco. I look up just in time to catch the flash in my face.

Kylian follows my gaze. "Do you want me to tell that guy to hit the road?"

I laugh a little. "If only that were all it took."

"Well," he says, "the best way to bore him to death is to make him watch you do math."

"Thanks." I try not to let my eyes get watery.

"I don't mean you in particular," he says with a tiny shrug. "I mean anyone. Think about it. Even chess has competitions people watch. No one wants to watch people figuring out math problems."

I bite my lip and nod.

"So, you're in l'option maths expertes?" This is the level of math that kids who want to become engineers take. In France, math is done differently than in the US. It's less focused on specific subjects like geometry or algebra and more focused on difficulty.

"Non, spécialité maths complémentaires," I say, which is the easier specialty math, but even this is way too hard for me. I'm not explaining that to him, though.

He juts his lower lip out a tiny bit as if he's surprised, in a disappointed way, while he contemplates this information. "I'm going to time you for twenty minutes, but just to get a sense of how fast you work."

It's all I can do not to make a face, even knowing the papo has me in his lens. Instead I take a deep breath and do my best to focus. I try to ignore the feeling in my brain, but it's there like the pea under the princess's twenty mattresses. It grows bigger and bigger.

I don't look up as I work, afraid of seeing the expression on Kylian's face, which probably is a mix of surprise and horror as I drag through the questions. When I get stuck, which happens on almost every question, I stare at my giant eraser and tell myself to focus and calm down. I spend more time thinking about that than I do about the actual problems. When I still can't get an answer in a reasonable time, I move on. But I'm only three-quarters of the way down the page when Kylian says, "Time."

He says it quietly, clearly concerned with how much work it's going to be to tutor me.

He pulls the sheet over to check my answers. I look for the papo but he's disappeared, for the time being, anyway. Two of my answers are right. For me, that's a win. To Kylian, I must seem like the dumbest person he's ever met.

When he's done, he stares at the paper for a few moments.

"Is this some sort of joke?"

"Excuse me?" My heart ticks like it might explode.

He rubs his jaw. "Look, I don't know you very well, or at all, really, but I don't have any doubt that you're pretty smart." He darts his gaze up to me and I'm suddenly back doing algebra in quatrième, or eighth grade as my friends from the States call it, and I've just been asked the train question. The one where two trains are traveling in opposite directions, and you're supposed to figure out the speed of one from the speed of the other. My breath catches and my mouth is hanging open and I couldn't be more paralyzed if a poisonous spider had just bitten me.

The memory floods me. My teacher asked me, the math-disabled girl, to answer that question in front of the whole class. She even made me come up to the board. I stood there, help-lessly clutching the dry-erase marker, until I hyperventilated and Diego Aubert had to give me the paper bag from his snack while everyone laughed. I cried. It ended two days later with me in the principal's office, but instead of the principal calling me in, my mother had called the teacher in. By the time my mother was through with her and the principal, the teacher never put me on the spot again, and I passed the class with a way better grade than I deserved. But my mom decided it meant that I'd be just fine having specialty math in high school, where I've struggled ever since, mostly faking my way through with mediocre grades and a lot of copied homework. But "Aurie and the train question" became a legendary joke at my school.

Kylian shakes my arm, and my breath rattles out. His eyes are seriously ridiculous.

"What's up with you?"

"Lille didn't tell you, did she?" I'm gripping my pencil so tightly I snap it. This is my fault. Lille was probably afraid I'd get mad if she told Kylian. But somehow, having to tell him feels a thousand times worse than if he already knew. I've spent my whole life hiding my disability. Most people think I'm ditzy, as my father calls it, and make jokes they think are harmless about how I should be blond. My great-uncle Chuck told me it's okay that I'm "on the clueless side" because a pretty face will take me further than a brain anyway.

"Tell me what?" Kylian asks.

And that's when I start crying. In the middle of Mamie's pâtisserie, on a random Saturday morning, just as Pierre Naillon walks through the door.

Ten

My heart is completely still, as if it's been turned to stone, but the pâtisserie erupts into chaos. Remy runs out from the kitchen and Kylian jumps up from his seat.

Remy grabs Kylian by the shirt. "What did you do to her? What did you do to Aurie?" he yells.

I stare at Remy because he's not the overly aggressive type. In fact, I can't think of when I've seen him this mad unless someone's safety is at risk, whether it's Mamie or me or his bandmates.

Naillon is firing on all cylinders, and Mamie runs out from the kitchen. She starts swatting at Naillon with her tea towel like it's some sort of ninja's nunchuck while he backs out of the store, banging into tables as he goes. Claudette has raced from behind the counter and is pulling Remy off Kylian, who is swearing he has no idea why I'm so upset. There's a lot of arguing that has Lille's name in it, but it's happening so quickly I don't process all of it. Mamie pushes Naillon onto the street.

Her lilting voice seems far away as she tells Naillon, "I'll call the police!"

"It's a public place," he argues with her.

"No, it's my shop. And you are never to come in again. Not for a tarte au citron, not even for a chocolate marquis!"

Mamie's chocolate marquises are famous all over Paris. She's using her big guns.

Naillon shrugs as if he thinks she's ridiculous and then slinks away while Remy and Kylian continue to argue about how ridiculous this whole tutoring situation is, the one thing they can agree on even though they've somehow made it into an argument.

Mamie marches toward us. Remy, Claudette, Kylian, and I stand in a cluster staring at each other, everyone talking at once except me because I'm crying really hard now.

Mamie snaps her towel at Remy.

"Ouch!"

"You're lucky that's all I'm giving you! Fighting in my pâtisserie as if it's some saloon from the Wild Western!" She says these last two words in English. Mamie loves to binge-watch American movies and shows. She's only four foot eleven, but it feels like she towers over her six-foot-two grandson. Her dyed blond hair is pinned up in a chef's hat, though, which helps the illusion.

"And you," she says, turning to me, "why are you crying? Are you trying to give the paparazzi a story?" Her eyes have the same green to them as Remy's. She seems like she could teach Lille some tough love techniques, but underneath her harsh exterior in a crisis, she's the sweetest, most reliable adult I've ever known. I shake my head no. A small gasp escapes me.

"Mon Dieu!" she practically yells, and hugs me as hard as she can. Which is surprisingly firm considering her size. Compared to her, I seem like a giant. "Your lesson for today is over," she says. She turns to Remy. "You will apologize to this boy and sit down and learn your English, and I don't want one word out of you that isn't from the lesson or a thank-you to this boy for coming here to teach you!"

"Oui, madame," Remy says, but he's not being sarcastic. No one has ever been brave enough to be sarcastic to Mamie. At least, not that we've ever seen.

"Allons-y," she says as she steers me to the kitchen and waves Claudette back behind the counter. I glance at Remy before I disappear. He and Kylian are sitting together, each of them glowering at the table.

I pull my phone from my miniskirt pocket, but Mamie scoops it out of my hand and slaps it on a shelf filled with sacks of sugar.

"I need to tell Lille," I say. "She has to start damage control."

Mamie shakes her head at me. "Non! You need to help me with the pâte sucrée for the tartes aux framboises. I need twelve, stat." She picked up the last word from streaming American medical dramas. Usually it makes me laugh, but not today. She nods toward the sink. "Wash your hands."

"But—"

"Non. There is nothing you can do to stop that photographer

from selling those photos to the tabloids." She pushes me toward the sink. Jean, a middle-aged pastry chef who works for her, nods at me from across the room to let me know I should listen. Then he goes back to cooking the lemon crème for the tartes au citron.

I pick up the soap and lather my hands.

Mamie busies herself around me, the way a bee hovers near a flower before going in to collect pollen. "Why did that boy make you cry?"

I shrug.

Mamie stops beside me and raises her eyebrows. Any principal would be grateful to have Mamie's penetrating stare.

"He said that I should be smart enough to do the math."

"Well, that's good," she says. "Of course you are capable."

"No, Mamie. He meant that I shouldn't need to be tutored because I should be smart enough to do it by myself." I grab a tea towel and dry my hands. A tear hits the towel.

"But no, he couldn't have meant that!"

"He asked if this whole thing was some kind of joke, because I shouldn't be so stupid."

She shakes her head. "He could not have said you shouldn't be so stupid."

"Well, that's what he meant." I blow out an angry breath. "And he did ask if it was all a joke."

Mamie purses her lips. She goes to the door and contemplates Kylian and Remy while I cut the butter into the flour, almond meal, and powdered sugar to form the dough. She watches them for a long moment, and then she turns and waves for me to get busy. "I'll speak to this boy later," she says.

"No," I say as I start to dissolve sea salt into the water for the tart shells. "I'll talk to him, but not right now. Lille didn't tell him about me."

She makes a *tsking* noise like a chipmunk. "You say this as if you have some sort of disease." She's slicing apples with quick, sharp motions but with a lot more force than she usually does.

"No. It's not a disease. It's a curse." I pound the dough into a ball, and she raises her eyebrows at me to be gentle with it.

I blow out a big breath and form the ball with my hands, gently this time.

"Enough," she says. She leaves the apples and comes and stands beside me and pets my hair, which is pinned up because I always put it in a clip when I come to the bakery so I'm prepared to help. Her fingers are fragrant with apples and lemon and cinnamon, but they're also sticky and we laugh. Then I sniffle.

"Come on," she says. "No more tears. You are better than this."

I don't think I am better than this, though. I'd like to be. I'd like to be the girl who can do these things. I'd like to be the girl who, to spite everyone, becomes an architect, or an astronomer who discovers some mind-blowing secret about the universe or redirects a meteor before it crashes into Earth. But I'm not. I'm just a girl who knows how to dress cute.

I make the twelve small tart shells that Mamie needs and help her to clean up since Jean has left for the day. I wipe down the counters, and then I plunge the sugar-coated mixing bowls and some bowls that had melted chocolate in them into hot water and soap and scrub them until they shine again.

"You didn't even finger-sweep any of the chocolate from the bowls," Remy says as he comes and stands beside me. He takes a tea towel and dries the bowls I've stacked on a drying rack.

I smile, but I don't look at him.

"Are you mad at me?"

I look up then. "I'm mad at myself. You were just protecting me." I'm a damsel in distress. A girl who needs to be saved. By her mother and her fake boyfriend and her fake boyfriend's grandmother. Deep down, I'm scared I'll always be that girl. I guess that's why it's so important to keep being good at being Aurélie McGinley, celebrity fashion vlogger. It's the one thing I excel at. Pleasing people with how I look and making them believe they can feel as confident as they think I am. No matter what the cost. We criticize girls for being princesses who need to be saved, but maybe some of us just don't have what it takes to save ourselves. Or, at least, being pretty is the only skill we have to do it.

"I shouldn't have overreacted like that," Remy says.

"That makes two of us. I'd better go explain it to him."

"He left."

"Oh. What did he say?"

"Nothing, really. He just said he had to go, and he packed up his stuff and left."

"I guess he's quit?"

Remy shrugs. "You know what? I don't care. Maybe we should run with this story and tell the tabs that you did like him a little and that I got jealous, but now we've patched it up and everything is fine. And then neither of us ever has to see him again."

Mamie doesn't look up from the chocolate mousse she's cooking, but she's listening. "All this lying is no good." She's the only one besides Lille who knows Remy and I aren't really dating.

Remy's gaze meets mine, his lips tight because we both know Mamie is right but that telling the truth doesn't work, either. Everyone thinks things about us that aren't true anyway and then we tell lies to try to make them happy and then we tell more lies to protect ourselves. It's completely ridiculous. Something has to change.

"I should go," I say as I hang up a tea towel. It's Camille's birthday and I promised my mom I'd be home by six.

"I'll come with you," Remy says.

I laugh. "You want to come to Camille's anniversaire?"

He shakes his head. "No, I really don't. But I don't want you to have to take the Metro so far by yourself. Not when you're feeling this way. We'll take the Vespa."

"It's too cold for the Vespa."

"Then the Peugeot," he says.

"Marcel is making deliveries with it," Mamie says.

"Okay, well, I'll at least ride the Metro with you and walk you to your house. I just won't come in." He grimaces, but it's playful.

I smile because he deserves it. "I'll be fine. Honestly. You

92

should stay and help Mamie and get to work on those songs for the Ed Sheeran entourage guy."

Remy laughs, but it will be a big deal if he pulls this off. "You're going to have to help me with the lyrics translation."

"You can count on it." I give Mamie a kiss and then pack up my barely touched math tutoring supplies and slip on my coat. Remy walks me to the door and pecks my lips in case anyone is watching or recording. "I'll text you later," he says.

I squeeze his hand and turn away into the chilly Parisian twilight. My mother will be expecting a progress report on my first tutoring session when I get home. And I haven't the slightest idea what I'm going to tell her.

Eleven

I don't know how three small children can make as much noise and chaos as a crowd of people six-deep lining a red carpet, but the TPs manage. It's a good thing I'm not the kind of kid who sneaks out of the house, because even if they somehow missed me sneaking out, they'd blow my cover every single time I tried to sneak in again.

"Aurie, Aurie!" they each yell as they pull at me and begin to recite some important story about the cat having discovered a box to play with or how the neighbors forgot to close their gate or that Daddy needed to go get more propane for the grill because it ran out and you can't have grilled aubergines without a grill. I'm not sure why a three-year-old turning four has her heart set on eating grilled eggplant for her birthday, but there are a lot of things I don't get about small children. I wonder if I was this weird when I was little, or if it's because there are so many of them. Or maybe they only seem weird because they're truly French, and I'm just an incomplete portion.

"Oh, Aurie," my mom says. "I'm so glad you're home. Could you make the Swiss meringue for the cake?"

I offered to ask Mamie to bake a cake, but my mom doesn't like to be indebted to people outside the family. So I get to make the icing since I'm the one who spends enough time at a bakery that I could win one of those amateur baking shows.

"D'accord, Maman."

"Merci, ma chérie."

I'm glad, though. She's so focused on Camille's birthday she seems to have forgotten about my tutoring.

Of course, it's a lot easier to make Swiss meringue at the bakery, where there isn't a forty-pound child attached to me like Victorian leg irons.

"Thierry, you're going to get burned," I say. "Please don't climb on me. Here, you can sit on the counter and measure the sugar."

"I want to measure the sugar!" Camille says.

Of course. There seems to be a rule that all small children want something as soon as, and only if, someone else has it. "Nope, it's bad luck for the birthday person to measure the sugar," I say. "You'll have to wait for Delphine's birthday."

"Daddy's birthday is next," Delphine reminds me. She's gone back to lying on the sofa in the living room, reading, and she pops her head up to correct me.

"Oh, right," I say, "You'll have to wait for your dad's birthday."

I stand at the stove and whisk the eggs and salt and sugar until the mixture reaches 120 degrees, and then I carefully sidestep Camille, who is still shadowing me like a papo on deadline. I put the bowl into the stand mixer.

"Can I taste it?" Thierry asks.

"No, it's still too hot."

He puts his arms out for me to hold him, so I do. I wish all men were this uncomplicated. He drops his head onto my shoulder and then sneezes into my hair. Or maybe not.

"Thanks," I say, and set him down. He giggles and runs off to see the cat, Chiara. I named her after Chiara Ferragni, the Italian fashion vlogger turned entrepreneur boss lady of her own fashion house, the original fashion vlogger before there even really was such a thing. I got to name the cat because she predates Armel and the TPs. Only by a couple of months, but she was my mom's consolation prize to me for moving here. She's a good cat. She let me cry on her. A lot. Until I met Remy. That was when my life here started seeming not so much like not-my-life.

We're just sitting down to grilled chicken and aubergines with roasted potatoes and carrots when the doorbell rings. My mother shoots me a questioning look. I shake my head to let her know I'm not expecting anyone.

"Will you cut my chicken?" Camille asks, because I'm the only person who, in her estimation, makes the pieces the precise size. It's kind of funny if you think about my dyscalculia. I really have no idea how I'm a master chicken cutter in her mind. Maman says it's just because she needs my attention.

I'm almost done perfecting her food proportions when I hear the chatter of my name and turn around. My mother is standing by the open door talking to Kylian. My heart nearly tumbles out of my chest at the thought of tonight's tabloid headlines. I jump up and run over, trying hard not to be seen from a window or the open angle of the door.

"What are you doing here?" I hiss.

"Aurie, where are your manners?" my mom says.

I scowl at both of them. "Maman, do you see any papos?"

My mother's eyes widen as it suddenly occurs to her that Kylian standing on our front stoop could get me in a world of trouble. She scans the front yard and street.

"Okay," she says quietly, "I don't see anyone, but we're just going to invite him in as if this is totally normal and everything is aboveboard."

I mouth "What?" at her as she says in a voice that could reach the street, "It's so nice of you to return Aurie's math book. Would you like to join us for dinner? We are just sitting down." She sounds like a robot. It's a good thing she didn't want to be an actress.

Before Kylian can answer, she pulls him inside and closes the door.

I throw my hands to my head.

"What were you thinking?" I ask him.

"Aurie," my mom says, to get me to be more polite.

"Maman, I can't risk any more bad press!" I fight tears. One more day huddled with Remy and Lille over my latest debacle just might kill me.

"I'm really sure no one followed me," Kylian says, with the nonchalance of someone who doesn't need to constantly curate

97

a public image. "And I had to talk to you about what happened at the pâtisserie."

"What happened at the pâtisserie?" my mom asks. Her mouth has twitched into an automatic frown.

Seriously, if this kid set out to intentionally destroy my life, he couldn't do a better job. It's like some archnemesis I didn't even know I had has given him the list of every one of my weaknesses. I shake my head. "Nothing, Maman." I glare at Kylian.

She straightens up because she's getting ready to cross-examine me. "Well, clearly something happened at the pâtisserie or this young man wouldn't be here now."

Kylian coughs as he shoots me a remorseful look.

"Is everything okay?" Armel calls from the dining room. "Dinner is getting cold."

My mother shakes her head like she's just remembered she has more pressing worries. "Kylian, come join us," she says, "and we can talk about this."

I don't know how I am ever going to explain this to Remy and Lille.

My maman leads the way. Kylian glances at me, his eyes a bit glazed.

"Lille 2.0," I whisper, and he puts his lips together in a silent whistle.

"You're here now. You might as well endure the torture with me. But there is a new invention called the phone you could have used." I gesture for him to follow my mom.

"I didn't ask to be roped into all of this, you know," he says before he glides past me to the dining room.

My mom has already pulled another porcelain plate and silverware set from the breakfront, because birthday celebrations require the good plates and real silver. I pull a side chair from against the wall and move over to make room for Kylian.

"Is he your boyfriend?" Camille asks. "I thought it was Remy."

"No, Camille, he's my math tutor." Or maybe I should have said archnemesis to be more accurate. I introduce my family to Kylian as we sit down. "And you've already met my maman," I say as she sets glasses of water and sparkling juice in front of him. There are a lot of *enchantés* going around, which makes Thierry decide this is a funny custom and he proceeds to say it until Delphine yells at him to shut up, which makes Armel shake his head at her with his most serious professor face and my mother correct her.

"We do not tell people to shut up in this house, Delphine."

"Oui, Maman," Delphine says.

"Enchanté," Thierry lets out one more time in victory, and I bite my lip to keep from laughing.

Camille then proceeds to explain that it's her birthday, which also requires a disclosure of everything she did today and all the presents she's asked for and a minute description of her favorite cake. It's a bit mind-numbing, but it keeps us off the topic of why Kylian has suddenly shown up, so I'm grateful for it.

When the kids are finally eating enough that their mouths are too full to fight for Kylian's attention, my mom shoots her volley.

"So, what happened at the pâtisserie?" she asks. "You didn't say there was any problem with your tutoring session." She says this and hands the aubergines around as if she's barely even interested in the answer, which even the TPs know can't be true as they fall silent and look at her.

"Something happened at the pâtisserie?" Armel asks. He tries really hard to step in for my dad not being here on the daily, but what he's really worried about is any fallout my life could bring to the TPs. Which is fair, I guess, but it doesn't do much to make me feel like I'm a full member of their family.

"It was nothing." Underneath the table, I play with a spinner ring I'm wearing. "It was just a little misunderstanding. Really, there was no reason for Kylian to come all the way out here. None at all. We could have just texted." I can't keep all the anger out of my voice.

"I'm very sorry to have interrupted your dinner celebration," Kylian says. I believe this as Delphine sends a bite of carrot flying across the table to land on his plate.

"Delphine!" my mother says.

"It was an accident, Maman," Delphine says. "Sorry," she adds to Kylian.

He pushes the slippery carrot mangled by Delphine's fork to the edge of his plate. "It's not a problem; please don't worry about it."

There's a lot of talk then about how he doesn't need to be sorry for interrupting us and how welcome he is. My mother forgets the pâtisserie incident long enough to start her cross-examination of him. I decide to settle in and enjoy this part of the meal. It serves him right for just showing up here with no warning.

I find out that he lives in an apartment in Bercy, which is in the southeastern part of the city. It's known for having a lot of bike-friendly parks. My mom already knows that his father owns the pharmacy where we met, so she moves on.

"What about your mother, Kylian? What does she do?" she asks.

Kylian sets his fork down. "My mom, well, we lost her when I was fifteen." He fingers the pink thread bracelet he wears, but I don't think he realizes he's doing it. So much for getting to enjoy my mother's cross-examination of him. Now, I just feel like an awful person.

"Oh, I'm so sorry," my mom says. "I didn't think, you're so young."

He gives her a diplomatic smile. "I get asked a lot. People don't expect it at my age."

"Where did you lose her?" Thierry asks. "I once lost my bear on the train. They have a lost and found. Have you looked for her there? I found my bear there."

"Hush, Thierry," I tell him, but Kylian chuckles.

"No, Thierry, we haven't looked on the train. But I'll be sure to check now that you've mentioned it."

My mom and Armel glance at each other and then at Kylian. "Thank you," I mouth.

Kylian nods. "It's just my dad and my little brother and me now."

My mother the attorney fortunately has more tact than

Lille the attorney and the inquisition stops after this faux pas. I'm worried she'll start back up on the pâtisserie incident, but Camille has finished eating and is ready to move on to her chocolate fudge cake with Swiss meringue, so the rest of us hurry to finish while Camille chatters on about her love of frosting flowers.

"Wow, that's beautiful," Kylian says when my mom brings it out from the kitchen, four little candles burning.

"Aurie decorated it." She says this as if Kylian is here to interview me to be the CEO of a bakery or as the prospective bride in an arranged marriage.

"Thanks, Maman."

She shrugs defensively. "It is, you're very talented at so many things." What she really means is that I could be doing anything other than what I already do. Although if I wanted to be a baker, she wouldn't think that was good enough unless I was going to the Sorbonne to become the world's foremost authority on the chemical processes of cupcakes. The thing is, I'm not incompetent, but I'm also not very good at anything besides fashion. My visual-spatial issues mean I can't draw, I can't dance or do any sports that require hand-eye coordination, and I can't fully understand music, even though I love it. I don't answer her; I just look down. But in my side vision, Kylian is tilting his head to study me.

After cake and presents, which Kylian suffers through much more good-naturedly than I expected, Armel herds the TPs to their baths while my mother cleans up dinner. Kylian and I offer to help her, but she's apparently decided he and I should discuss whatever brought Kylian here. Not that I won't have to give her a thorough debriefing after he leaves, but for now it's just us. I take him to the living room and close the shutters.

"Listen," we both say at the same time as soon as we sit down. We laugh.

"Go ahead," Kylian says.

"I'm sorry I overreacted, it's just that, well, see, I am slow in math. I actually have—"

"Remy told me. I'm really sorry I treated you like that. It was just because your math wasn't lining up with what I already knew about you, so I thought . . ." He stops and shakes his head. "I honestly don't know what I thought, but ever since I met you, it seems like whatever I've thought is wrong. Or at least something other than what I expected, and I guess I didn't know what to think. It seemed like all this must be some sort of publicity stunt or something."

I nod. Or at least I try to nod enough to make it seem sincere. I think he is genuinely trying to be nice, even if he's not very good at it.

"I'm sorry, that wasn't a very eloquent apology." He flushes.

This softens me. "It's okay. It seems genuine."

He smiles.

"So, if you want, we could try again, and I could not be a jerk next time?"

I smile. "As in you won't be one, or just that you'll try not to be but there are no guarantees?"

He laughs. "Probably the latter." He holds out his hand to me in truce.

I slip my hand into his. It feels different from when I'm holding hands with Remy. It feels unknown, and a little scary. It feels a little bit like being at the top of the London Eye. Remy and I went there once when I had an invitation-only Stella McCartney event. I pull away as soon as politeness lets me.

"I don't usually have to apologize to people as much as I've had to do with you," he says. "I'm usually a pretty nice guy."

I contemplate him. I think he is an okay guy underneath.

"Are you and Remy all right?" I ask.

He bites his lip and bobs his head. "I think so. I understand why he reacted the way he did. I'd probably do the same if you were my girlfriend and someone made you cry like that. Even if they didn't mean to."

I still don't know if it's okay to tell this kid the truth about Remy and me, so I just nod. Besides, I wouldn't tell him here with my mother's bat ears pulsing in the next room.

"Well, I should go," Kylian says, and stands, so I follow.

I walk him to the door.

"Do you want to try tomorrow?" he asks.

"Okay. But maybe the bakery isn't the best place after all."

Kylian rubs the side of his head. "We could meet at the Parc de Bercy, at the picnic tables by Les Grandes Pelouses?" He picks up the backpack he dropped by the door when my mom yanked him inside.

"That would probably be better. Then, even if we're being watched or photographed, it's all out in the open. I promise not to cry."

"I promise not to be a jerk."

I smile.

"I can do it," he says.

We both laugh.

"Good night," he says.

"Good night," I say as I close the door behind him, and I get the same little rush I had that first day, when I closed the door on him at his father's pharmacy.

Twelve

The Parc de Bercy is remote enough that paparazzi will only spot us if they followed us, or if someone recognizes me and posts it in real time. But we aren't doing anything we aren't supposed to, so it's a chance I need to take if I'm going to get my mom off my back about Le Bac, let alone pass it. And I need to graduate from high school if I'm ever going to do something with my life other than fashion influencing. That sounded way too much like my mom, but maybe all her harping has finally gotten to me. Or maybe it's seeing people like Remy and Kylian doing something that changes the world for the better, but fashion just doesn't feel like quite enough anymore.

We're at a picnic table under some tall sweet gum and oak trees, books and notebooks and calculators spread out around us. The spring day is still a bit crisp. The trees are fully in bud, and the sun streaks down between the newly green branches to the grassless, dry dirt surrounding us, warming us. It's chilly enough that none of the other tables are occupied, but not so cold that it's unpleasant. I'm wearing an Anatomie running jacket with thumb holes in the sleeves to keep my hands warm that I got for doing an ad for them last year. Kylian is wearing a cotton beanie with the logo of the University of Edinburgh on it.

"Are you going there?" I ask, pointing to the logo.

He shrugs "It's on my list. They have a lot of sustainability programs. It all depends on where I get accepted."

"I know your grades. You'll get accepted wherever you apply."

He scoffs. "There's a lot of competition out there."

"So school strike isn't just a movement for you, you want to make a career out of it?"

"Well, I wanted to be an astrophysicist, but since I lost my mom, I'm planning on either going into medicine or chemical engineering. I want to do something that ends cancer. We pump so many chemicals into our food and water and air, and we don't seem to care what they're doing to us."

"I'm sorry you lost your mother to cancer, and about Thierry."

"Well, lots of things get lost on trains. It was honestly a pretty sound suggestion, for somebody who's not three yet." We share a weak smile.

"Is that what your mom would want?"

"What do you mean?"

"Would she want you to change what you wanted to be to find a way to stop cancer?"

He looks at me and I shake my head. "I'm sorry, that is really none of my business."

He doesn't say anything for a moment. "No one has ever bothered to ask me that before. I don't think she would. I think she'd tell me to go be an astrophysicist. We used to go camping and she would tell me stories from all over the world about the constellations. I think she would tell me to go discover something amazing about the universe, like how to stop entropy." He pushes the bracelet around on his wrist.

"Entropy?"

Kylian smiles. "It's the concept in physics that basically says everything falls apart eventually."

"Oh, I see." Silence overtakes us.

"Your English is really good," I say.

"I have England to thank for that. My mom was a professor of history at the University of Leeds. But she missed France and got a job back here, which was better for my dad anyway. And then she got sick."

"Do you mind talking about it? Remy never talks about losing his parents. Except sometimes to me when we're traveling and he thinks I'm asleep."

Kylian contemplates me. "I don't mind talking about it with someone who genuinely cares. But Remy had it much worse than I did. I can understand why he wouldn't talk about it." He shakes his head. "I had time to prepare, and I only lost one parent. And it wasn't like the whole world was watching."

I nod. When Remy's parents died, all of France mourned, but they weren't mourning their mom and dad. Remy was.

"He's lucky to have a girlfriend like you."

There's a small tickle in my stomach when Kylian says this, and I think about telling him the truth. I feel like we could trust him. "So—" I say, at the same time that he starts to say something, and we both stop and laugh a little.

"Go ahead," he says.

"That's okay, you go."

He clears his throat. "I hope you won't be upset with me, but I did some research last night."

I incline my head, on full alert. "Research?"

"You know, on dyscalculia and what it's about. Honestly, I had never heard of it before Remy told me you have it. So I looked it up to figure out how to help you."

Right. I'm someone you have to "figure out" how to help. A research project, a lab rat. I can just imagine how that conversation between him and Remy went, complete with "discal-what?"

"I got you this," he says, sliding a very girly notebook from his backpack and slipping it in front of me. It has a fun drawing of the Eiffel Tower on it with a girl wearing haute couture floating beside it, surrounded by flowers and a blue sky.

I half smile. "What's this for?"

He catches my gaze and holds it. "I read that you should make a dictionary of terms, to make it easier to remember math terminology. The articles said that making your own list is better than just trying to memorize them. I thought it might be good to have a notebook just for that."

I'm kind of surprised by how hard he's trying. He's a lot

nicer than I've given him credit for. And I'm definitely embarrassed that I need his charitable opinion of my dysfunctional brain.

"You struggle with that, right? The articles said it's common." His eyebrows pinch together.

I nod. "It's a strategy I've been using for a while."

"Ah, I'm sorry, I must seem like such a precocious débile."

I shake my head. "I've never had a notebook for it that was this fun. It was very thoughtful. Thank you."

"I figured I owed you by now. I made a list of some other ideas the articles talked about, but I guess you probably know all these." He unfolds a piece of graph paper and hands it to me. He's written out a list of compensation techniques in small, neat print, like highlighting or circling key words in a problem to help me focus on them, something I've done since I was diagnosed in sixth grade, or reviewing the last learned skill before moving on to the next.

"Are any of them new to you?"

"A couple," I say. "Or it's more that I know them, but my teachers don't usually bother to do them." I decide I should spend a few minutes before each math class reviewing on my own. I want to show Kylian I can do this. I want to show myself I can do this. His generosity is making me feel like maybe I could.

He's brought us hot chocolates from a nearby American-style café in a little cardboard caddy, and I take mine and sip as he pulls a small paper bag from his backpack. "Croissants."

I laugh. "Is there anything else in your magic backpack?"

"No, sorry," he says, his smile lighting up his face. He opens his math book. "So, I thought maybe we could start at the beginning? And if it's too easy for you, then we can move on?"

"It's never too easy for me." I can't believe I just admitted this to him, but it's best to set the expectation bar as low as I can. The buttery croissant melts on my tongue, and I hope he doesn't see the flush I feel on my cheeks.

"Well, we've got a few months to get you ready for Le Bac. We'll make sure you pass with flying colors."

I shake my head.

"I mean it," he says. "I'm sure you can do it."

He sounds so sincere, but reality has settled back down on me. This is the part where I'm supposed to nod like I believe him. Still, it's not like he's expecting me to become an architect or a veterinarian or something meaningful. I just need to pass Le Bac, with a high enough score to make my parents not be too disappointed in me. I give him the obligatory nod.

"Alors," Kylian says, and turns his book so I can see it better.

I take a deep breath and we start.

We're slowly working our way through a session on estimating limits from graphs when a little girl around eleven years old comes up to us and stands beside the picnic table. A woman watches us from a nearby path.

"Would you like a photo?" I ask the girl.

A smile spreads across her face and she nods. Her blond ponytail swishes behind her. "S'il vous plaît, mademoiselle."

I return her smile. "You can call me Aurélie." I look over at Kylian. "Will you take the picture for us?"

"Yes, of course," he says. She unlocks the phone, which is probably her mom's, and hands it to him.

"What's your name?" I ask.

"Anna."

"Enchantée, Anna."

She giggles. I motion for her to sit beside me, and we pose for Kylian.

"Say 'differential,'" he says.

I groan. "Smile big," I tell her.

"Got it," Kylian says.

"Let's do another," I say, and make a peace sign, which Anna imitates. Then Kylian hands the phone to her.

"Anna, can I ask you for a favor?"

She nods. "Anything!"

"Would you wait to share that until this afternoon? I'm trying to study, and I don't want people to know I'm here right now or they won't let me get my homework done."

"Oh, yes," she says, "I promise." She crosses her heart.

I lean over and hug her. "Thank you so much!"

"You're my favorite person in the whole world!"

"That's very sweet, but I think your favorite person should be someone who takes really good care of you. Is that your maman?"

Anna nods.

"You have a wonderful day, and give your maman a big hug, okay?"

Anna's head bounces up and down so hard I'm not sure it

won't pop right off her neck. "Merci beaucoup, Aurélie!" she says, and runs off.

When I turn back to the books, Kylian is watching me.

"What?"

"Do people do this to you a lot?"

"All the time."

"That must feel so weird." He taps the eraser end of a pencil against his lips. "I could never deal with that. You were really sweet to her, though."

"It used to be easier. Before Remy and I became so famous. But the more famous we become, the more people want from us, and the harder it gets."

"Inverse proportions?"

I nod. "Wouldn't you ask your celebrity hero for a photo?"

He frowns. "That's not really a thing I have."

"Fair enough." I look past Kylian to the tall trees beyond. "I think most people do, though."

"I don't get it. I mean everyone is just a person. I get admiring someone for something they do well, but half the people who are celebrities don't even do anything that matters. At least, not in a good way. Private jets are really bad for carbon emissions."

"Well, Remy and I don't have private jets. In fact, he hates to fly, so at least that's one thing you don't need to dislike me for." But he's right. I don't do anything that matters much.

"I don't dislike you," Kylian says. He brings his gaze up from the table and lassos it onto mine. For a moment, it feels a little hard to breathe. "But I think you dislike me, especially since I have to keep apologizing."

I look away. "You just make my life a lot more complicated, and it's already complicated enough." I think about Remy. Everything with Remy is easy. It's just our celebrity lives that are too much.

He smiles. "You've definitely made my life more complicated, too."

I glance at him a moment, but I'm pretty sure that looking too long at Kylian is a bad idea. I pick my pencil up and, for once, I'm happy to hit my math homework.

Thirteen

My leg is bouncing under the table while I'm expecting Kylian to get frustrated with me like he did at Mamie's pâtisserie, but if he has any desire to beat his head against the table at how thick I am, he doesn't let me know it. I start to take more chances with my answers, and I hesitate less. But even when I get it wrong, Kylian doesn't show it if he's annoyed. It's just because he feels sorry for me, though, so I fake it as if I'm understanding, the way I've trained myself to do.

After the fourth time I fake it, Kylian challenges me. "I don't think you really got that."

I look up. "I do." The words are automatic. Dyscalculia has made me a habitual liar on this score. This isn't the first time someone's tried to help me, after all. Sooner or later, we reach the point where I just can't get it, and I end up feeling like the least intelligent person on the planet while the person trying to help me is so frustrated that they give up on me.

"I don't think so," he says. He doesn't say anything else. He just stares at the paper.

I take a deep breath. He's mad at me now. I hate this feeling. This is the part where I have to make someone else feel better about not being able to teach the unteachable.

"I get it," I say, "it's fine."

"Non."

"Non?"

"It's not fine." He flicks his blue gaze up to meet mine. "Why do you tell people it's fine when it's not?"

I shrug and look away.

"If you aren't going to be honest with me, then I can't help you."

Wow. He really knows how to push buttons.

I exhale. "Because, eventually, you're going to get mad because I can't understand and then I still won't understand, and you'll think I'm a total moron and I'll feel like one. It's easier for both of us if I just pretend."

"So you've spent your whole life letting people think you understand even when you don't?"

I nod, but I don't look at him.

"You can't do that with math. It's a building block. All the concepts are pieces in the architecture of the cosmos, and if some of the pieces aren't fitting properly, then your universe will have structural defects, so eventually it will collapse."

"Entropy," I say.

Kylian laughs. "Exactement. Entropy."

"But you're going to get frustrated with me. Some things I just can't understand. Especially calculus."

"Nonsense. Do you know what the great physicist Richard Feynman said about calculus?"

I shake my head.

"He said, 'Calculus is the language God talks.'"

It takes me a moment to answer Kylian because this seems way more profound than my little dyscalculia brain can process. "I don't really believe in God."

Kylian smiles. "You don't have to. That's not the point. The point is that calculus is the language of the universe. You believe in that, don't you?"

"Yes, of course I believe in the universe."

"And you believe that you are part of the universe?"

I nod, a little reluctantly. This feels like a trick question.

"Well then, math, calculus particularly, is your native language."

We just look at each other. How does this kid, this stranger, make me feel like I somehow belong in these spaces I've never belonged in before?

"I never thought about it that way."

"You must never have had a tutor who was a total math geek."

We smile at each other. "I suppose not."

"So, from here on out, you will tell me, no matter how many times we have to go over it, when you aren't understanding. It just means that I haven't explained it well."

I look at him.

"I'm serious," he says. "If you don't understand, then that's my fault, not yours. Everything about the universe is understandable, even if we haven't yet figured out all the ways it communicates to us."

I'm still taking all this in. No one has ever treated me this way. Why is he being so nice when he didn't even want to tutor me in the first place?

"Oui?"

"Oui," I say, and nod.

Kylian smiles, satisfied, and backtracks to the first place where I faked it as if I hadn't fooled him at all.

I pull the math book closer, willing my face not to flush. After a while, Kylian comes over to my side of the picnic table to better see the calculations I'm writing down. I glance around for papos, but I don't see anyone with cameras, or anyone even watching us.

At one point I get stuck and hesitate. I'm getting that feeling in my head like I just can't face this anymore.

"What's wrong?" Kylian asks.

I don't answer.

"Aurie, you have to tell me if you want me to help you."

I catch his gaze. I do want his help. I want it so desperately I could cry. I don't want to be the girl who is always looking in on a world run by math with no idea how any of it works.

"It's just . . ." I stop. How do I explain the way I feel? I don't even fully understand it.

"It's just what? You can tell me."

I rock a little bit, until I realize I'm doing it. Kylian takes my hand. "Breathe, and then tell me."

I take a deep breath. "So, this is going to sound made up and crazy, like I'm just being dramatic to get out of studying, but when I start to get overwhelmed with math, I get . . ."

"Get what?" he says when I hesitate again. "Afraid a ridiculously handsome math genius won't come to tutor you?"

I laugh.

"Seriously, tell me?"

So I do. It comes out all rushed and jumbled and messed up, but Kylian listens. He asks me questions no one has ever asked me, like where it feels that way, and what do I usually do when it happens, and I tell him about Aurie and the infamous train question, and when I'm finished I'm a little breathless.

"I haven't read anything about what you're describing, but I did read that math anxiety is a really powerful obstacle to people with dyscalculia," he says.

"I don't know how to get past it once it starts. I just shut down."

Kylian nods. "Maybe when that happens, you could acknowledge it and honor it, because anxiety is concern for ourselves, and then set it aside and think about your math problem as if it's a necklace that's gotten tangled. Something like your grandmother's necklace, something precious and worth saving. And little by little, you can unravel the tangles until it's all free. If a step doesn't make sense, then take a break, phone a friend, or whatever you need to do to clear your head, and then untangle that necklace."

I shake my head at him, but I'm smiling. "How did you get so wise about stuff like this?"

He laughs. "I've been in therapy since I lost my maman. Going to a hospital gives me anxiety now. Even the smell of disinfecting alcohol does. So, different trigger but same sort of problem. Only instead of my head feeling like it's shrinking up, I get nauseated."

I nod slowly.

"Do you think you can try again?"

"Yes." We start over. Very, very slowly the necklace starts to unravel.

We're just finishing up the lesson when my phone buzzes. It's my American granddad.

"I'm sorry," I tell Kylian, "I never don't answer my grand-dad." I guess I should be more that way with my dad, but I'm not. My grandfather would lecture me until I was twenty-five if I didn't take his call. Kylian motions for me to go ahead, but I take a deep breath because the chances of this getting awkward are statistically high enough that even I can guesstimate them.

I tap accept and the video of my granddad in his study in Marblehead, Massachusetts, pops onto my screen. "There's my doughnut!" he practically shouts when he sees my image. In my peripheral vision, I catch the smirk that darts across Kylian's face.

"Hi, Granddad, how are you?"

"I'm good. Just missing my little bean." He always uses nick-names for me that invoke New England's finest. He smooths his gray mustache even though it's always neatly trimmed. Then he squints at the screen. "Where are you?"

120

"In a park, studying for the Bac." I add this last part in the hope that he won't keep me too long if he knows I'm doing homework.

"Oh," he says. "You should just take the SATs. That's what the good universities here use."

"I need to pass the Bac to graduate high school, Grand-dad. And American universities take the Bac. And I took the SAT twice last fall." He knows all this, because I've explained it enough times that I sound like a commercial when I say it. What I haven't explained is that I did pretty badly on the math part of the SAT. I did well enough on the rest of it. But the math, not so much. It was like two different people took the exam.

"Oh, right," he says. His eyebrows collapse together. "Who's the fellow?"

Somehow Kylian has ended up in my video feed. I'm pretty sure I didn't accidentally let that happen. I angle my phone so my grandfather can see him better. "This is my tutor, Grand-dad, Kylian."

"Enchanté," my granddad says extra loudly and slowly, which is pretty much all the French he knows.

"Enchanté, monsieur," Kylian answers.

"So, is this a new boyfriend?" my granddad asks. "I thought you were dating that Apollo singer guy."

My face burns with the force of a rocket launch. "Kylian can speak Eng—"

"Did I tell you about the kid I met at Whole Foods the other day? O'Reilly, Patrick O'Reilly. He was stocking shelves in the oatmeal aisle. He's a freshman at Boston College—"

"Granddad, please say you did not give him my number?"

Kylian at this point isn't even trying to hide his smile.

"I'm telling you, Aurie, he'd be great for you! He wants to be a knee surgeon. I'm gonna need a good knee surgeon in a few years."

"Granddad, you cannot give my number to total strangers! Even if you want them to be your doctor someday."

"He's a nice boy, Aurie. He helped me find the oatmeal with the most fiber content. His grandparents belong to the rowing club where your dad used to crew, although I don't think I've ever met them. It's amazing what a small world it is, isn't it?"

"Remarkable, Granddad."

Kylian coughs.

"Do you want his number? I have it here." He starts rummaging through the papers on his desk. "And something he called Snapit. Hold on, maybe it was Snapback? It's one of the social sites." He waves his hand around to let me know that my generation is a bunch of weirdos, while he tries to pick up guys for me in a supermarket on a totally different continent by getting advice on fiber content. Beside me, Kylian looks away as he tries not to burst out laughing.

"No, Granddad, that's okay. Listen, I really need to get back to studying. Kylian is getting paid by the hour. But I'll call you later, okay? I love you!" Before he can answer, I send him a bunch of kisses and hang up.

"That was the best conversation I've ever eavesdropped on in my whole life."

I look around, expecting a papo to jump out of the bushes,

but there isn't one. For once there's no audience to canonize my humiliating moment on the internet.

I turn my gaze on Kylian and try to ignore how hot my face feels. "He really wants me to move back to the States. He thinks that if he gets me an American boyfriend, then I'll come."

Kylian nods, but he's not laughing anymore.

"What do you want?" He's watching me intently. So intently that my stomach flips a little.

"I don't know. I don't really fit in there anymore, but I've never fit in here, either."

"You speak French fluently, even if not like a native. You go to school here, have friends here, family. What do you mean you don't really fit in?"

"I mean exactly that. I speak French fluently, but not like a native. Because I'm not a native. I never will be. I'm someone who has family here. Someone who lives here. To my friends in Paris, I'm the American girl. In Boston, I'm Aurie, the French girl who visits her American dad. I live in both places, and neither is home."

"But you're a Paris celebrity!" He isn't even being sarcastic. I think.

"Yeah, that's kind of like being a Paris Original," I say, referencing the baseball hats they sell at the Eiffel Tower. One of which I do own and wear when I go back to Boston, but there's nothing authentically Parisienne about touristy baseball caps. Just like there's nothing authentically Parisienne about me.

"What about your boyfriend?" he asks.

"What do you mean?"

Kylian shrugs. "Sometimes people worry about absence not making the heart grow fonder."

Remy might not be my real boyfriend, but whenever we are apart, which isn't often, it feels like part of me is missing because we spend so much time together. But Remy has his dreams, and I have mine, even if I'm not really sure what mine are. I guess it's a good thing we aren't for real because sooner or later we're bound to be separated anyway.

"Remy and I are solid," I say. It's not a lie, just a bit mis-leading. "It's everyone else who wants me to be different than I really am." This, at least, is true.

Kylian purses his lips a moment. "Maybe you just need to look at it differently. Instead of one home, you have two. Home squared."

"Or instead of one home, I have two halves, with some missing shards where they're supposed to fit together." As soon as it's out of my mouth, I clamp my lips shut. Those are the kinds of things I think, not say out loud. Not to anyone. Not even Remy.

Kylian watches me.

"Sorry," I say. "I don't usually say things like this."

"I believe you," he says. "That sounded like a whole lot of pent-up frustration spilling out."

"Well, I'm sorry I spilled it all over you. It's not your problem."

"It's fine. Sometimes it's easier to tell people who don't really know us about the things that are eating us up inside." He smiles. "At least you're talking in fractions."

My gaze darts up. Catching his blue eyes is like catching a wave. Suddenly you're surfing and everything is somewhere else where you don't need to think about it. I kind of wish I could stay right here in this moment forever, and never have to think about any of it again. I return his smile.

Someone calls my name and I turn just in time for the flash of a paparazzo's camera to crash me down off that surfboard right back under the water.

Fourteen

The hum of Lille's office refrigerator is the only sound as she paces from the window to the sofa to her desk and back to the window. The carpet beneath her is ridiculously plush, but I still don't know how she manages this in stilettos. Not for as long as she does, anyway.

Remy and I sit there like students called into the principal's office. Again.

I swear he's starting to sit like all the bad boys in movies, laid-back and feigning indifference. It's honestly supercute. I sit there wondering which one of us will crack first.

"I could be writing songs now," Remy says, raising his eyes to Lille. There's a reason girls scream when they see him. I hope he never learns to believe they should. It would ruin the whole effect. For Remy, though, music is about music, not about scoring girls. I couldn't say the same about most of the other musicians I know.

Lille brings her hand up and quickly closes her fingertips together to tell him to shut up.

"I could be studying for Le Bac," I say to help him out.

Lille turns to me the way the interrogator in a spy movie turns to confront the mole. She even rests her fingers on her desk and leans toward us. I'm pretty sure this is where the sidekick we didn't trust to come along is supposed to break in and rescue us with a zip line he's somehow already installed from the window to a waiting van.

"And that is exactly why we are all here now. Do you think I have nothing better to do with my time than run interference for you two?" She taps a pile of contracts sitting on her desk.

Beside me, Remy is squirming as much as I am, even though this is all my fault.

"Look," Remy says, "this weekend was a total public relations disaster. We get that. But in those pictures from yesterday, there's nothing except the angle to suggest there was anything going on besides studying between Aurie and that Kylian kid." Remy can't quite bring himself to say just *Kylian*. "You can even see the books and calculator in it. They don't look like props, no matter how the shooter made it seem. And who has a date like that, even if they are trying to fool the papos?"

I nod hopefully.

Lille crosses her arms, not convinced.

"I don't know what I'm supposed to do," I say. "I can't study in private with him because people will think we are secretly making out. I can't study at the pâtisserie with him because people will think we might secretly be on a date even though my real—supposed, anyway—boyfriend is in the next room. And I can't study in a public park with him because we might be covering for the fact that we'd rather be somewhere else making out." I turn my palms up. "Where exactly are we supposed to study?"

"You need to study with him in public *with Remy there*," Lille snaps, while Remy asks, "You don't secretly want to make out with him, do you?"

"Remy was at the pâtisserie," I snap back at her.

"Where he tried to beat Kylian up!" Lille practically yells. "In front of a papo!"

Remy is still staring at me. "No," I answer him, and hope I'm more convincing to him than I am to myself, because honestly I'm not so sure.

"That was my fault," Remy says, satisfied enough that he turns to Lille.

"No, it was mine," I say.

Lille pinches the bridge of her nose a moment and then reaches into her drawer for her ibuprofen. She gulps down the off-white capsules and exhales.

"While I'm glad you two are so willing to accept the blame for one another, you are *both* responsible."

"I've been thinking," Remy says.

Lille and I look at him. Remy doesn't say things like that without having something monumental to add to the conversation. He's going to say we should fire Kylian, and I already know I don't want to. I was somehow understanding the stuff he was teaching me yesterday. Sometimes he had to try two or three, or more, different ways to explain it to me, but I did eventually get it. No one has ever bothered enough to get through to me before. He didn't have to take tutoring seriously, the way we practically blackmailed him into it. I just wish his eyes didn't have to be the color of a dream vacation destination. It makes me worry that math isn't the only reason I don't want him to stop tutoring me.

Remy reaches over and catches my fingers in his hand. "I think we should go all-in."

My mouth drops open. "You think what?"

"What exactly does that mean?" Lille says. The crease between her eyes deepens, but her head falls sideways. She's ready to grasp at any solution.

"I think we should go all-access. Aurie and I documenting everything, so there's nothing left for the paparazzi to find. If they don't have anything to scoop, then they'll back off."

Lille holds her chin as she contemplates this. "Like Chiara and Fedez," she says, referring to my thirteen-year-old self's idol and the musician she married. They went all-access before they even got married because it was better than being hounded by the paparazzi. But that meant their kids had to live in a spotlight they didn't even choose.

I jump up and start to bore my own path into Lille's expensive carpet. "It won't work."

"Why not?" Lille pivots toward me so quickly I don't know how she doesn't topple over in her stilts.

"I can't grant all-access. My mom and Armel would never

go for me filming anything at home that included my family, especially the TPs, which is totally fair. And school isn't going to let me film anything there, either. Plus, I wouldn't want to. Some of my classmates would act so weird if they thought it could get them famous."

"Okay," Remy says. "All-access except for your family and school. That's not what the tabloids care about anyway. They want to know about us."

"This could work," Lille says.

"But us isn't the us they think it is," I remind them. Maybe it would be easier if it were. I study Remy a moment, and it feels like I've suddenly seen something I shouldn't have. I turn to the window as my face heats up.

"Nobody needs to know that," Remy and Lille say together. They can't be serious.

"It's one thing to pretend to be boyfriend and girlfriend in public," I say, turning to face them. "It's another to pretend every minute we're together."

Remy gets up and helps himself to a water from Lille's fridge. "You want one?" he says as he turns to me. I nod.

"Lille?" he asks, but she shakes her head no, lost in thought. Or scheming, I should say.

Remy comes over and slips the cold glass bottle into my hand. I'm wearing booties with a heel today, and he still towers over me. When I look into his eyes, I see what I always see. A place that doesn't care whether I'm American or French. A place that isn't only looking at one half of me or the other. Remy sees all of me, even the parts he doesn't get. Remy and fashion vlogging have been the only places I've felt like I belong for as long as I can remember. Until yesterday, when Kylian started all that stuff about math being my native language in the universe. Maybe that was all a bunch of nonsense just to get me to trust him. I should look up that Feynman guy he talked about. But I did understand the math we did.

This is your fault. Lille doesn't say the words, but I hear them as if she did. Just like I always do.

Remy takes my hand. "We can make this work."

"Even movie night?" I don't want to share movie night with anyone outside of Mamie. Remy belongs to me. Like Thierry belongs to me. That's why my heart is ticking faster than it should be right now. There's so much on the line. I have to get this right.

Remy's smile reaches the grouchiest part of me. "Especially movie night. So easy."

"Kylian would have to agree to it if we're going to get the full effect," Lille says. "We need to be transparent about the tutoring."

Remy frowns.

I look at her and then back at Remy. "I really don't think he'll go for it."

Remy turns away from me. "Well, we'll have to work around him, then. Because this is our only chance to get control of this situation. We've tried protecting our privacy and they just keep coming for us." He sits down on the sofa and puts his elbows on his knees. He's wearing an Elton John T-shirt I found for him in Stockholm. Remy is lean, but his muscles tug at the old cotton. My heart melts a little. I want to make him happy. But this idea seems beyond impossible to pull off.

I take a breath. "The pressure has been way worse since we told them we were dating. Maybe instead of going all-in, we should have an amicable breakup? I just don't see how we're going to pull this off. We already live in a fishbowl." I take a swig of water. I haven't had nearly enough to drink today.

"They're never going to believe that now," Lille says. "Especially if you two continue to be best friends." She studies us a moment. "You two are still best friends, right?"

"Of course. What else would we be?" I ask. I can't imagine a world, my world, without Remy in it.

She shakes her head, dismissing whatever idea she was concocting.

Remy isn't saying anything. But I can tell from the way he crinkles his eyes that breaking up is the last thing he thinks we should do. This fake dating thing wasn't my idea, but I did agree to it. It wasn't his idea, either, for that matter. It's Lille I should blame. But I can see now how bad it will look if we suddenly break up, even if I don't ever see Kylian again. And I want to see Kylian again. I need to see Kylian again. He's my only chance to pass Le Bac. And for the first time, I'm starting to believe it might be possible. I just hope that's the only reason I feel so desperate about seeing him again.

Remy's beautiful eyes track me from the sofa. I walk over and sit beside him and sink into the citrus-and-amber scent of his Bleu de Chanel aftershave, as familiar to me as my own pillow. This will always be my favorite cologne because it will always make me think of him. I have to make this work. But I can't look at him when I answer.

"Okay," I say. "All-access."

Lille reacts to this news with an excessive amount of enthusiasm. So much so that, for better or worse, it raises my suspicions. She even claps her hands. She was barely this excited about the commercial Lancôme offered Remy and me when we announced our couple status. And Lille was really excited about that commercial because she's putting her double commission on a down payment for her dream Majorca vacation villa. A commission she'll get in a few weeks when we do the photo shoot.

"What?" she says when I contemplate her.

"You seem . . ." I search my brain for some vocabulary that belongs in books. "Exuberant," I say at last.

"It's a good decision," she says, but she turns toward the window as she says it.

"Lille?"

She turns back, her lips pressed into a pout.

"Lille?" Remy says.

She shrugs. "Your mother has me under a deadline." She spits the words out as if saying them fast enough might take away their meaning.

Of course she does. Me doing well on Le Bac is as important to my mother as my first steps or my first words. It's the promise of a life to come. And a goodbye to all my fashion influencer nonsense, as she calls it.

I let out a breath. My mom and I aren't completely at odds here.

"She just worries about you," Remy says.

"It bothers me that she and Armel can't acknowledge or appreciate what I've built for myself, but I get why she worries. I mean, I really do want to pass Le Bac and go to college."

"I know," Remy says.

For every successful teen influencer who transitions their celebrity into a real-world career, there are a flock of people who lose all relevance, or worse, become unrecognizable in a desperate attempt to stay relevant. And, if I'm being truthful, while fashion vlogging gave me an identity when I felt like I'd lost myself in every other way, I'm starting to feel like I've outgrown it. I mean, I still love fashion and being part of this world, but I want my life to be about more than just trending optics. If I said these words out loud, everyone in fashion would pull away in horror. Fashion, they'd inform me, is about self-expression and self-esteem. It's about creativity and being our best selves. Which is all true. But it's also about creating exclusivity. It's about creating a sense of enviable rarity, a dreamscape others can almost reach if they follow your lead, buy the same clothes, or live the same lifestyle, even though all of that costs more than most people will ever be able to spend and few of us will ever be as tall or as skinny as a runway model.

When I was younger, that sense of being able to get backstage in the fashion world, of belonging in it, seemed like everything to me. But now I see that the people on the inside aren't really any different than the people on the outside. Prettier and thinner, maybe, but still with the same insecurities and flaws and unfulfilled dreams, even if it's just to eat an entire pizza by themselves. There's something missing. I want my life to mean more. I want to make the world a better place. Remy's music does that. People cry at his ballads and dance like waves at his concerts. Kylian's school strike does that. Remy and Kylian are making the world a better place, while I'm just stalled. I want Le Bac. I want to pass and go to university, and I want to do something that matters. I don't know if that's possible, though, or if I'm just fooling myself. And I can't even tell Remy that because it would just add to the pressure he's already under.

Remy waves his hand in front of my face. "Earth to starship Aurie?"

"Sorry, what?" I dart my gaze from Remy to Lille.

Lille sits at her desk. "Are you fully on board with this? Because it's going to mean opening yourself up."

I slip my fingers under my thighs to stop squirming. "You mean about Le Bac?"

"I mean about everything," she says. What she means by everything is my disability, I think.

"What she means," Remy says, "is that people are going to be coming on the journey with you, and they're going to want to know when you succeed."

"Or fail," I say.

Remy shakes his head. "You aren't going to fail."

"You can't know that. Lots of people fail Le Bac."

He pulls my hand out from under me. "Lots of people aren't you."

I nod, but my face is doing that pressed-down thing where it's saying something completely different.

"It's a lot of pressure," I say, my voice not very loud. "If I don't pass, I'm going to lose a massive amount of credit with my followers. Success, at everything, is part of the dreamscape." I could lose my livelihood and college, all in one big bottom-of-the-ninth at bat.

Remy and Lille nod. I want to tell them what failing would mean to me, too, but I don't.

Remy strokes my head like I'm some pampered golden-doodle. "It's a lot of pressure, but I'm here for you now and after the results, whatever they are. We rise or fall together. But I really do believe it's going to be fine."

He's so beautiful. For the first time it hits me why. His face is ridiculously handsome, but he has an inner beauty that just flows out from him, like when sunlight hits a waterfall and makes a rainbow out of it. It's the reason everyone loves Remy without guardrails. I wonder how he can be this way after everything he's been through, and I promise myself I'll pass Le Bac because, on top of all the other reasons, I can't let Remy down.

"Okay," Lille says. "Our next step is to try to get Kylian on board. But, if not, we go ahead with all-access where we can."

"My mom is not going to be pleased," I say.

Lille shrugs her little pouty-face shrug. "No, but I don't think she will stop you, as long as you aren't putting anything out there that's damaging to you or that violates the family's privacy. And you can definitely spin it that getting the paparazzi off your trail enables you to concentrate more on Le Bac."

"I hope so." It seems like too much to ask from a bunch of vlogs, that they will appease my mom and keep the public at bay, but at this point it's all I've got to work with. I need to be studying, not running damage control every day.

Remy and I leave Lille and make our first all-access vlog when we get to his Vespa, which is parked by a tree.

"Do I look okay?" I ask before we start, showing him my face as if I'm looking in a mirror.

"Of course you look okay." But he dutifully tucks in a slip of hair that's gone astray and smooths one of my eyebrows with his calloused thumb. Then he hits record as I glom onto his other arm. It's hard to get us both centered in the shot since I'm not the usual height guys like him date, so he sits on his scooter while I stand close to him.

"Salut à tous," Remy says, and launches into an explanation of our new plan to give our fans more access. We leave out the part about doing this so the paparazzi will give us some peace, and make it sound like a gift we want to give everyone. It feels a bit narcissistic, but that's a feeling I had to come to terms with a long time ago. It's not really me, after all. It's radiant me. An image I create, the way a painter makes a self-portrait. Except I'm not trying to capture the real me, just some aspect of my unique style that translates into what my audience wants to see. No wonder my mother thinks what I do is messed up.

The words roll from Remy's mouth. He has a slight Toulousian accent that he gets from Mamie, who moved to Paris after high school. The beginnings of his words are soft, yet still formed enough to be a standardized Parisian accent. It's all part of his unique Remy St. Julien charm, another way he surprises and delights everyone he meets. Sometimes French sounds harsh or ridiculous to my American ear, but when Remy speaks it, I believe it's the most beautiful language in the world.

We're halfway through when a papo jumps out in front of us, camera poised.

"Remaurie, give us a kiss." It's Pierre Naillon, who has been everywhere we are lately.

Remy laughs and looks at his phone. "So, this guy who doesn't really know us wants to tell you the story of us," he says to his camera. "But we think we should be the ones telling our story."

Naillon hesitates and lowers his camera a moment.

Remy continues as if Naillon isn't there. "From now on, Aurie and I will be letting you have all-access to our lives, not just the scripted parts. Like right now. Let's meet this paparazzo." He smiles and turns his camera so that we're filming Naillon. The guy stares at us.

"What's your name?"

Remy's not giving an inch. He knows who Pierre Naillon is. Lille and Remy and I have studied his professional life like it was a school assignment.

Naillon shakes his head. "It's not important who I am." He shuffles on his feet. I doubt any celebrity has ever done this to him. He has a beard and spiky hair and wears a silver ring on his thumb. Lille's type if she were in a grunge mood. Sometimes I wonder if she's fully left her teen years.

"It's important to us," I say. "You've been following Remy and me as if you're with the Directorate-General for External Security or something."

"CIA," Remy adds in English for our American fans. Which, because of his accent, sounds like ceh-ee-ah.

"Pierre, isn't it?" I ask.

"Well," he says, and then doesn't add any more.

Remy laughs and turns the camera back to us. "I can see why you'd be more interested in us. He doesn't seem to want to tell his own secrets, just ours." He says it so good-naturedly that it makes Naillon look like a total crétin. Which he is.

"We'll do it for him," I add with a smile. "This is Pierre Naillon. He likes to follow us. Everywhere."

Naillon snaps another photo or two, but he's lost his edge. He turns suddenly and goes down the street as if he's caught sight of some other high-profile target and disappears around a corner. It's a good omen, maybe, for how this might work.

"Don't you want to ask about my Versace dress?" I call after him, but he doesn't turn around. "It's fit-and-flare silk!"

Remy laughs and turns the camera off for a moment. "That worked pretty well."

"Better than I expected. I wish we could do that to all of them."

"There's too many," Remy says. "We make a great team, though. We're good for all-access?"

"Full steam ahead." I'm still nervous about the whole thing, but I'm also out of decent options.

"This is going to work, Aur, I know it." He clicks his camera back on and pulls me close. "Listen, Aurie and I are headed to band practice. She comes pretty much every time, and now you can, too."

"I'm their unofficial manager," I add, "because I always tell them whether a song is working."

Remy laughs. "She's a very tough critic."

He has his arm around me, his hand on my hip, and I'm leaning into him. I look up at him and he kisses me. Not our usual kiss, which is a modified version of la bise for the papos when we say hello or goodbye to each other. A real kiss, his lips soft on mine, where they linger so long that I forget where we are.

Is he kissing me for show or for real? I'm not even sure if he still has the camera rolling. I'm suddenly not sure of anything, really. All I can think about is how soft his lips are and how he tastes like spearmint and how my stomach feels like waves crashing against the shore.

But the thing I'm most not sure about is why I find myself absolutely kissing him back.

Fifteen

When I come up for air, my eyes pop open. "What was that?"

"Now I have to edit that out," Remy says, tapping pause. His eyebrows contract. "Are you mad at me? I just thought it would be better access than what Pierre took. I should have checked with you first. I'm sorry. Honestly. I didn't mean to take advantage of the situation." He wipes his index finger across his lips as if he's trying to erase the kiss. He can't quite look at me, and I could swear his cheeks are flushed.

My face turns scarlet. I can't see it, but I sure can feel it.

"No, of course not," I say. "Why would I be mad? We were just putting on for the Remaurie Show."

So why is it so hard to breathe right now? It's like my dress has shrunk two sizes in the past ninety seconds.

I glance around the street, unable to look at Remy. What's he thinking? Surely he could tell I was kissing him back? For real? God, what is wrong with me? It's like my insides have instantly caught fire. I put my hand on my side to steady myself.

"I just, I wouldn't want my mom to see that," I say, looking down at my boots as I tilt my toes upward. "Me putting on a show like that," I add, to try to cover that I kissed him for real.

"Yeah, she doesn't like me as it is."

"She likes you." I'm probably lying. I'm honestly not sure what my mom thinks of Remy. She gets weirdly quiet whenever I talk too much about him. So I've stopped.

Remy gives me a soft little scoff.

"She doesn't *dislike* you," I say. That, maybe, is true. She is, however, absolutely thrilled with Kylian, ever since she grilled me after our tutoring session in the park the other day and I could explain about estimating limits from graphs like a reasonably informed person.

Remy shrugs, but it's not a defensive shrug. It's more a shrug of acceptance. My mom isn't going to easily accept anyone she thinks I'm dating, and especially not Remy, my coconspirator in fashion influencing.

"I'm going to be late for practice," he says without looking at me.

I nod and slip on my helmet. I think about asking him to drop me off at a Metro stop so I can just go home and pretend none of this happened, or more practically, do an internet search for the top ten destinations to become a hermit, but it's probably better to act like I always do and go to practice with him. Usually I work on our social media pages in case I have posts to schedule that I want to show him first.

Remy turns and kisses my nose and rests his helmeted forehead against mine. "I'll edit it out as if it never happened." He says this last bit so quietly and sweetly that it hits me exactly what he's saying. He knows I kissed him for real, and he's telling me it's okay but not to do it again. He just wants to be friends. Because that is, after all, what we are. It's amazing how you can talk to someone you know so well without ever using words to say what you mean. Sometimes we have whole conversations using just emoji. The fact that he tries so hard to reject me in a way he thinks won't hurt my feelings even more just makes it all seem as horrible as it could get. Rejection + Pity = Mortification^2. That's an equation I can understand.

He sits on the Vespa, still not looking at me.

"Merci." I squeeze out the word with the last bit of pride I still possess and hop on behind him before he sees how puddled my eyes are. It's the first day he's had the Vespa out since early November, and now it feels awkward to put my arms around him like I usually would.

Remy clears his throat and then closes his hand over the brake and pushes the start button, and the familiar putter of the little red Vespa starts to rumble beneath us. He turns his head so I can hear him. Even his profile is beautiful.

"Are you going to hold on or were you hoping to get swept off like a kite, since it's already a windy day?"

I laugh, but it's almost a cry because being swept away might not be so bad right now. Still, I need to at least try to pretend I don't know that he knows that I just kissed him as if we are really boyfriend and girlfriend, so I slip my arms around him. It feels so familiar because I've done it thousands of times, but it also feels weird and wrong because I've never done it after acting like such a complete loser.

I can't quite hold on as tightly as I usually would, though. Remy notices about halfway to the studio. He turns his head at a stoplight and asks me if everything is okay.

"Yes, of course." I plop my chin against his shoulder blade just like I did all last summer. I wish he didn't smell so good. Remy nods as the light turns green and pulls out onto the busy avenue. The studio is in Montmartre, and we dip and twist through the streets as Remy follows the path he knows so well. It's chilly on the Vespa, so I lean into him for warmth, but now I'm conscious of it. Remy dives into a parking spot in front of the studio and kicks down the stand. I hold on to his shoulders as I jump off because that's what I would have done before I threw myself at him like one of his desperate groupies. I move right into taking off my helmet, though, so I don't have to catch his green eyes studying me to figure out why I went all fangirl on him. But I can still feel his gaze as if I looked up to meet it.

I need to calm down. He kissed me first and I wasn't expecting it. That's all. I must have overreacted because of the surprise. No big deal, just a spur-of-the-moment reaction, which means absolutely nothing. It could have happened to anyone in that situation, best forgotten as if it never happened.

Besides, he's made it pretty clear that his kiss, no matter how scorching, was just another publicity stunt. I just don't get why he made it feel so real.

Remy hops off the bike and holds out his hand for me in case there are any stray cameras around. I slip my hand into his, the way I always do, and he strides into the studio while I practically skip along to keep up with him. The rest of the guys are here already. The rehearsal room is arranged with a drum set and piano, but the band brings their own guitars. Since Remy only has the Vespa, his bassist, Simon, brings a rehearsal guitar for him. Remy keeps the guitars he plays at gigs or recording sessions at home. Mamie has most of them displayed on the wall like fine art. Some of them belonged to his dad, but two of his dad's iconic guitars were lost in the plane crash that took his parents. Along with their other band members and manager. A group of people who had been like family to Remy growing up.

When I consider that he found out after it was in the news, it's not that surprising he would ask me to go all-in to fool the papos. Or that he would kiss me as if it were real to make that charade believable.

"Let's get started," Théo, the drummer, says. "I have a date with a girl from Mexico tonight." He grins and it makes his oval face seem longer. His spiky dirty blond hair and shadow beard make him look like a kid you'd see busking on the streets near the Eiffel Tower. Then he stops grinning. He looks from Remy to me. "Is everything okay with you two?"

"Of course," we both say, way too eagerly. Remy coughs and grabs his guitar from Simon. The guys exchange looks. They're all four or five years older than us, put together by the record label when they heard what Remy could do at thirteen. I try to think of anything that will get my face to cool off, but all I can think about is how kissing Remy St. Julien is nothing like kissing Jean Dalliere in seventh grade after the history decathlon, or Alain Archambault under the Eiffel Tower when I was fifteen.

I plop myself down on a sofa in a corner and whip my computer from my backpack to work on our social media feeds. Everything I consider posting, though, seems to suddenly have some double innuendo that I'm afraid will make Remy think I've abdicated my role as his best friend to become the president of his international fan club. Like the photo of Remy crooning into the mic that I take and then delete, or the selfie of my Versace dress that's as red as my lips, which still feel like they've been rubbed in paprika. So the only thing I post is a picture of a croissant from breakfast. Remy knows I only post pictures of food when I'm out of good ideas. But I have to post something.

I do some research for my #FridayFashionFauxPas hashtag, and then I switch to working on my French history homework to get my mind off what Remy must be thinking, but I end up doodling. I draw a picture of a heart and immediately scratch it out. Then I draw a hockey goalie in net, but I'm not very good at art and it mostly looks like something Camille would draw. Sometimes I stream American hockey, to feel closer to my dad. The Atlantic Ocean is a lot bigger when some of the people you love are on the other side of it. Most of my cousins, including the girls, play hockey because New England is all about hockey and doughnuts. It's a lot of fun when we're all together rooting for whichever team is cousined up, or when my dad and granddad and I go to the Bruins games and stuff ourselves with pretzels and nachos. Or when Remy comes with me on my twice-a-year New York Fashion Week trips, and we catch an Islanders game where hardly anyone recognizes us. When I watch hockey by myself, though, it usually just makes me feel farther away from my American family.

But I'm lucky. Remy would give anything for the privilege of calling his parents with the tap of a button. Even though they're gone, he still worries about letting them down. But his talent is so big he could never disappoint them. I don't really take after either of my parents. No matter what choice I make for college, I'll always have one foot in another world and be disappointing one side of my family. Maybe I should go to the States, before I get any crazier and seriously start to catch feelings for Remy.

"Aurie? Aurie, what do you think?" Remy says.

I shake my head to clear it. This is always what we do. One of them will ask what I think, and Théo will say I wasn't even listening, and then Max, who plays guitar and some piano when Remy doesn't play them, will tell Théo that I absolutely was paying attention and then they all insist I tell them what I think. It's as if they're afraid to veer from this playbook and lose the game, as if music is soccer and you have to follow superstitious rituals.

Today it takes me way too long to focus on what Remy is saying. When I finally realize they want my opinion, I sputter.

"It was good," I say.

Everyone except Remy shakes their head at me, wanting a real answer.

"Maybe Simon was a tiny bit ahead?" This isn't totally made-up. He does tend to do that, and it's possible I noticed it somewhere in the back of my mind. The front of my brain was totally consumed with the emotional chaos of trying not to think about kissing Remy St. Julien. My best friend. Someone who slurps the last of my milkshake if I don't finish it. Someone I've drooled on as we've slept in a heap on trains and planes. God, that's like kissing your cousin! What is wrong with me?

"I was not fast," Simon says, his eyebrows cinched as he glares in my direction.

"I don't know," Théo says, "I think you were." Simon wears beanies all year long and has tattoo sleeves. Mamie says he thinks he's an American, which she doesn't mean as a compliment. Max, second guitarist, has curly brown hair and speaks with a Czech accent because his family immigrated here when he was nine.

"Whatever," Remy says, "we've got five gigs next month and I need you guys to be ready. Let's do it again." He moves his hand in a circular motion to tell them to set up again.

They start the song over. It has a soft piano introduction before it builds. Remy does what he always does when he sings during practice: He focuses on me. He does it at concerts, too. I'll look up to see him searching for me until his eyes rest on me a moment longer than anywhere else. I'm his security blanket, and he's mine. At least, that's what we were until today. Now I don't know what we are. His eyes pinch together like he's wondering if I'm an alien inhabiting the real Aurie McGinley's body. I go back to scrolling on my computer as I try to keep my face from turning the color of a pomegranate.

I need to get ahold of myself before I completely blow my life apart.

When the band finally wraps up, they want to get something to eat, so I tell Remy to go ahead without me.

"Come with us," they all say. Max tugs at my sleeve to convince me.

"It's Tuesday," I say.

"Laundry day," Remy tells them. He turns to me. "I'll give you a ride."

"I can take the Metro. You should have dinner with the guys."

Remy shakes his head, but he seems to be stretching for nonchalance. "I'll eat at home later with Mamie."

The guys nod collectively as they glance at us, obviously trying to figure out what's up while they pretend not to be looking at all.

They pack up their gear and we all head out. I'm afraid Remy's going to say something once we're alone, like *Hey, sorry I gave you the wrong impression earlier, but I just want to be clear that we're only ever going to be friends.* I try to act normal as we walk to the Vespa, but I feel so weird I don't know how he doesn't see it. My palms are sweaty, and my heart feels like it might leap out of my chest and take off running down the street. But he doesn't say anything. At least I don't have that humiliation to deal with.

We climb onto the bike, and I make sure to hold on to him the way I always do. Tightly. I rest my chin on his shoulder, watching the street coming at me as if it's a carnival ride. I'm never scared when Remy drives. He knows what an accident can cost better than most people.

We don't really talk on the way home. Rush hour traffic has died down and it's after seven when he pulls up in front of my house. He cuts the engine, but he doesn't get up. I slide off and hand him my helmet.

"I'll text you later?" he says.

I nod.

"You can give me an update on whether the tiger pajamas with the holes in the toe made it through another wash." He smiles. Thierry has a passion for those worn-out PJs that most supermodels can't inspire in a man. My mom keeps telling him they don't fit, but then he starts to scream like Camille so she lets him wear them "one more time."

"Sooner or later, my mom is going to make them disappear."

Remy grimaces. "I hope it's not on a school night because you will not be getting any sleep when she pulls that trigger."

I laugh. "Thanks for the ride."

"Absolument. À demain." He pulls me in and gives me la bise. A little more tenderly than usual, it seems. Because Remy wouldn't ever intentionally hurt my feelings, and he wants me to know that.

I nod and turn up the sidewalk to my house as the Vespa revs Remy back to Le Haut Marais.

Sixteen

I expect the house to be in the full chaos of cleaning up dinner and laundry night, complete with an ongoing chase over the tiger pajamas, but it's eerily quiet. This isn't good. It means my mother is upset with me and Armel has conveniently disappeared with the TPs to the rare treat of a restaurant. Well, it won't be a treat for Armel, but the TPs will be in all their glory. So much that I feel sorry for him. Armel's not a bad guy. He's just not someone I'm particularly close to. It's like we orbit one another's lives, each of us trying to give the other some respectful distance.

"You're late," Maman says, her voice coming out of the dusky living room. She's watched too many film noirs.

I drop my backpack and take a deep breath as I walk in and sit down across from her.

"Remy's practice ran a bit late. They're getting ready for some shows next month."

My mother's head moves but the rest of her face stays frozen.

I hesitate between trying to beat her to the punch by apologizing for whatever it is I've done this time and deciding to wait her out. I honestly don't know why she's mad at me. I haven't done anything lately. Aside from fake dating my best friend and kissing him for real like I was auditioning for a bachelorette show. But my maman doesn't know any of that. Unless there's been a tabloid report I don't know about.

She slides her phone from the coffee table and pulls something up. Then she flashes it at me. I squint in the dim light. Why do parents always have their phones so bright?

My eyes focus. It's a social media post with a photo of me locking my lips on Remy St. Julien's as if I just won a contest for most obsessed fan on the planet. No, make that the universe. Remy wasn't the only one filming us, apparently.

The room may be practically dark, but I could swear my face has just illuminated it like the Stade de France during a World Cup night game.

"I can explain," I say. Although, really, I can't. Not even to myself.

My mother exhales. "Aurie, I understand that you like Remy. He's very handsome and can be very charming. And he's always been kind to you."

"He is, Maman, he's always looking out for me." I like it when I don't have to lie to her, but I don't like that I have to defend him. Remy didn't get me interested in fashion vlogging. It's not his fault I became an influencer.

My mother's eyebrows constrict. It isn't enough to make her like Remy.

"However," she says, "photos like this are forever."

She stares at me, her lips pressed together, like she's a statue.

"I'm sorry. We just got caught up. It wasn't as . . . bad as it seems." Correction, I just got caught up. Remy wasn't any happier about the situation than my mother is. For just a moment, I think about coming clean to her. I so much want to tell her everything and have her say it will all be okay. And that I'm not a bad person, and that I haven't just ruined the best friendship I've ever had. I want to tell her how scared I am, about letting her down, letting Remy down, letting Lille down, letting Dad down. The list goes on, but it ends with letting myself down.

"If you're going to chase celebrity, then you can't afford to get caught up in the moment, Aurie. You chose this. I'm not a stage mother insisting you become rich and famous."

I nod, but I don't raise my eyes to meet her gaze.

"I know, Maman. You don't want me to be an influencer. I won't kiss Remy like that again." There's a small pang that goes with this, and it makes me angry with myself. I should be disgusted by kissing Remy, but instead I'm remembering how impossibly wonderful his lips were. I shouldn't feel sorry for myself that our kiss meant nothing to him. I should be glad.

Ridiculous teenage hormones.

"I hope not," my mom says. "You're seventeen years old, Aurie. I can't make your choices for you. I couldn't even do that when you started all this at thirteen. But how are your teachers, your fellow students at university, or the graduate schools you'll apply to supposed to take you seriously when your biggest goal in life is to be seen in a pretty dress kissing a pretty boy?"

Ouch, that stung. I'd like to remind her that it was me who made vintage brooches the rage of Fashion Week last fall, but she wouldn't be impressed anyway.

"You're being unfair, Maman. I got caught up kissing my boyfriend. It's not like I was doing anything so wrong." Okay, well, not theoretically, if you don't include all the lies.

"Aurie, women may be able to rise to the highest offices now, but that doesn't mean that we don't have to battle every day to be taken seriously as intelligent, capable leaders. You can't act like a pop star and expect to be respected when it counts."

I think that was a dig at Lille, but I'm not entirely sure. Lille is pretty professional, aside from when she acts like my friend rather than my manager. But my mother thinks Lille is a little too good at keeping my influencer status climbing with some of her shenanigans.

"Maman, I know you've faced a lot of barriers in your career because you're a woman, but I don't think I'll be blacklisted at law schools because of a silly picture of me kissing my boy-friend at seventeen."

My mother raises her eyebrows and shows me her phone. Okay, the photo does look pretty ludicrous. Tomorrow there will be memes with a steam cloud over our heads and people writing captions like *Aurie McGinley tries to show the world that Remy St. Julien belongs to her* or *Aurie McGinley tongue-wrestles Remy St. Julien to the ground.* God, this is so bad. But I can't help wondering if she would be this upset if she liked Remy. Like if boy-math-genius Kylian were in this photo in-stead of Remy, would she care this much?

"Would you be this upset if you liked Remy more?"

My mom pulls away a little. She hesitates, the way she does when she's weighing her words carefully. She's always a lawyer, even when she fights.

"I don't dislike Remy," she says.

Right.

"I just think he distracts you from the things that matter."

I nod slowly. "Like school, and math."

"You can't spend your life as a fashion vlogger, Aurie!"

No, of course not. Because the thing that I'm seriously good at isn't good enough for my mother. Never mind that I've got a worldwide following or that brands come to me to make their image sell. I get this isn't something that changes the world for the better, but it's not nothing, either.

"Chiara Ferragni has."

My mother exhales hard. "And is that the life you really want? Having to orchestrate every single day of your life around a camera so that the paparazzi don't find a scoop? Not even being able to have a disagreement with your partner because it will become front-page news? Having to share every private moment with a worldwide audience?"

I drop my gaze from hers. She's right. The more Remy and I live in this fishbowl, the less I'm liking it. But I don't really have a way out. Not without letting Remy and Lille and maybe even myself down. It seems like no matter what I do with my future, someone is losing because of me.

I stand up. "Well, you don't have to worry about me getting caught kissing Remy again." I turn to go to my room.

"Did you and Remy break up? Is something wrong?" This time, there's genuine concern in her voice.

I turn back and shake my head. "No, Maman, we didn't break up. I just promise you that I won't be kissing him again." I should add *in public,* but I don't. My mother studies me.

"You're sure nothing has happened?"

I look her in the eyes to try to convince her.

"I have homework to do." I hesitate for just a moment in case she's going to keep harping at me, but she doesn't. I grab my book bag and climb the stairs to my room. It's in the back of the house on the third floor. I like it because it still has the original door and windows from when the house was built. It reminds me of being at Remy's, cozy and bright, with almost lemony walls and a white painted canopy bed.

I drop my bag on the floor, but I don't sink into my unfinished math homework like I should. I need to create content for tomorrow's vlog first. It's my fashion history day of the week, where I recite some anecdote from the annals of fashion lore, so I dig around on the internet looking for material. It doesn't take too long before I choose how Alexandra, Princess of Wales, made a fad of choker necklaces in the 1860s when she wore them to cover up a scar on her neck. In fact, she was such a style icon that women would wear mismatched shoes to imitate the limp she developed after a bout with rheumatic fever. I still need two more post ideas when Armel and the TPs come home. The house bursts with sound for about an hour until they are finally all in bed. I putter around taking makeup off and changing my clothes. I haven't returned

Remy's a-ha T-shirt yet. I hold it for a moment, but I don't put it on. Somehow everything has shifted, and nothing feels right anymore. I slip on an old graphic soda company T-shirt instead and finally settle down to do my math, but I'm as lost now as I was at the studio. Normally I'd FaceTime with Remy and have him walk me through the problems while I pretended to understand them. But that no longer feels like an option.

I text Kylian instead and ask him if he has time to help me. He answers quickly. *Video chat?*

Sure.

My phone lights up as he calls. Before I can even answer it, Remy is calling me, too. I see the two calls competing, and my thumb hovers over them.

Math is what I should be focusing on. Not on Remy and how I've messed things up. There's nothing I can do about that now beyond pretending I didn't kiss him back for real. But I can still pass Le Bac. I can still get into a decent college and make my parents happy. Our fans would be happy, too. And who knows? Maybe then I could find a way out of this suffocating glass box I'm sitting in. I tap decline on Remy's call and pick up the video chat with Kylian.

Seventeen

'm in my second class of the day, philosophy, when my phone vibrates incessantly, which means it's Lille texting or calling. We aren't allowed to have our phones out at school, even on our breaks, so I do my best to ignore the slight humming that comes from my Burberry backpack as regularly as Lille double-parks. Lille knows this rule, but like anything else she finds inconvenient, it doesn't stop her.

No matter how much I try to concentrate on Proust, though, her insistence on reaching me when I'm at school can only mean that she's seen the photos of me kissing Remy as if I'm some desperate contestant on a reality dating show.

I dread dealing with her. It was bad enough last night when I had to face my mom. And I still feel guilty about choosing math and Kylian over Remy. I can't put off facing Remy forever. But even without talking to Lille, I hear every word she wants to say to me.

Aurie, what the hell is going on in these photos?

I wish I knew, Lille.

Aurie, if you're thinking of catching feelings for Remy, then you'd better think again because you're going to ruin everything for us.

Yes, Lille, I get it. Us.

And I mean EVERYTHING.

My philosophy teacher breaks up our imaginary conversation just before I start to cry. "Aurélie, are you with us?"

"Oui, Madame, je suis désolée." I blink back the swimming in my eyes and try to shut out the whispers from my classmates that I must be thinking about kissing Remy as if I'm devouring my favorite gâteau au chocolat.

The only bright spot in my morning is when I turn in my math homework, and it's truly been done by me. Well, with guidance. Kylian doesn't just give me answers like my other tutors and friends have done. He forces me to backtrack when I make mistakes and figure out where I went wrong. It's a painstaking and super-frustrating process, but he hasn't complained, even when I have. He's even put some fun into it, inventing stories about the equations to help me remember them better. They're like the stories that ancient societies told about the stars, except Kylian's variable heroes are traversing the universe to save it from greedy and obnoxious people. He doesn't tell me directly that those people are mostly celebrities, but it's definitely what he means. I don't know, maybe he's right. Celebrities do take too many private jet rides and spend way too much on designer handbags.

When I get to my locker at lunch period, the alarm on my phone goes off and it hits me that I'm supposed to be leaving now for the Lancôme shoot. I forgot all about it in the misery of my public display of inappropriate affection. Remy and I are contracted to shoot a major international ad campaign while pretending to be the perfect couple. Great.

Normally I'd be celebrating an afternoon off school, but I'm pretty sure this day is only going to get worse. When I unlock my phone, it takes at least a minute to get through Lille's onslaught of frantic texts and messages, which, not surprisingly, all sound like the conversation I invented for us in my head. She's also been drilling into Remy's day apparently, as I have multiple messages from him asking me if everything is okay.

Way to make things even worse for me, Lille. Thanks a bunch.

Remy's last message says he'll pick me up at school, as Lille is going to meet us at the shoot. It's at a photography studio in La Défense, the commercial district in Paris, which is a neighborhood that looks more like Wall Street than what people think of when they imagine Paris's cute little cafés and crooked old houses on cobblestone streets.

I pack up the books I'll need for my homework tonight and head to the school office to sign out. The principal wasn't any more happy about me missing afternoon classes than my mother was, so I had to promise not only to make up the work I'd miss but also do extra credit. People glide past me in the hallways with more than a couple of side-eyes thrown my way. One guy I don't really like tells another, "If I had known she could kiss like that, I'd have gone for her the first day of premiere."

As if. I shake my head and keep walking, while the second boy giggles like this is middle school.

When I get outside, Remy is just pulling up to the curb. I

run down the steps, and he hands me my helmet. The bright midday sun makes me squint.

"Are you sure everything is okay?" he asks, without saying salut. He pecks me tenderly on the cheek for any invested observers.

"Of course," I answer as I hop onto the Vespa behind him. I haven't told him about the grilling I got from my mother over our kiss. Correction, my kiss. But I saw plenty of the memes that exploded all over the internet. As expected, they all centered on me as the girl in the relationship. Remy can kiss in public any way he wants with his automatic guy pass.

"Why didn't you answer my call last night?" Remy asks.

"I was working on my math homework."

Remy's face is turned so that he can just catch my expression. "You did it by yourself?"

It's hard not to squirm. "No, Kylian helped me. Over video chat."

Remy turns around. I think I've hurt his feelings. He should be relieved not to have the burden of helping me anymore, but instead he gets quiet. I slip my arms around him, maybe a little too tightly to make sure I'm doing enough, and he pulls the Vespa into the stream of traffic.

We don't talk on the way to the shoot, we don't point out interesting people or comment on everything from the traffic to the latest hot spots we pass. We don't make our endless inside jokes. The ride takes longer than it should, or really it's just that my time with Remy now drags along like a Segway with a dying battery instead of a supersonic jet.

When we finally get to the studio, Lille is talking with the photographer, Roberto Santilli, to make sure his setup is what was laid out in the contracts. Santilli is a big score. Lancôme must want this ad to do really well internationally, which is perfect for getting people interested in Remy's music. Lille's right, there's a lot riding on this. As soon as Lille spots us, her gaze is glued to me. Thankfully the stylists come to get us before she has a chance to start her interrogation. She still manages to mouth "What is up with you?" as I go by, though.

I shake my head as innocently as I dare and follow the stylist to my dressing room. Lancôme often partners with up-and-coming fashion designers for their ad campaigns. For this one they've chosen a relatively new British designer, Dani Meadows. There are several dresses for the stylist to choose from, and the fashion house has sent a seamstress in case any last-minute alterations are necessary. But first I'm popped into the makeup chair, where one of Paris's reigning salon masters styles my hair, and then a makeup artist as famous as her clients decides how my face will look. When she's done, I barely recognize myself. I look like I'm closing in on my midtwenties instead of seventeen. My nose is skinnier and my cheekbones are higher. My mother is going to hate this shoot. I take a deep breath, but it feels like all of Paris is hounding me, crushing me. No matter what I achieve, everyone always wants me to be something else, something more, something they imagine rather than the real me.

"Photographer wants precheck," a young guy says, darting his head into my dressing room without knocking. I slide out of the chair and follow him down the hallway.

The studio has some natural light, manipulated by blackout curtains on remote control. There are soft boxes and umbrella lighting, as well as setups that mimic daylight, placed at various angles for Santilli to choose from. Remy is already there, leaning against a table off the staging area. He's looking down at his phone, but the screen isn't lit. When the photographer says my name, Remy looks up, his gaze searching until he finds me.

I try to send him a goofy smile, the way I always would, but it feels off, and it's almost like he doesn't even recognize me for a second. Then his mouth softens to a slight smile.

Lille comes marching over from the coffee and pastries table, but the photographer is already directing us to the positions he wants to check. We don't have to do anything except stand there, and sometimes turn while he decides if the lighting is right for the look he wants. We'd normally banter, but today we just follow directions like good little robots.

Then we're swept back to wardrobe. The next time I see Remy, he's looking pretty otherworldly in a Raf Simons suit that's been tailored to exaggerate every detail of his guitar-shredding muscles. It captures an element of indie rock grunge while also making him look like he's just about to step out on a runway.

"Don't forget to breathe," Lille whispers in my ear dryly. I turn to look at her. Okay, it's possible I forgot she was even here for just a second.

I shrug. "He looks nice." I sound pretty nonchalant, but she's right, it is a little hard to breathe. There's something seriously wrong with me. But it's just because I made such a fool of myself.

"Mmm," she says, narrowing her eyes at me.

"Aurélie," the photographer's assistant says, saving me from any further cross-examination, "we need you here next to Remy."

I nod and comply.

"You look . . . ," Remy starts.

"Not at all like me?" They have me in a strapless green velvet dress with a golden-age-of-Hollywood vibe, sophisticated and hot without showing anything. My mother has Lille under strict orders not to put me in any outfit that's too revealing.

"I was going to say beautiful, but not really like you."

So I'm not normally beautiful to him. Check.

He's studying me. I turn my gaze to Santilli. He walks over and poses us, checking the result in his camera as he goes. He puts Remy's arm around my waist and tells him to gaze down at me. I'm instructed to look into the camera "as if it's the sexiest man alive." I'm so glad my mom isn't here, although my cheeks are burning anyway with Remy pressed up against me.

The rest of the shoot goes pretty much the same way. Remy is supposed to smile at me as if he's thinking "about what happens next" while I gaze at the camera with "the pent-up passion of a girl in a nunnery."

Remy and I have had shoots together before, but they were lighthearted when the world only suspected we might be more than friends. Now everything is awkward and tense and way too suggestive. By the time we get to the shots where Remy and I are supposed to be gazing into each other's eyes, I'm so nervous my hands are clammy as I clutch the sleeves of his jacket.

"Okay, Aurélie, laugh as if Remy has just told you the most

wonderful news in the world," Santilli says. He speaks French with an Italian accent. Click, click, click. The camera is beating faster than my heart.

"Okay, Remy, kiss her," Santilli says, constantly moving around us like a mini-hurricane.

Remy grimaces.

Now would be a really good time to fake my own death and go live on an uninhabited island somewhere in the South Pacific.

"Come on," Santilli says, "time is money!"

"Sorry," Remy whispers, and very gently places his lips on mine.

"No, no!" Santilli says, "Like you kissed her in that viral photo a few days ago."

Remy pulls away from me. "I don't think that's a good idea." He says it quietly as he looks the photographer in the eye.

Santilli stops and lowers his camera. His bald head shines in the studio light. "What do you mean? She's your girlfriend. Just kiss her like you kiss her when no one is watching."

Oh boy.

"My mom's not going to go for that," I say, my voice shaky. For the first time in my life, I'm super-grateful for how overprotective my mother is. The last thing I need is a repeat of kissing Remy St. Julien. I'm not sure I wouldn't get caught up all over again. Or else I'd be so stressed that the whole thing would look staged and fake. There's no middle ground anymore. It's like my heart and I are on those separate roller coasters that race each other.

Santilli's eyes are almost as wide as his camera lens. "I'm sorry, what did you say?"

Remy steps forward and in front of me. "She said her mom isn't going to let her take the kind of photos you want of us kissing."

Santilli stares at Remy.

Yep. Faking my own death and vanishing from society is definitely my best option at this point. And then Lille intervenes.

"There's nothing in the contracts about them making out for the cameras," she says, with so much nonchalance it seems like a ridiculous ask in the first place. I could seriously kiss her right now, even though she's just doing it to keep my mom happy.

Santilli turns to her. They face off for a moment or two, and then Santilli breaks. Lille eventually breaks everyone except the guys she dates. "Okay, we'll go for an innocent kiss, something subtle and sensuous."

Remy turns, questioning me with just his raised eyebrows. I nod.

The next thing I know, Remy St. Julien, my best friend, is brushing his lips against mine as tenderly as you'd pet a kitten you didn't want to frighten away, and for more than a moment it feels like everyone around us has completely disappeared.

Eighteen

Whatever grace Lille was giving me before the shoot started is over as soon as I get back to my dressing room. I'm still washing my face at a small sink when she clicks her heels into the room. The hairdresser and makeup artist have left, but the stylist is standing by to help me undress. She's not that much older than me, but she seems closer in adultness to Lille. She unhooks a gold necklace they've had me in while I take out some diamond earrings and hand them to her.

"You may go," Lille says to her. The young woman nods as she grabs the boxes for the jewelry and leaves.

I think Lille's about to launch into me when she says, "Wait a minute."

She disappears, so I struggle out of a sequined bodycon dress I wore for the last segment of the campaign and slip on the Amiri T-shirt-style top and midi skirt I wore to school. I'm barefoot and my hair is still ultra-coiffed, but otherwise I'm almost me when Lille returns with Remy. He looks a little sheep-ish. I have the sudden urge to yell "You're fired!" at Lille. The last thing I need right now is her riding me about acting weird around him.

The hallway is quiet. Everyone has cleared out already, except apparently the photographer's assistant, who must be packing up the lighting equipment based on the muffled thumps that come from the studio.

"What the hell was going on out there?" Lille says. She's wearing a crisp lilac suit and her nails are painted a complementary teal, which I notice when she crosses her arms.

Remy and I mumble replies about not knowing what she means. I'm not sure if he looks at me, because I can't bring myself to look at him. This is so weird. Usually when Lille yells at us, we're in it together as coconspirators.

"Look," she says with the intensity of a drill sergeant, "you are my two biggest talents, and I need you to be in sync with each other. That doesn't seem to be happening right now." She frowns and it somehow ends up feeling like weights pressing on my chest.

"We're fine," Remy says. He turns to me. "We're fine, right?"

"Of course we are." Even I don't believe me.

"See, we're fine," Remy says as he turns back to her.

Lille slams her hand down on the makeup counter, which makes the little bottles rattle a bit and me cringe. "That," she says, pointing toward the studio side of the building, "was not fine!"

"Santilli seemed happy; the Lancôme rep seemed happy," I say, but it's hard to sound convincing when I know she's right.

Lille just stares at us. "The photos will suffice, but whatever is going on with you two needs to stop." She wags her finger between us for emphasis.

Remy shrugs and I turn away.

"See! This! What is this? And neither of you has made fun of me in days!"

I glance back at Remy. Do we really make fun of Lille that much? We should work on that. As for the rest of it, I don't even know where to start.

Remy loosens his green tie and pulls it slowly from his neck. It's past seven. They brought in dinner for us, but we barely had time to eat it. "You get mad when we make fun of you."

"Stop changing the subject," Lille says, spinning toward him as she paces. "You two haven't been normal since those very real-looking photos of you kissing outside my building surfaced. What is going on?"

My cheeks burn. I still have tutoring and homework to get through, and there's the dull thud of a headache banging around the backs of my eyes. Maybe I should just confess and get it all over with. It's not like Remy doesn't know already that I got sucked in. But if keeping my maybe-feelings for him secret can cause this much havoc to our friendship, then I don't want to know what confessing would do. Besides, whatever I feel is probably temporary. Or imagined. I honestly have no idea what I'm feeling. All I know is that now when Remy stands close to me, it's as if someone stole all the breath from my body. He's just a boy. The same boy I watch get yelled at by his mamie every Friday night when he forgets to take out the trash. The same boy I fall asleep on when we watch K-roms. But he's not just that boy anymore. He's also the boy who kisses like it's an Olympic event he's been training for his whole life. Where did he even learn to kiss like that? Is that like playing the guitar? It just comes naturally to him? Because that cannot be how good it is to kiss someone usually. The few kisses I've had before don't even compare. I just wish everything could go back to the way it was. I wish I could go back to the way I was. Before that impossible kiss.

"It's just that I improvised that kiss, and I made Aurie uncomfortable because of it. This is all my fault."

I can't believe he's covering for me like this. Actually, I can, because Remy has looked out for me from day one. I don't deserve him.

Lille studies us, then takes a turn around the room, heels clicking lightly on the laminate flooring. "Non."

"Non?" I ask.

She shakes her head. "Non. There's more to it than that." Her gaze zeroes in on me. "And I think it's all centered on you, Aurie."

She stops in front of me. I sidestep her and cross the room toward the door to pick up my backpack, but really to get farther away from the intensity of her gaze. It's totally creeping me out. Lille says her great-grandmother was a resistance fighter in World War II. If she was anything like Lille, I believe it.

"Aurie, have you changed your mind about this fake dating thing?" she asks.

I don't turn around. "I don't know what you mean." Did she really just ask me that in front of Remy? Since when is Lille harder on me than my mom is?

"You need to be honest with us, because we all have too much riding on this for you to keep secrets. Do you wish you were dating Remy for real?"

My eyes are stinging and it's hard to breathe. "Of course not!" I spin around to face them. Remy's cheeks are ashen. "I, I mean, it's something else," I say, in a sad attempt to buy enough time to invent a plausible excuse for myself.

"Like what?" Lille presses me. "Because it seems to me like you're falling for Remy."

I laugh. Or at least, I try to. It sounds more like a maniacal hamster having the hiccups. Why is she doing this? She's supposed to be on my side.

"Aurie, you don't have to—" Remy starts, and that's when I snap. I can't handle any more pity from him.

"I'm dating Kylian," I blurt out. "I just didn't know how to tell you guys. But I'm dating Kylian."

Did I seriously just say that? What is wrong with me? That's not a lie I can even sustain. But it's all I could come up with under Lille's relentless cross-examination. I could never be a criminal.

Their jaws drop, and neither of them says anything. Maybe I can say it's a joke. Then they'll believe that I'm just being regular, goofy me and Lille will drop this whole microscopic exploration of my heart. A joke might throw them off the scent and make them as unsure of what goes on in my head as I am. I open my mouth to insist it's all a prank, but Lille and Remy aren't looking at me. They're looking past me.

I turn around.

Kylian is standing in the doorway, staring at me.

Nineteen

Kylian gives us a small, lopsided smile. "Lille told me to meet you guys here, to save time."

"Oh, that's right, I did," Lille says, kind of absent-mindedly, which is very un-Lille. She's staring at Kylian and me as if we're strange sea creatures washed up with the tide.

Remy's frowning. The last time I saw him frown like this, he walked out of a gig after a concert promoter tried to cheat him.

Still, if Kylian didn't hear me, this is salvageable. I can tell Lille and Remy later that I was joking. As long as neither of them says anything weird in front of Kylian, I might get out of this with a little bit of dignity.

Kylian steps forward and drapes his arm over my shoulder. So much for my he-didn't-hear-me theory. I bite my lip. He must be pranking me, getting ready to ask what the hell I'm talking about in front of Lille and Remy.

"So, you told them about us, huh?"

I stare at him. He sounds completely serious.

He smiles. "It's okay, they were going to figure it out sooner or later." He glances at Remy and shrugs a little. I don't know why they antagonize each other so much. They actually have a lot in common, like being good at math and caring about other people and dead parents.

"I guess so," I say.

Lille and Remy look like they've just witnessed a car accident. Maybe they have. Why is Kylian playing along with this?

Remy clears his throat. "When, uh, when did this all happen?"

If my heart were beating any faster, it could outrun a jet taking off.

"Just yesterday," I say at the same time Kylian says, "A couple of days ago."

We look at each other. Then we each mumble something about the other one being right. We don't seem very convincing.

"Well, I mean, we talked about it the other day," Kylian says, "but it wasn't official until yesterday." He's much better at this than I am.

I nod.

Remy narrows his eyes. "What's going on, Aur?"

"It just sort of happened." My voice is squeaky. Remy and Lille are never going to believe Kylian and I are a thing.

Instead of being suspicious, though, Lille is immediately taken with strategizing the situation. She's apparently gotten so used to dealing with my messes lately that damage control mode is the first reaction she has now.

"How on earth do you two think this could work?" she

asks. "I mean, you can't ever be seen together like that." She flails an arm in our direction. Her eyes dart to the windows, but we're seventeen floors up and the curtains are still drawn from when I was changing.

"I hadn't thought of that," I say. "It's nothing serious. I mean, really, it's nothing."

Kylian and Remy are studying me. Why do I keep making things worse?

"It seems like something," Remy says, so quietly that I would wonder if he'd actually said it, except that when I look in his eyes, I know he did.

"Lille, you said you had a place for us to have our sessions?" Kylian asks. The tension in the room shifts, but it doesn't go away.

"Yes, there's a conference room down the hall they said we could use. Follow me."

We traipse out of my dressing room and follow Lille in single file, with me in the middle, until we find it. It's small, with overstuffed chairs surrounding a shiny black oval table. Floor-to-ceiling windows line one wall, and prints of African wildlife decorate the rest. Lille goes to the studio and grabs us some waters and the remnants of the pastries while Remy and Kylian and I settle in.

"So, who's going first?" Kylian asks.

"Lady's choice," Remy says, looking at his fingers instead of me. He's definitely upset that I didn't tell him. Not that I could have, since I invented the whole thing five minutes ago. But of course, Remy doesn't know that.

"Um, I guess I could go first," I say.

I sit down and pull out my math book and notebook.

"How was class today?" Kylian asks.

"It was good. I was able to follow a lot of it." I glance at Remy. His jaw is jutting out just a tad.

"Did you write down your questions?"

I nod and push my notebook over to Kylian. Anything I don't understand in class, I write down so that he can help me with it when we study.

He reads over my list. "Hmm, I think you're having trouble recognizing the variables in these linear differential equations."

"I thought I understood the other night when you went over them, but today they seemed unrecognizable."

Remy makes a small sound, and I look up. Does he think I'm unrecognizable, too? He turns away when my gaze meets his. He pulls his songwriting notebook from his backpack and opens it.

"You need to find the integrating factor first," Kylian says, drawing my attention back to him. For the next forty minutes, I do my best to learn what he's trying to teach me. But everything I say feels like a performance now. If I thought I lived like a circus monkey for the public, it's ten million times worse doing it for Remy. And Lille. She sits in the corner on her phone, but her face twitches like cat whiskers every time Kylian says anything too quietly.

When I pause over an equation, Kylian leans in and says, "You're so cute when you're concentrating."

Lille immediately looks up. I appreciate him playing along,

but does he really need to flirt with me in front of them? And the worst part about it is that he's cute doing it.

"Switch," Lille says. She really could have been some dictator's favorite general. I'm not through with all my homework problems that are due next class, but I have a good start.

Kylian smiles. "You can video chat me later if you need more help."

"Thanks."

"I'm really tired," Remy says. "Let's just call it a day, huh?" He slaps his song notebook closed.

"No," Lille answers. "We go on as usual. You two do your lesson. I need to talk to Aurie."

I knew this was coming, but to hear her say it is so much worse than anticipating it. She gets up, and I follow her out of the room. We go to the darkened studio, and she turns. There's just enough light to catch her expression.

"What are you thinking?"

"I think you mean why aren't I thinking?"

She shakes her head almost convulsively. "This isn't something to joke about. But, oui, you could put it that way."

I let out a breath. Maybe I should tell her that kissing Remy was a huge mistake. But if I do, she's just going to be more convinced than ever that I've fallen for Remy. If I even have. I don't think I have. That would be way too weird. Unnatural and weird.

"I don't know, Lille. It just happened." My chest is so tight. I need to start meditating or something.

She shuts her eyes dramatically. "We cannot afford for

things to just happen, Aurie. Everything you do, everything you say, every decision you make, from what you eat to what you wear to whom you like, has the potential to blow up on all of us."

It used to be that the word "us" made me feel supported and safe. Now it's like an elephant I'm supposed to carry on my shoulders. An elephant with a bomb strapped to it. We sit down but neither of us says anything for a while.

Then Lille leans in so close I can see the color lines running through her brown eyes, even in this dim light. "Do you understand how much is riding on people believing that you and Remy are a couple? This Lancôme ad is just the beginning!"

I shake my head. "What's the endgame, Lille? Are Remy and I getting married? Having kids? How are we ever supposed to get out of this mess?"

She frowns. "You didn't think it was a mess before Kylian made his move."

"He didn't make a move, Lille. Trust me."

"You and Remy need to keep riding this train, or it's going to derail. And it won't just be you who gets hurt. I understand, Aurie, that you're having big feelings about going to college and what comes next for you, and I do understand how hard it's been this last six weeks or so, but adding a real boyfriend to a fake boyfriend is like booking a flight on the *Hindenburg*."

"The what?"

She shakes her head. "It was an early blimp that blew up. Don't they teach you kids history?"

I'm hoping Lille's done with transportation metaphors. If

I'm the one booking the flight on this doomed blimp, then she's the one who designed and built it. I blink back tears.

"Aurie, since you and Remy got caught in that kiss, your social media analytics have been off the charts, and engagement is up across all your platforms. As well as your number of followers."

I've seen the analytics, too.

"Everyone's invested in you two being a couple. And now you want to risk, how do you say in English, putting an orang-utan hammer in our plans."

I frown. "I think you mean throwing a monkey wrench in them."

Lille shrugs. "It's not important how you say it. Just the meaning."

"Trust me, Lille, I completely understand that every single decision I make from here on out is going to ensure that at least one person I care about is incredibly unhappy with me. And that I'm one misstep away from alienating 4.6 million people who believe they know all about me."

Lille bites her lip and studies me.

"Do you really like Kylian?" she asks. "I could have sworn something changed between you and Remy."

I look away. Maybe I like Kylian. It's better than liking your best friend. Whatever I do, I can't lose Remy. "He's very thoughtful. And even you think he's cute. An hour ago you were upset because you thought I had feelings for Remy. Now you're unhappy that I'm dating Kylian. I can't win."

Lille exhales hard. "Teenagers and hormones. Why can't you just not like either of them?"

"I don't know, Lille. Hearts do what they want."

Lille scoffs, but in an agreeing way.

"We're done," Remy says from the doorway. I look over and he and Kylian are standing there watching us. I really hope neither of them heard any of our conversation.

"Okay," Lille says. "It's showtime. We all walk out of here together, making sure that all backpacks are prominently displayed, and Remy, you will take Aurie home. Kylian, you leave without looking at Aurie. Just say a general good night."

"Yes, ma'am," Kylian says like a soldier, and even Remy has to suppress a smile. Lille gives Kylian a look that could down a charging rhino.

"Come on, Aur," Remy says. He pulls my book bag from my shoulder to carry it and waits for me to go ahead of him, just like he normally would, even before we started "dating."

Out on the street, we say good night to Lille and Kylian. I'm going to have so much to explain to Kylian when I get home. Remy's Vespa is parked across the street, so Remy slips his hand into mine as we cross the boulevard. It's dark out, but camera flashes come from our right, and Remy pulls me close to him and smiles as if I'm some long-lost treasure he's found. Whatever version of Lille's cross-examination he wants to launch into is going to have to wait, and I've never been more grateful to the paparazzi in my life.

Twenty

I worry the whole way home, but Remy doesn't ask questions. He doesn't speak at all. I hold on to him as the Vespa darts and surges across the darkened streets of Paris, iridescent from a spring rain that came and went while we were at the photo shoot and studying. I lean my cheek against his shoulder blade, like I used to, wishing for just a few moments that we weren't famous at all. Just a couple of teenagers without so many expectations. Without fans wanting us to be one thing or another. Without paparazzi perched to catch us doing something that would shock our fans into hating us. Without worrying about where our different destinies might lie. But I don't know who we would be then. Probably we never would have met. Maybe we wouldn't have been friends even if we had.

Remy slows the bike for a red light and sets his left foot down to keep us steady during the stop. He turns his head as if he's going to say something, but before he can, we're recognized by some teenagers in a rideshare beside us. They shout for us to wait and ready their phones for pictures. Remy chucks his chin up to say hello, and then he places a hand over mine as it rests against his stomach. The light changes. Remy pulls his hand back to the handlebars and zips us down Avenue d'Eylau into the heart of Auteuil.

When we get to my house, the rideshare is long gone. The Vespa sputters to a stop as Remy's long leg stretches to the ground again. The house is dark except for my mom and Armel's room. It's after ten and tomorrow is a school day for both of us. I wonder if he's as tired as I am.

I slip off the bike and put my helmet in the top box.

"Text me when you get home," I say.

He nods.

"Thanks for bringing me the whole way home."

He nods again.

We look at each other. But he doesn't say anything, so I turn away. Remy grabs my hand and turns me back.

"Are you sure about this?" he asks. "You barely know this guy."

I take a deep breath. "I know you don't like him."

"I don't trust him, Aur. At all. And you've handed him information that could ruin both of us." He doesn't say it meanly, which makes it worse than if he had.

I try not to wince. "He wouldn't do that."

"I hope not," Remy says, echoing my thoughts. What if I'm wrong about Kylian? I didn't tell him on purpose that Remy and I aren't for real, but I shouldn't have been so careless. I completely forgot he was coming to meet us for tutoring. I really need to learn how to strategize like Lille, instead of always reacting to things and making them worse. I knew she was worried about me liking Remy. I should have had a plan for her insistence on knowing my heart. As if such a mystery is even knowable.

"I'm sorry."

Remy sweeps his gaze to the sparkling street.

"I know you'd never hurt me on purpose." His voice sounds gravelly. "But you should have told me something like this."

I take a breath to stop the tears. "No, I'd never hurt you on purpose." I pull my hand from the warmth of his and walk to my front door.

The Vespa starts up as my key flips the lock. I don't look back.

My mom and Armel are lying in bed reading, their door open.

"How was your shoot?" my mom asks, looking up from her book.

I try to smile, but I've used up my allotment of fake smiles for the day. "It went well."

"Did you have dinner?"

"They brought food in for us."

"Well, there are leftovers in the fridge if you're still hungry." My mom smiles at me, a little tentatively. "Aurie, I need you to watch the kids tomorrow night. Armel and I have that reception for the visiting professor, and the babysitter just canceled."

I nod and take a breath. "I'll ask Kylian and Remy if we can have tutoring here, and if not, I'll just skip."

"How's that coming?" My mom's hazel eyes are locked on me.

My jaw gets tight. "Well, I'm definitely understanding more."

She and Armel share a smile, clearly relieved.

"I'd hate for you to cancel. If they can't come here, I'll try to find another sitter."

I shake my head. "No, it will be fine." I could use a break after tonight's fiasco, but I can't tell my mom that.

"Good night," I say.

They tell me good night, and I go brush my teeth and wash my face. I'm exhausted. Too exhausted to try to finish my homework, but I'll have time tomorrow after lunch. When I crawl into bed, I finally face my phone. Kylian has texted.

Are you all right?

Where do I even start? I've messed everything up and he's worried about me. *I'm so sorry.* There are already dots jumping but I keep going.

I type *It was all I could think of in the moment,* but that sounds like I've had Kylian on my brain way more than I should have, so I erase it. He answers me.

Don't worry about it. I know you didn't realize I was standing there.

I really want to move back to Boston and live in my dad's basement.

It's just, Lille has this crazy idea that I've fallen for Remy, and she wouldn't let it go. So I thought if I said that, then she'd shut up about it.

So you and Remy aren't dating?

No, not really. It's complicated.

Well, you had me fooled. You two are like chocolate and crois-sants. Sounds like a Lille idea, though.

I laugh. *It was. But also, our fans were already convinced we must be. If anything, they gave her the idea. She just grabbed it like those batons that relay runners use.*

Lille obviously knows the truth. Anyone else?

Just the three of us, Remy's grandmother, and you. You won't tell anyone, will you? It would make this even more of a mess.

No, I won't tell anyone.

Merci beaucoup.

De rien.

Technically, de rien, means "of nothing." But people use it to say no problem. Or no worries. It's nothing. But this is some-thing. This secret is holding my whole world together.

Or is it? Remy and I have never been further apart. Lille has never been weirder with me. And I've never lied to my mom before this started. I just want to sleep.

Could we have tutoring here tomorrow night if it's okay with Remy? I have to babysit my siblings.

Sure, no problem.

Thank you. I'll see you tomorrow. Good night.

There are no dots coming. I get the feeling that Kylian wants more answers than I have, but I'm so tired I can barely think straight.

Good night, Aurie, he finally answers.

I haven't heard from Remy yet, so I text him to ask if he got home okay.

Not yet, he replies. *I took a drive.* He does that, sometimes, when he's upset. He drives past Notre Dame and finds a place to park that overlooks the Seine. Usually, he takes me with him, though. Sometimes we talk and sometimes we just watch the lights on the water. Sometimes we listen to music and sometimes we try to imagine our futures. Somehow we always get stuck at the part that separates us.

It's late, I text.

Yes, Maman, I'm heading out now. I'll be fine. You go to sleep. Text me.

Please, I add.

Ouais. Yeah. Remy doesn't usually say "yeah" to me. It's not that we're formal with each other, it's just that "yeah" is such a halfhearted expression. It's amazing how one little word can carry so much weight. But he's never been so dismissive with me, either. *I'll be fine. You go to sleep.* It's just not how we are with each other. And he's never made fun of me for worrying about him before. Since when is it motherly to check on your best friend?

He has every right to be mad at me. Even if all we are is friends, and even if that's the way he wants it, he's right. I at least owed it to him to tell him I was dating Kylian. Except that I'm not, and I found out about it at the same time Remy found out. And Kylian. God, I should superglue my mouth shut! How can someone be such a colossal disaster without even trying?

I lay my phone on the nightstand and turn out the light and wait. When Remy finally texts that he's home, I mark it with a heart and close my eyes. I try to let go of all the stress of the day, but it takes me a long time to drift off to sleep. How am I supposed to sleep when my conversation with Remy is the start of a great divide with him, and my conversation with Kylian is only the beginning of a lot of explaining?

Twenty-One

When I open the front door, Remy and Kylian are standing together like a pair of gargoyles, if each one wanted to scare the other off. Lille's made sure they'd show up at the same time so that any paparazzi skulking around my house have nothing to work with.

"Come in—" I say, only to be drowned out by the TPs running to drag them inside, complete with a shouting competition to be recognized first.

Kylian's brought them chocolate croissants.

"What do you say?" I ask them.

"Merci, merci, Kylian!" they cry.

Camille flashes her brown eyes at Remy. "Didn't you bring us anything?"

Remy's mouth drops open. "Um, no, sorry, Cam, I didn't. I will next time." I glance at Kylian, but I can't tell if the smile he's wearing is smug or not.

"Eat those at the table," I say. "I don't need Maman mad

at me for letting you get chocolate everywhere." They troop over and sit down. I help Camille and Thierry take theirs from the bag, and then the three of them proceed to send croissant flakes all over the place.

"I guess I should have brought cookies instead," Kylian says.

"They don't really need all this sugar anyway," Remy tells him, handing Delphine a napkin. I send him a pleading look and he shrugs in reply.

"Aurie, will you get me milk?" Thierry asks.

"I'll get it," Remy says. It's not that Remy wouldn't get Thierry milk if it were just the two of us here, but it feels a little weird today, like he's a cat rubbing his face against the furniture to leave his scent on it. He knows where everything is here. Kylian doesn't. Somehow it feels like we're all thinking this. But maybe I'm just being hypersensitive, since I know how he feels about Kylian. And me. He might not want me, but he still thinks he has to protect me as his friend.

"So, who's going first?" Kylian asks.

Thierry is already taking care of that answer. "Remy, will you play football with me?" he asks, his giant hazel eyes and long lashes doing most of the asking as he rushes to slurp some milk.

Remy groans. He's just teasing them, though, and they know it.

"Play with us, play with us," the girls chime in, giggling and sputtering their food everywhere. Camille nearly falls off her chair as she kneels on it.

"Sit down," I say. "You aren't a monkey."

They all make monkey noises then, until Remy tells them it's time to go outside. "I'll keep them out of your hair," he says, looking at me. "For your lesson," he adds, as if he thinks I plan to use my tutoring session to make out. Even my mom wouldn't have said that.

If my face were any hotter, it could heat an igloo. But if I'm as red as clown lipstick, Remy doesn't seem to notice as he ushers the TPs to the yard, with Thierry on his back while Camille pulls at his shirt and Delphine holds his hand. I really hope none of them are harboring some hidden pathogen that's going to get Remy sick.

"Ready?" Kylian asks.

I had forgotten he was even standing beside me. "Yes, of course," I say, and we sit down at the dining room table. He unpacks his things and organizes them neatly.

"Listen, Kylian, I don't know why you're going along with this, but I really do appreciate it. I know it's . . . awkward."

Kylian chuckles. "It's a little past weird. But one thing about you, Aurie McGinley, is that you're never boring."

"That's not intentional."

He shrugs, but he's smiling. "Maybe not, but it's still interesting."

He pulls my homework notebook toward him and looks over my latest notes.

"So, why are you going along with this?" Maybe I shouldn't ask and make him rethink it, but I kind of owe it to Remy and Lille to find out. I don't think I'm wrong about him the way Remy does, but my record hasn't been stellar lately.

This time when he looks up, he's not smiling.

"You seemed pretty upset by the little I heard, so you must have had a reason to tell them we were dating."

It's hard to look into his eyes, which sounds ridiculous considering how beautiful they are.

"And you were just willing to go along? I mean, you didn't even want to tutor me. Us. You didn't even want to tutor us." I pick up a mechanical pencil and roll it around in my fingers. Early evening sun filters through the long windows and lights up the blue and green watercolor abstract paintings that line the walls.

Kylian pushes his auburn hair from his face. "Look, I don't know how you really feel about Remy. I mean, he seems to be the kind of guy every girl goes for, so why not you? But, for whatever reason, you went out of your way to tell him a lie so he would think we were dating. I mean, unless you're a pathological liar, there must be a reason."

Neither of us says anything for a moment. It's kind of amazing he has this much faith in me. Remy doesn't seem to have any faith in me anymore.

"You aren't a pathological liar, are you?"

I smile. "If I said no, would you believe me?"

We laugh, and the tension dissipates.

"It's just that Remy and I are so tight that we've been like—" I stop, my mind drawing a blank to explain how close Remy and I are. Or how close we used to be until I screwed everything up with that meaningless kiss. That unforgettable, heart-achingly-good, meaningless kiss.

"Chocolate and croissants," Kylian supplies.

I smile a little. "Like chocolate and croissants. At least, we were, until it got weird because Lille started all that stuff about me catching feelings for him."

"And have you?"

I look up. Right now there's an entire amusement park operating in my stomach, and I don't even know why. All I know is that my life has never been more complicated. "No, of course not."

Kylian smiles as if he doesn't quite believe me.

"It's just weird between us now, that's all. And having two fake boyfriends is two fake boyfriends too many."

"One of them could be real. If you want."

My eyes widen. "Pardon?"

Kylian's face turns red. "I just mean that, if you wanted to, you know, date for real, we could."

I stare at him. Is he serious?

"Or not, you know," he adds hastily. "It was just a thought." It's adorable how embarrassed he is. I can't believe he just put himself out there like that. Has he liked me all along? I think back to the pharmacy, and there was definitely a current that passed between us. I didn't think much of it then, but maybe it meant something after all. Still, dating Kylian for real is not something I had even considered.

I bite my lip. Maybe I should date him? He is really cute. Maybe the fastest way to make sure I don't have feelings for Remy is to have feelings for someone else? And Kylian has done so much for me already. I wouldn't even have a prayer of passing Le Bac if he weren't helping me. Maybe if Remy really believes that we're dating, then he'll get over his distrust of Kylian and his fear that I want us to be real and everything can go back the way it was before I ruined it all.

"Honestly," Kylian says, "let's just forget I said that and worry about you doing well on Le Bac. It's cool, really."

Muffled shouts of joy slip through the closed windows as the TPs play soccer with Remy.

I shouldn't even be contemplating this. "It's just that my life is already so complicated, and I don't think I'm very good at juggling all these balls. I'm barely managing with one relationship, and it's fake." I can't quite look at him. I don't want to hurt him. He's such a nice guy, any girl would be happy to be his girlfriend. The way that Reine girl watched him the day we met, she'd jump at this chance.

Kylian clears his throat. "Ce n'est pas un problème, honnêtment."

For just a moment, I let myself linger in the blue of his eyes, on some immaculate Grecian isle where no one knows who I am except people who love me for me. The real me, who can't plan in reverse or do carpentry or clap in time to the music. The real me, who is just a little out of sync with the rest of the world so that the safest place for me to be is in the fantasy world of high fashion and social media dioramas. He lingers there with me, and I wonder if he can read my thoughts as clearly as it seems like he can.

"Alors," he says at last, and we both look down at my notebook and start going over my homework. We work steadily then. When we've gotten through my homework, Kylian helps me get ready for the next lesson that's coming up on derivatives.

The door to the backyard opens. Remy and the TPs flood into the kitchen. The TPs all need water. Kylian and I finish up the lesson as the kitchen bustles with the commotion of my siblings and their endless tiny demands, while Remy tries to shush them so we can finish. I place my things into my book bag. When I look up, Remy is watching me from the dining room doorway.

"Second shift is all yours," he says with the same smile he uses for our inside jokes about Lille.

I smile back automatically, and it feels good to be in sync with him, even if it's just for a moment. I don't need to be in step with the rest of the world. But Remy St. Julien is another story entirely.

I herd the TPs upstairs for their baths so that Kylian and Remy can study. The next hour is filled with bubbles and water splashed everywhere and giggles and tears. I don't know why bath time requires so much drama. I don't remember ever being like them, but I guess I must have been, because it's not just one of them, it's all of them. Then again, maybe they set each other off like Pavlov's dog. One minute it's all fine and the next Camille is crying because Delphine has her favorite rubber ducky, or Thierry is crying because he's got bubbles in his ear, or Delphine is crying because Camille used her hooded panda towel. All I know is that I'm in no hurry to have kids of my own.

Thierry goes last. When I've rubbed him dry and tugged his PJs into place over his sticky damp skin, he leans into me. He smells of lavender and mint in a way that only little children smell. I'm kneeling beside him, and he throws his arms around me.

"I love you, Aurie," he says.

"I love you, too," I say, my heart as soft as a caramel from À la Mère de Famille, the oldest chocolatier in Paris.

"What about me?" Delphine says from the bathroom doorway.

"You too," I say. Camille straggles in behind her and plunges into a group hug, and Delphine follows. Camille clutches her favorite stuffed animal, a purple platypus she named Pauline.

"Aurie," Delphine says.

"Yes?"

"I like it when you watch us."

"Me too." I really haven't spent much time with them lately.

"And Remy," Thierry says. "He hasn't played with us for a loooooong time."

I laugh. "That's because you guys always make him sick when he plays with you."

They shrug and giggle.

"I like Kylian," Camille says. "He brings us chocolate croissants."

"But Aurie kisses Remy like this," Delphine says, and proceeds to smash her face into Pauline the platypus, which makes

Thierry shriek with laughter and Camille pull Pauline away as if the stuffed animal could get cooties. Then they all make kissing noises at me as they laugh uncontrollably.

Even the TPs think I'm Remy-obsessed.

"Do you love Remy?" Camille asks. "Are you going to marry him?"

This child watches too many Disney movies. "We're a little young to get married."

"But you loooove him," Delphine says.

"Don't you love him?" Thierry asks, so seriously you'd think he was a scientist writing a thesis on love.

"Of course I love Remy," I say to shut them up.

"Remy loves you, too," Delphine says.

He does, but I'm so far in the friend zone that the only internet is dial-up. "Okay, well, let's go tell the guys good night and I'll read you a story before you go to bed."

They run down the stairs whooping louder than a stadium full of soccer fans. I clean up the towels and clothes they've strewn across the bathroom and hallway and then I follow them back to the dining room.

Camille is in Kylian's lap and Thierry is in Remy's. Delphine is sitting next to Kylian as if she's the grown-up in the group. Sometimes, she's so much like our mom I expect her to tell me which chores to do.

"I hope you thoroughly disinfected them," Remy says.

Thierry laughs and makes little jumps in his lap.

"I did my best," I say.

"Aurie loves Remy," Camille says, just before she starts

giggling like some amusement park automaton gone haywire. She hugs Pauline and starts to kiss her the same way I kissed Remy in the photo.

Remy swallows like he has a tuba stuck in his throat. He doesn't take his eyes from me, as if he's afraid I'm about to morph into one of his hysterical fangirls and jump him. It always embarrasses him when some girl starts crying all over him.

Thierry chimes in. "Aurie's going to marry Remy."

Remy coughs.

France has nineteen volcanos. Maybe I could throw myself into one.

Thierry makes a bunch of noisy kissing sounds before he almost falls off Remy's lap and Remy has to catch him. Delphine cackles, too. "Ewww," she says. "Kissing is so gross."

"Did you see the picture?" Camille asks Kylian. She's laughing so hard I'm hoping he can't understand her.

"They're just being silly," I say, but my palms feel clammy.

"You said you love Remy," Delphine says. "Upstairs. You said you love him. Don't you love him?"

"You said that?" Remy asks. He pinches his brow.

Everyone is watching me now, like a group of cats waiting for a bird to jump just a little closer.

"Well, not exactly," I say. I'm completely trapped. I can't say I love Remy like a friend, because the TPs will want to know why I don't love him like a boyfriend, and I can't say I don't love him because it's three against one and besides I did technically say it. And I do love him. He's my best friend. My first real friend in France. My first fake boyfriend, in the now-growing

197

collection. Besides, isn't a girl supposed to love her boyfriend? It's normal for the kids to think I would love him.

"It's, I mean, what I said was—" I stop. Remy is silent, his face twisted into some cross between concern and horror. I get it, really, I do. He doesn't want to hurt me. But do I really need a good explanation for saying I love him? Isn't being best friends enough? Maybe we aren't even that anymore. And why does it bother him so much? I mean, would me being in love with him really be that horrible for him? It's not like he would be forced to love me back. And maybe he found kissing me to be horrible, but he started it.

"Why are you mad, Aurie?" Thierry asks.

I adjust my face. "I'm not, I'm just tired. And you three need to get to bed." And I need to get out of this room before I have a Camille-style meltdown.

Kylian stands up. The cute boy who doesn't get sick at the thought of dating me. "I should get going," he says. He slides his black backpack off the table and slings it over his shoulder.

"Yeah, me too," Remy says, no longer looking at me.

"Tell the boys good night," I say to the TPs.

They jump around and hug Remy and Kylian. Thierry insists that Remy give him a piggyback ride up to his room, so he does. Camille and Delphine chase after them.

I walk Kylian to the door.

"Listen," I say. "The kids asked me if I love Remy, and I said yes because of course I do. He's my best friend. But I can't explain that to them. They think we're dating."

Kylian nods.

"You know what, this is all a mess. I shouldn't involve you in it."

Kylian smiles and pulls my hand into his. "Well, I admit that in the beginning I was reluctant, but . . ." He trails off. His blue gaze holds me, gently, the way waves rock you. The way he looked at me that first day.

"I'll see you tomorrow," he says as his kiss lingers on my cheek. "And if the answer is yes, then I'm in."

My stomach drops just a bit, like an elevator jumping.

Remy clears his throat as he comes down the steps. He looks tired. And annoyed.

"Listen, Aur, maybe we should talk." He has his gentle face on, his mouth soft around the edges, his eyes sincere and dark. The face he uses whenever he has to give me bad news. He glances at Kylian. "Privately."

"There's no need," I reply. "The kids misunderstood. I just meant that I love you like a friend. Like my best friend. I said it to shut them up because they think we're dating and were being silly."

I expect to see relief rush over his face, but instead he just looks from me to Kylian and back again. He doesn't trust Kylian and he never will. But at the moment, that's the least of my problems. I need to get them out of here before I full-on cry.

"Good night," I say. They exchange wary glances.

"Good night," they both reply, a little grudgingly. I open the door and practically shove them through it.

Twenty-Two

I wake up the next morning with a sick feeling in my stomach. Remy didn't text me to let me know he got home safely until I texted him to ask. He's definitely mad at me. I can't picture my life without Remy in it, at the center of it, but I also can't stop thinking about the way he looked when he thought I might like him, as if he'd just stepped off a bad roller coaster ride. Maybe we weren't as close as I thought we were, if the thought of dating me is so repulsive to him.

And why shouldn't I date Kylian? He's cute and kind and super-smart. Besides, it's not like you can only date someone if they're the love of your life. How would you even know if someone is the love of your life until you date them? My parents were sure they were each other's forever love, and they both got it wrong. And they dated for three years before they got married. I just wish Remy didn't dislike Kylian so much.

The other problem is that I don't know how Kylian and I are supposed to date while keeping it a secret from the whole world, even my family. We can't go anywhere and be seen together, so it's not like it's really dating anyway. When Lille started all this fake dating stuff with Remy, I didn't even think about how we'd end it. We were so focused on the beginning, and it was such a natural fit for Remy and me, that I totally forgot to have an exit plan. Another aspect of my disability. I'm great at analyzing things, like why something has happened, but I'm terrible at strategizing. I never win board games unless it's just luck, and I never think to ask questions like "What if?" I should ask Kylian how to get better at this, before I make any more colossal mistakes in my life. He's probably great at strategizing. Math and strategy are definitely related.

Calculus is the language the universe talks. I think it must be, and that's why no matter how many languages I speak, I still walk through the world like a foreigner. I hate being disabled.

I wipe away a tear and focus on my day. It's Saturday, and Kylian and Remy and I are getting together later at Mamie's for our lessons. I've already promised Mamie I'd come early and help her, but first I have to help my mom with some chores and schedule our social media posts. Remy and I have been vlogging a lot of our routine activities, and it seems to be working. At least, I haven't seen Pierre Naillon since before the Lancôme shoot the other day. After I've showered and dressed, I give my fans a quick plan of my day, show them my Gucci polo dress and tennis shoes outfit, and then go help my mom.

"This is the first Saturday you haven't been booked up since before Christmas," she says as I help her organize the pantry. She does this every spring to get rid of expired food and try to get more balance between the number of cookie packages (never enough) and the number of hazelnut chocolate spread jars (always too many).

"It's just been really busy this year."

She nods. "Have you thought any more about where you want to go to school?" She tries to pretend she's not really that interested in the answer as she roots around for all the un-opened packages of food. "Why are there three boxes of these same crackers opened?" she adds.

I shake my head to both questions. "I wish I could clone myself and one of me could stay here, and one could go to the States."

"You used to call it home. When we first moved here. You'd always ask me when we were going home."

I laugh. "I thought you'd lost your mind, and we weren't really going to stay here."

She smiles. "And now?"

I shrug. Now no place is home. I take a deep breath. "It feels so huge. As if my whole life depends on this one choice. Like I have to pick a side and stick to it." I don't say things like this to my mom. I can't look her in the eye.

She releases the box of cereal she's about to pick up and turns to me, her gaze locked on me. "You're not American," she says. My eyes get misty.

"And you're not French."

So at least she gets it?

Her face softens. "You're both, Aurie. No one can take that away from you."

Our gazes meet in some no-man's-land, like we're suddenly in Liechtenstein. But we don't live in a neutral country, and sooner or later my parents are going to make me choose a side.

She strokes a lock of hair from my face. "Ma chérie, I can see that you don't believe me."

"You can visit anywhere. But to really live someplace, to really belong someplace, that's something else entirely."

"Maybe," she says, "but to belong somewhere, we must first believe we do."

I twist my face into a maybe.

"Aurie, no one can take your identity away from you. But no one is going to proclaim it for you, either."

I bite my lip. She's right about that.

She smiles. "It is a big decision, I understand that. But it's not written in stone. People move to Europe and America all the time. It's not another planet." She flattens her expression. "Even if it sometimes seems like it."

I laugh.

"I would love for you to stay. The kids are still so little, it's important for them to have you in their lives regularly, not just when you can manage to get home for a holiday. This past year, it's already seemed more like you were halfway out the door than here. I want you and the kids to be close, even if you aren't close in age. You'll remember these years, but to them there will be a big divide once you go, and these early years will get foggy."

I hadn't thought about that. Another variable to add to the equation. Wow, Kylian wouldn't believe I just thought in math terms. I'll have to tell him. I didn't know variables could hold so much pressure, though.

"I promise, Maman, I'll think about that."

She hugs me. "I love you so much."

"I love you, too, Maman."

"Help me get them lunch, and then you'd better get going."

I nod. We finish tidying the last shelf of the pantry. I think she was trying to make me feel better, but this decision still feels huge. It might even feel more huge. Yes, I can always change my mind, but there's so much riding on what I decide. For my family, for Remy. Even for Lille. I'm sure she could find another talent to represent to make up for not having me on her list, but it's because of Remy and me that she's almost got her Majorca vacation home.

I help my mom make the TPs some macaroni and cheese. It's not like mac and cheese in the States. Instead, you cook the pasta and then add diced ham, Gruyère cheese, and butter. Sometimes, when Maman isn't home, I make them American mac and cheese. They think it's "weird but kind of good." Maman says it's disgusting. Armel calls it "barbaric."

When I go to leave, I kiss Thierry on the head.

"What about me?" Camille asks.

I laugh. "You told me kissing was gross."

"That's only when you kiss boys like this," she says, and proceeds to kiss the air like she's the star of a French movie.

"Okay, I get it." I kiss her on the head. Then I kiss Delphine, too, who, like Maman, is very dignified with affection. Maman is laughing.

"Au revoir," I say, and grab my backpack and go.

I take the short bus ride to the Billancourt Metro station. The entrance is marked the way they all are, by a distinctive streetlamp with a red *Metro* sign. I go in on the Avenue du Général Leclerc side and weave my way to the platform. Line 9 will take me straight to Le Haut Marais. I vlog myself on the way, and get stopped a few times by adoring fans, while other people who don't know me give that look that says *Oh God, another wannabe influencer.* Billancourt is a busy terminal, but the trains run every ten minutes, so even on a Saturday, it's only a little crowded.

As soon as I get on the train, I text Remy to let him know. It's thirty-seven minutes to the Architect's Duplex station at Le Haut Marais. Remy will be waiting for me. Not because it's too dangerous to walk to Mamie's alone, but because that's what we've always done. The first time I ever went to the pâtisserie, Remy met me at the station and it became our tradition.

I haven't talked or spoken to Kylian since I shoved him and Remy out the door last night. I wonder if he's changed his mind about wanting to date me. I wonder how dating when no one can know you're dating, while you already have a fake boyfriend, can even work. When I was thirteen, it seemed like being famous would be wonderful. Now I can't imagine why anyone would choose to have their livelihood and happiness depend on what other people think of them. It's different for Remy. He creates something tangible, and he needs people to like it to make that something he can do as a full-time job. But an influencer just creates appearances completely reliant on the approval of others.

When I emerge from the Metro, Remy is standing near the lamppost sign. I don't know how either of us really feels, but we act as if everything is completely normal between us. He's even brought me a bouquet of violets from a nearby florist shop. Violets are my favorite flower. He flings my backpack over his shoulder.

All through Le Haut Marais, spring is blooming. Bakeries and bistros are bustling, and shops are starting to sport outside tables filled with the things they sell, like books or clothes or candles. Even the little grocery down the street from Mamie's has a table filled with jams and jars of honey and saucisson sec, which is like Italian salami. People scurry around with long baguettes in their totes as they do their Saturday shopping.

Remy vlogs us most of the way. I show the audience my beautiful violets, and everything feels normal between Remy and me. We walk hand in hand and tell our fans what's new in the neighborhood or point out the places we love the most. Hearts float up the screen on our live stream faster than we could count even if we tried. I haven't been this happy in days. Remy tells them au revoir as we near the pâtisserie and turns off his camera.

Kylian is standing out front, waiting for us.

"You two start," Remy says. "I've got to fix the dishwasher."

"Again?" I ask.

Remy does a half nod. He's offered a hundred times to buy

Mamie a new one, but she's convinced that nothing new could be as good as the ones she has, even though one of them breaks down so regularly that Mr. Dubois at the hardware store has started to order random extra parts ahead of time. Remy says that dishwasher is more dramatic than an American reality TV star.

"Don't you need help?" I ask. I usually hold the flashlight and hand him tools while he works. He looks so cute when he's fixing it, with it half pulled out from under the counter and him lying on the floor, his hair flopped across his forehead while he squints to see what's wrong.

Remy shakes his head. "You need to study." He doesn't look at me, just turns and glides into the kitchen.

Kylian motions for me to sit down.

"Listen," I say as I unpack my math book and notebook, "I'm really sorry to be like this, but you can't smile at me in public like you just did outside."

Kylian stares at me.

"Like that," I say.

He laughs. "So how can I smile at you?"

"You know," I say, glancing around to make sure no customers can hear us. "Just normal."

He nods, and it reminds me of when we first met, and he thought everything about my life was ridiculous.

"I'll be more careful," he says, a hint of sarcasm in his voice.

"I'm serious."

He holds up his hands in surrender. "I promise."

"Thank you."

"So does this mean you still want to say yes?"

I will my face to stay its normal color. "Yes. Also, I've been thinking about what I could do to help you with your climate stuff, but I haven't come up with anything good."

"You could convince the fashion world to stop generating so many clothes for landfills."

"Very funny. You might as well ask me to wave a magic wand and have all the oil companies decide voluntarily to go solar. I'm serious, though. I promised I'd help you, and I will."

"Well, we are trying to raise money to send people to the next COP. Maybe you could use your celebrity to help us fundraise?"

"You mean those United Nations conferences on climate?"

He nods.

"Yes, I could do that. How much do you want to raise?"

"How much can you raise?"

"A lot, I think. If we have a good plan for how it will be spent."

"Really? I was thinking like bake sale funds." He opens my notebook and pulls it over to look at my questions.

"I mean, we could have a fundraiser as big as you want. We could have a whole music festival to bring awareness and raise money."

"You could put that together?"

"With some help, sure. Remy could be one of the headliners. And between us, we could get some more stars to come out for it. Remy knows a lot of people in the music industry, between his parents' old friends and his own music. And we could get corporate sponsors. Every big fashion house is part of an international conglomerate these days, and I have contacts at all of them."

"So get the worst offenders to pay for us to fight them?" he says, smiling. His eyes look really beautiful in the afternoon light of the pâtisserie. Mamie has tartes aux citron, lemon tarts, in the oven, and the whole place smells like summer even though it's not quite May.

"Why not? Like how they all talk about supporting LGBTQ causes or women's rights in the States and then donate to conservative politicians who want to make us live like we're back in the fifteen hundreds. They never walk the walk, but they'll pay to line it with roses so that people think they do."

Kylian chuckles.

"Okay, don't look at me like that," I remind him.

"Because some paparazzo might think I like you and take a photo?"

I nod, but that's not the only reason. When he looks at me like that, my stomach gets as nervous as it was that day at the Parc de Bercy, when he made me believe that I might not be completely unteachable in math.

"So, your assignment is to put the numbers together," I say. "How many people you want to send, what it would cost for transportation, hotels, meals, and passports if they need them. Aren't these things held all over the world?"

"Well, they're supposed to happen in Bonn every fall, unless a party offers to host, but some country always does. It's great tourism money. The last couple have been in the Middle

East, so it will probably be in Europe this year, but they haven't announced it yet."

"Why do they call it COP? Shouldn't it be the CCC, Conference on Climate Change?"

"It stands for Conference of the Parties."

"Very UN of them," I say, and he laughs. He opens my math book to the last set of problems I did.

"This is really great of you."

"I do care about the planet, despite what your friends think."

"I get it. And I'm sorry about them that day, honestly."

"You didn't seem to think much of me then, either."

Kylian's face colors. "We'd better get started on your math if we're going to keep you on track for Le Bac."

I let him change the subject. Flirting with someone feels, I don't know, risky. I want to like Kylian. I do like him, I just don't know how much. But I'm not sure how I feel about risky. I choose the safe side of adventure. I don't take big risks. Not with school, not with fashion, and not with my life. But now I seem to be walking a high wire with no net. And no Remy St. Julien to catch me if I fall.

Twenty-Three

After my lesson, I head to the kitchen to help Mamie. Today, she wants me to make *le fénétra,* a pastry from the Toulouse region, made with shortbread, apricot jelly filling, candied lemons, and an almond-based biscuit known as dacquoise. It's not normally a thing you'd find in a Paris pâtisserie, but lots of transplants from Toulouse know to come to Mamie for a taste of home. She doesn't make it all the time.

"Are you feeling homesick, or did someone ask for this?" I ask.

She smiles. "Both. I need four."

"Oui, Mamie."

She busies herself beside me, making a confit violet, or violet jam, also a specialty of Toulouse. Maybe this is why violets are my favorite flowers. Maybe it's because they make me think of Remy and Mamie. Or maybe it's because they're so delicate and strong at the same time.

"So," she says after a few minutes, "is everything okay between you and Remy?"

I nod.

"Hmm," she says, lifting herself a little to stir the violets as they cook.

"Why, did he say something?"

"Non, and that's why I think something is up. He's been very reserved lately."

Well, he would be since he's (A) worried about me, who is disgusting to him, liking him, (B) mad at me for not telling him I was dating Kylian when I made it up on the spot, and (C) sure that Kylian is a villain come to destroy us. I don't really get that last part. I mean, Kylian boarded this *Titanic* reluctantly, and he hasn't done anything that should make Remy distrust him besides liking me. In fact, he's gone along with all of it, sooner or later. I think it's because Remy has such a hard time letting anyone get close to him. Between his fear of losing people and his fear of our fans finding out the truth, he's become a little paranoid.

"Which planet have you flown to?" Mamie says, nudging me.

"What?"

"Well, if you were making those shortbreads any slower, we'd need to start the bûches de Noël." Christmas cakes.

I laugh. "Je suis désolée, Mamie. I have a lot on my mind lately."

She sighs. "I don't think you should go to America."

"No?"

She shakes her head. "It's not just anywhere I can find a pastry sous-chef who will work for free." She says this completely deadpan, as if that's the only reason she would be sorry to see me go. My eyes instantly mist up.

"Well, I was planning to ask for a raise anyway," I say, forcing a small laugh.

She catches my gaze and smiles. "Double?"

I nod. "Double what I get paid now."

She laughs and wipes a tear from my cheek. "You always have a home here."

I kiss her cheek and we go back to baking. I hope Mamie will always feel like home, even when Remy doesn't. I'm starting to understand that Remy and I were destined for splitsville, fake dating or not. I was always going to go to college and Remy was always going to be living the life of a musician, traveling more than he isn't. I just don't think my heart is ever going to be as accepting of that fact as my head may someday be.

"How do you know, when you have a big decision to make, if you're making the right one?" I ask.

She laughs. "You don't. When you choose one path, you will never know what would have happened if you had taken another."

"But we know when something is a mistake."

Mamie shrugs. "Sometimes right away, sometimes after a very long time, and sometimes never."

"How could we never know if something we decided is a mistake?"

"Because you will never know what else might have been. You could have what seems to be the best of outcomes, but you will never know if another choice might have been even better."

"But then it's not a mistake, it's just one of two good options."

"Perhaps," she says as she pipes out pâte à choux dough into profiteroles for some St. Honoré cakes. My favorite thing about Mamie's pâtisserie is that, while there are some pastries, like her tartes au citron, that she makes all the time, her menu also changes each day. She only makes St. Honoré cakes when she's in the mood to honor the patron saint of bakers and pastry chefs.

"How did you decide that you'd change your menu every day instead of only having the same menu like most places?"

She laughs. "I would have lost my sanity if I only made the same pastries every day for a lifetime! I don't know how people do it!"

I guess some things aren't really a choice. "How did you know that opening a pâtisserie was a good decision?"

She almost bristles. "I didn't. In fact, Remy's grandfather was absolutely against it!" She wipes her hands on a tea towel.

"Really?"

"Mais oui! He said it was the silliest thing I'd ever said and that he'd leave me if I did it. He was sure we were going to lose all our investment. He said I didn't know anything about running a business even if I was a decent baker!"

"But he didn't leave you."

She stops piping a moment. "No, not until he died. But that was after he had admitted it was a good idea."

She loved Remy's grandfather, but he's been gone so long that she smiles over her victory.

"Ma chérie," she says, her voice becoming as soft as pastry cream, "life is a journey, but the destination is never where we believe it will be. It always lies somewhere else, no matter how hard we try to chart our course in a certain direction. And we spend our lives rerouting our carefully planned-out paths."

"My grandmother McGinley had a poem about that, framed in her house," I say, remembering for the first time in a very long time my grandmother's entry hall. "Something about how whales follow whale roads and geese follow roads in the air, but how the heart headed for Peru will somehow end up in China." I try to remember the poem and poet's name. I close my eyes and envision myself standing in my grandmother's entryway, with its Scandinavian-blue walls, almost white, and that poem torn from a book and put into a gold leaf frame. Just beyond the glass door, there were apple trees lining the driveway. *By Jane Hirshfield.*

I suddenly feel like crying because, for just a moment, it was almost as if I'd been back in her house. But my grandfather sold that house when he had to put my grandmother in the home, a couple of years after my mother and I moved to Paris.

"We're all done." Remy's voice comes from the doorway like a shove and brings me back to reality. "Kylian's surprisingly good at translating song lyrics."

Kylian stands beside him. For once they don't look like they want to kill each other.

Remy's face gets serious, and he crosses the kitchen to me. "Aur, what's wrong?" He slips his hand around my wrist the way he always would have, but then pulls away.

"Nothing." I shake my head and smile at Mamie. "I just realized that even though my grandmother is basically gone, she still has things to teach me."

Mamie nods.

"Listen," I say, "Kylian and I need to talk to you about something."

Remy raises his eyebrows.

"It's about helping Kylian with his climate action stuff. Like I promised when he agreed to tutor us." I add this last part because Remy hasn't told Mamie that Kylian and I are dating now. Even though she knows Remy and I aren't.

We sit down at a sturdy oak table Mamie uses to organize the trays for the glass cases in the shop, and I explain our idea to Remy. He watches me as I talk. It's never unnerved me before, but now I keep wondering what he's thinking.

"So, what kind of festival are you imagining?" he says when I finish. He leans back in his chair and waits.

"Kylian's going to make us a budget of how much he needs to send a group to the next COP. Anything over that can be for used for awareness. We could make it a whole publicity campaign."

"Go big or go home?" Remy says with a smile, making fun of my American side.

I smile. "Yes."

"All right, if it's something you'd like. How many acts do you want?"

"I don't know. We could make it an all-day thing. Or even a weekend. Where should we have it? Somewhere open-air and meaningful."

"What about Hôtel de Ville, on the plaza out front?"

"But they have huge concerts there," Kylian says.

Remy presses his lips together patiently.

"It's perfect," I say. "Right in front of city hall. Where else would you hold a concert to fight government inaction?"

Kylian glances at Remy as if he's looking at him for the first time.

"We're going to need Lille," I add.

They both grimace. At least they can agree on one thing.

"Well, she's going to be in charge of all the contracting and permits for the venue. I'll handle the general planning and logistics, and I'll reach out to my corporate contacts for sponsorships and my celebrity contacts for support. Remy, most of the acts will have to come through you, since you're the one with the most musician contacts."

"Okay," Remy says, "just let me know how big we're talking, and I'll take care of it."

Kylian beams at us. "This is amazing. If you can pull this off, I'll be so grateful!"

Remy laughs in a scoffing way. He doesn't have any doubt we can pull it off. "You've never seen Aurélie McGinley put her mind to something. Problem-solving is her specialty."

I smile. It's good to see them at peace with each other. And to get a compliment from Remy. I just hope I can deliver on this promise and still keep them both happy, because I'm pretty sure that my relationship with each of them could be riding on it.

Twenty-Four

ille was less than pleased when she found out that I'd volunteered her to handle all the permits and contracts that we'll need for our climate festival. And to figure out a budget for the venue.

My mother, on the other hand, was quite excited when I told her about our plan. She thinks it's a great idea for me to use my celebrity for "something that matters."

We hold our first meeting to organize the festival at my house. Remy and I are still vlogging as much as we can outside of school and family, and on camera we continue to look like the perfect couple. But when the camera is turned off, there's a distance between us that feels awkward and disappointing, like when a movie you were loving goes in a different direction than the one you wanted it to take.

My mother has taken the TPs to the park so they won't disrupt our meeting. It's a warm day for early May, and when I think about the world my little sisters and brother will inherit, it makes me extra glad I've agreed to help Kylian. I don't want any of us living on a scorched earth. Especially just so that some people can be very wealthy for a short time.

Lille is the first one to arrive. She has on casual clothes, which for her is a black Louis Vuitton pantsuit with a peach-colored blouse. For once I'm in jeans, and it's heavenly. When I'm in the States, I almost live in them.

"I brought some boules de Berlin," she says as she hands a box of small cake-like doughnuts to me.

"Thanks, but I didn't think you believed in sweets, especially at meetings." Lille says that snacking during meetings, especially on sweets, will make you put on weight. And being overweight doesn't give you credit in the fashion world. When I first started fashion vlogging, my mom was paranoid that I'd develop an eating disorder, so every time Lille said something about my weight, my mother emphasized the importance of eating healthy. And we do. My mom and Armel make sure that every dinner at home is filled with vegetables and fresh fruit.

"Well, when in America," she says.

"Okay, Lille, why is this an American idea? Europe is pretty famous for its rock festivals."

"Yes, but not to fundraise for charity."

Okay, so she's still mad that I've volunteered her for this. I'm about to launch into a rant about how she won't be able to finish paying for her Majorca vacation home if Remy and I don't have a livable planet to work on when Kylian shows up.

219

He's brought his dad and that Reine girl from his school strike group. From what he told me, they started the group together. He introduces Reine to me, nudging her as he does.

"I'm sorry I was rude to you that day at the pharmacy," she adds to her enchantée, looking like a guilty puppy.

"It's not a problem," I say. She looks prettier than she did the first time I ran into her. Maybe because she's not scowling now.

Kylian introduces his dad to Lille, and then Remy shows up and he gets introduced to Reine and Kylian's dad, too. Reine is all smiles at Remy. Apparently, it doesn't bother her when a hot guy wears designer clothes, just when I do.

We all sit down at the dining room table, but not before Lille pulls me aside.

"You should have told me the dad was better-looking than Kylian," she whispers. "Do you think he'd want to model?"

"I think he's happy with his pharmacy." I have a fleeting hope that she won't make things weird, but then I remember she's Lille, so it's kind of inevitable. She spends most of the meeting contemplating him, and while I get that it's as a potential talent, I doubt that's how anyone else will see it.

Kylian's brought his budget. He wants to send a contingent of thirty students from around the world to the next COP. It's a little hard to gauge, since we don't yet know where that's going to take place, but he's made a spreadsheet of all the information we need. Kylian's determined a budget per student of five thousand dollars for registration, travel, lodging, meals, and incidentals. We guess high on the budget, but travel costs could be a lot less for many participants, which would let us use the extra money to bring more kids from places that have been hit the hardest, like indigenous communities in Alaska or Central Africa.

"I think we could blow well past this goal if we can get enough musicians on board," Remy says.

"Still," Kylian's dad says, "we should plan conservatively and then broaden if we are able. It's going to be a big outlay for the venue."

"Monsieur Chenault is right," Lille says, smiling at him.

"Please, call me Louis," Kylian's dad says.

Remy's face contorts into the same one he makes when we're in the States and I ask him to eat American fast food, like he might get sick.

"The guys and I will donate our time," he says, "but if we're bringing in talent from outside Paris, then we'll probably have to at least pay their travel and lodging. And they like to stay at five-star places."

"We can't have anyone coming here on a private jet," Kylian says.

We all nod and murmur that he's right, except Reine, who says, "Absolutely not!" Remy shoots me a look, asking me if she's always this aggressive. I give him a quick nod to say yes.

"Let's target acts who we think will be sympathetic," I say. "And we have a lot of good local talent, plus we can bring in other European acts on trains cheaply enough. What kind of music are we even featuring?"

"Remy's music is a fusion of singer-songwriter, indie rock, and pop," Lille says, "so we should stick to those genres."

We all agree on this.

"I'll get corporate sponsorships to cover the venue management and fees, but I don't know that I could get enough to cover travel and lodging for groups, especially if they are coming from overseas and want suites in luxury hotels."

"Maybe we could get the hotels to donate some of the lodging?" Reine asks. She looks straight at Remy as she says this, even though she's sitting next to him.

"It's worth an ask," Remy says. "Another way we could make some money is to have food vendors there. They could pay a fee to rent space from us and then keep the rest of their profits."

"Mamie could have a booth," I say, "and we could make all the pastries for it. She'd only have to donate the ingredients and let us clog up her kitchen." Remy laughs, because we will get scolded a lot, but she'll still do it to make us happy.

We brainstorm like this for so long that my mom comes back with the kids and we're still huddled around the table ironing out our ideas. I've been taking notes in the notebook Kylian gave me but starting from the back and upside down. It's like an empowerment notebook now.

"Stay for dinner," my mom tells everyone.

Kylian's dad protests that he doesn't want to intrude, but Kylian and my mom and Lille persuade him. Kylian's little brother is with friends tonight anyway, so there's no reason for them to rush home. This is the longest Kylian and I have ever spent in the same room, even if it is with a lot of people who have no idea we're dating. I'm not even really sure we are dating. I mean, we say we are, and Kylian video chats me every night, but we were doing that anyway for tutoring. It's just now he tutors me and then we talk about other things until I'm too tired to keep my eyes open. He hasn't even kissed me yet.

At some point during dinner, both Remy and Kylian pull me aside to mention how chatty Lille is being with Monsieur Chenault.

"Is she hitting on my dad?" Kylian asks me as we go into the kitchen to get the dessert. "I do not need Lille as a stepmom."

I laugh. "I doubt it. She always goes for flashy guys. I think she wants to make him a client."

"Pardon?"

We carry an apple tart and whipped cream into the dining room. "Your dad's a hottie. I mean, for his age."

Kylian pulls away like I've just said something impossible. Then he looks at his dad and presses his eyebrows together in bewilderment.

"Lille thinks he'd make a great client."

"I swear, if she turns him into a model, I will never forgive you," he says, but he's laughing.

I shrug playfully.

Remy watches us. He doesn't seem happy, and it reminds me that it can't seem like I'm flirting with Kylian. Armel is also watching me and sends a curious look to my mom, but she's helping Delphine tie her hair up so she doesn't get it in the dessert like she usually does. Reine, still perched on Remy's left, doesn't look very pleased with me, either. I stop smiling and take my seat next to Remy.

It's weird, but it felt more real to date Remy when I was

fake dating him before I started to date Kylian than it does to date Kylian for real. But that's just because no one knows but Lille and Remy. Everyone thinks I'm dating Remy for real, so it made it feel like it was true, at least when we were still best friends. I sigh and dig into my tarte aux pommes. I don't know what it's like to be a normal teenager, but it has to be simpler than this.

Twenty-Five

May whirls past as if I'm on one of those swing chair amusement park rides where you spin superfast in a circle and the people below shift and repeat but you can't touch them. There's so much to do that I don't have time to think about anything beyond the festival and Le Bac, which looms in my nightmares like something that wants to devour me. I'm kind of glad, though, because it also means that I don't have time to think about my status as a fake girlfriend or a real girlfriend or a daughter who has to decide which continent and parent to choose.

We're calling the festival Rock the Climate, a riff on the popular American campaign to get kids to vote. Remy has put together a pretty amazing lineup for the three days. Day one will focus on singer-songwriters, day two will focus on indie rock, and day three will focus on pop, but we have different acts slipped in each day to keep things interesting.

We've mostly been meeting at my house or the pâtisserie

twice a week, but today we're at Kylian's apartment. It's in a newer building, and its big picture windows overlook the Parc de Bercy. The park looks beautiful in its late May finery, all the trees decked out in bright greens. I expected Kylian's home to be very masculine without his mom, but instead it's as if she were still here, everything apparently kept the way it was when she died. There are family pictures lining the walls, and lots of colorful fabrics in modern prints. I stop before a photo of Kylian and his brother when they were little with his mom.

"You were so cute," I say, looking at the pictures. "I always thought you looked like your dad, but I definitely see your mom in your smile."

Reine comes over and studies me as if that's a totally inappropriate thing for the girlfriend of Remy St. Julien to say to another guy. She's probably right.

"We should get started," I say.

We sit around the dining room table, and Reine rushes to the chair beside Remy. I pull out my notebook, which I've filled with an excruciating number of details. This whole project is a lot bigger than even I envisioned, and I had a pretty good idea of what it entailed when I suggested it. I've seen enough of Remy's gigs and fashion shows and corporate parties to know how much it takes to pull off a big event.

Remy is wearing a green vintage concert T-shirt from Boston's *Don't Look Back* album that I bought for him. The green highlights his eyes, but I can't help but wonder if he's sending me a message, and not just with the album title. *Don't Look Back* was the beginning of a lot of trouble for the band, especially the guy who had been the main catalyst for the whole thing. Maybe wearing this T-shirt today is Remy's way of telling me where he thinks our friendship is headed. Unfortunately I already know.

"I think we should have some surprise acts," Remy says, "to help build interest and curiosity. It could be another marketing tool." He leans back in his chair, and it reminds me of all the hours spent in Lille's office strategizing my latest mess-up.

"What do you mean?" Reine asks. She's taken to sitting next to him at every meeting. Even I don't do that, and I'm supposed to be dating him. When they stand up together, she's almost his height. Guys like tall girls. At least they do in country songs. Now that I think about it, the girls that Remy dated when I first knew him, before we became best friends, were very tall.

"You know," he says, "acts we bill as an unnamed special guest, to build curiosity."

"That's brilliant," Reine says, and smiles adoringly at him. Remy's face colors. It still amazes me how he can be such a showman onstage, but one-on-one he's so humble and sweet.

"Are we going to get anyone to agree to that, though? The whole point of donating their time is to get the publicity," I say.

Remy shrugs. "I think I can get one act, at least."

"Who?" I ask.

Remy smiles his inside smile. "It's a surprise."

I laugh. But maybe two can play this game. It suddenly occurs to me how awesome it would be to get a-ha to come and have them play "Take On Me" with Remy. If they'd do it.

"Okay," I say, "let's reserve two of the last Sunday slots as surprise acts and see if we can fill them. But what will we do if we can't?"

"I can repeat, and Vaillancourt would take the other slot, I'm pretty sure. They were really happy to join," Remy says.

Vaillancourt is a local group named for their lead singer and guitarist. They play a fusion of pop and rock and are making a name for themselves across Europe, just like Remy.

"I like that," Kylian says.

"I'll work on one of the surprise acts," I say to Remy, "and you work on the other. But if we bill it as a surprise, then I don't know that two acts already in will be enough to keep people happy if we can't get the acts we want."

"Well," Remy says, "it's still a surprise if we repeat. And I haven't even asked any of the local jazz bands. There's no reason why that couldn't be the surprise. If we could get a big-name jazz band, that would be cool."

"I'll help you," Reine says, with so much excitement you'd think she was saving his life. "I'm sure we can pull it off." He smiles at her. Is there something going on with them?

Lille and Louis come in from the kitchen, both of them laughing. Kylian gently kicks me under the dining room table. I look at him and shake my head. It's not my fault his dad is flattered by Lille's attention.

They've made jambon-beurre sandwiches with arugula for dinner, along with roasted potatoes in a cream sauce and green beans almondine. I'm pretty sure this is the first time Lille has ever set foot in a kitchen, let alone made anything in one. When I look up, Remy is widening his eyes at me, obviously thinking the same thing.

"This looks so good, Monsieur Chenault," Reine says as Kylian's dad sets down the platter of sandwiches.

We all echo her. I haven't eaten since breakfast. I tried to have lunch at school, but I had snuck away to make a couple of phone calls for the festival, and by the time I'd finished, afternoon classes had started. I dig into the meal like a starved kitten, fully expecting Lille to start on me about eating and how I need to look more like a model than not, but she doesn't.

Remy nudges me, and when I look up, cheeks bursting, he tilts his head toward Lille, who is completely absorbed in pouring wine for her and Louis. Remy and I look at each other, our faces scrunched up. Very un-Lille. I swear it's like we're all under some *Midsummer Night's Dream* fairy spell.

On my other side, Kylian taps my arm and nods his head toward Lille and his dad.

"Sorry," I mouth. He knows it's not my fault, but still, I don't blame him for being unhappy. I wouldn't want my dad dating Lille, either. I mean, she has a lot of great qualities, and she can even be fun sometimes, but that's a lot of intensity to bottle up into one relationship.

We go over our progress during dinner. I've gotten enough sponsorships to cover most of our costs, and I haven't tapped out my resources yet. My mom has pitched in to help Lille, the venue and management company are booked, and we've almost sold out our vendor slots. The management company is taking care of the stage, backstage, and security, although Remy always brings his own small security team since Oslo. Eighty percent of our acts are either committed or looking like they'll commit by our June 15 deadline, which also happens to be the date of Le Bac. Just in case I needed a reminder. The festival is the weekend of July 4.

Remy and I have been splashing social media with the details, and ticket sales have started.

When I've gone through our status report, we're all quiet for a moment.

"I wasn't sure you could manage all this, Aurie, but you've done a great job," Lille says, raising her wineglass to me. Lille hardly ever tells me I've done a great job, especially for something she wasn't on board with to start. It feels weird but also ridiculously satisfying.

"Hear, hear," Remy says, raising his water glass, and everyone chimes in. It makes my eyes tear up.

"Aur, what's wrong?" Remy says, slipping his hand onto the back of my neck.

I shake my head. "I don't know." And I really don't. Why would a little praise make me so soft? People shower me with compliments all day long on the internet. But maybe that's it. That praise is from people I don't know, who don't really know me. Now I'm getting compliments from people who honestly care about me. Well, I don't think Reine really likes me. And I guess I was wrong about her having feelings for Kylian, because she is definitely Remy-obsessed. She hasn't looked away from him all night. But the rest of them care about me. Kylian touches my knee under the table and smiles at me. And even though nothing is the same with Remy, I know he still at least cares about me.

We help to clean up dinner and then Remy and I start our tutoring with Kylian. I go first, and Reine stays to "keep Remy company." I should have said I'd go second and then she would have probably gone home.

Kylian's dad and Lille leave for a stroll in the neighborhood. Another thing I have never seen Lille do, stroll. I didn't even think it was possible. Walking with Lille is like walking a husky. Reine and Remy sit in the living room. We can't see them from where we are in the dining room, but we can hear them. Reine talks to Remy about music because she plays, too. If you can call the flute and ukulele playing. I know this isn't fair to people who play the flute and ukulele, but it crosses my mind anyway.

"Hey," Kylian whispers, "where are you? You're a thousand miles away tonight."

"Sorry," I say. "I'm just tired."

Kylian brushes back a lock of hair that's fallen from behind my ear. He smiles at me. "You've been working so hard. And I hate that I can't even take you out for a break. Or out at all."

It's almost weird to think of dating him in public. I can't even imagine what that would be like. "Well, at least Le Bac will be over in a couple more weeks, come what may."

"You're more ready than you think you are."

I shake my head.

"Hey, I mean it. You need to believe in yourself." He smiles at me, close enough to kiss. His beautiful eyes are calm like the Mediterranean ocean.

"About most things, I do. Just not math."

"You've come a really long way in such a short time."

Reine's laughter bursts from the living room, high-pitched and a little forced. This is probably as alone as Kylian and I will ever be in person.

"Kiss me?" I ask.

Kylian smiles and my heart races.

"No way!" Reine says from the other room, as Remy tells her about the time we got lost in New York without enough money, so Remy started busking a Niall Horan song for cab fare back to our hotel, and Harry Styles was in the crowd and gave Remy a hundred-dollar bill.

Kylian and I laugh softly, and then he leans in. I'm finally kissing my very real boyfriend, even if practically no one knows that's what he is.

Twenty-Six

Kissing Kylian isn't anything like kissing Remy St. Julien. I mean, why would it be? They're completely different people. Besides, how is anyone supposed to concentrate on kissing their boyfriend when their fake-boyfriend-and-once-upon-a-time-best-friend is in the next room flirting with a girl who hates them?

I'm not saying it was a bad kiss. It definitely wasn't a bad kiss. It just wasn't as monumental as I thought it would be. It didn't knock all the breath out of my body, and I didn't completely forget where I was. Although, how could I, with Reine shrieking with laughter in the next room?

Maybe Remy isn't like some Olympic gold medalist in kissing. Maybe the whole thing was the element of surprise. I was halfway through that kiss before I even realized it was happening. Or maybe he is just an amazing kisser and that's why I got caught up. Maybe some people are just exceptional kissers, and some aren't. But it's not about how well someone kisses; it's about who they are, and how they feel about you. Kylian is a great guy, and he actually wants to kiss me.

"We should be studying," Kylian whispers when he pulls away with a smile. His eyes are so beautiful.

I smile back. I don't care what Remy thinks. I trust him.

"Seriously," he says. "You only have a couple more weeks, and then I'll kiss you all you want." He links his pinkie into mine like we're making a pact for future kissing dates. He grins at me like a little kid. He's so happy to be with me, it's almost overwhelming.

I nod, and we start studying again. He doodles little hearts in the margins of my notes as he waits for me to solve a problem. He really is adorable. I'm almost able to ignore the ridiculous amount of giggling coming from the living room. I mean, Remy is very charming and funny, but come on. He's still Remy St. Julien underneath all that. He's just a boy like any other. Who kisses like a Greek god.

When I finish my lesson and it's time to switch with Remy, Kylian and I both sigh, but mine is relief and his is filled with an obvious wish to get the next hour over with. I feel kind of bad about that because he'd never have had to tutor Remy if it weren't for me.

Reine hangs around with me in the living room for a few minutes, but we don't really have anything to talk about. Kylian's and Remy's voices drift in as they go over how to use gerunds. Every time I hear Remy's accented English, I have to smile.

"Well," she says, "I guess I should get home now. I'll see you next time. Tell Kylian and Remy I said good night, will you?"

"Of course." When she's gone, I take a deep breath. My life used to be predictable and dependable. It was in perfect balance. Well, almost perfect. I guess Remy could have started to date someone else before we agreed to fake date, but he never seemed interested in anyone and I never worried. We were so close, it seemed like what we had was unbreakable, even if one of us did eventually date someone else. That was pretty naive of me. Sooner or later, one of us was going to meet someone we wanted to date, and fake boyfriend and girlfriend or real best friends, we were destined to separate, like molecules splitting. Guys and girls may be best friends in the movies, but in real life it just doesn't work that way, especially when they start dating other people.

The physicists are right. All things end. Eventually. Entropy doesn't discriminate between the good and the bad. Everything we build, everything we work toward, everything we want, eventually it has to balance out and begin to fall apart. For every action there is an equal and opposite reaction and all that. It's the way of the universe, and now, thanks to Kylian, I speak the language the universe speaks, even if I'm a novice at it.

When I think about Remy St. Julien, though, sometimes I wish I weren't learning the language of the universe. There are some lessons it wants to teach me that I just don't want to learn. Like when we first moved back to France and I didn't know what escargot were. I still wish I didn't know that one. Sometimes, it's better to be a foreigner and not understand a place. Especially when you suddenly find yourself crossing the badlands of entropy.

Twenty-Seven

On Saturday we meet at my house so that I can teach our pastry contingent to make pastries. But first I do a quick vlog on sustainable fashion and a review of some of the best outfits I saw at the charity gala Remy and I attended last night. Tom Ford and Missoni have been crushing it lately.

We aren't beginning the pastries until eight days before the festival starts, so there won't be time for anyone to learn as they go. We're sticking to some simple tarts for the booth, but we're going to need a lot of them. Kylian and Reine bring a couple of friends from their school strike group, a girl named Olivia and a boy named Daniel. Remy's bandmates Max and Simon also come. Théo says he's terrible in a kitchen, so he's volunteered to help with making sure the sound checks are all done properly. That's one less thing for me to do, so I'm grateful. I've written so many notes that the festival half of my notebook is almost meeting the math part of it.

Before we start, Remy asks everyone if they're okay with

being on our vlog. "We'll be able to edit it," he tells them. "We aren't live streaming anything." We can't afford to. We have too many secrets to spill. Besides, Remy and I struggle to be in sync these days. Where we used to finish each other's sentences, now we sometimes collide when we talk, or miss each other's cues we would have gotten easily before.

I've chosen tartes au citron, chocolate praline tarts, apricot-pistachio tarts, and raspberry tarts with shortbread crust for the pastries. We're also going to sell langues de chat, or cat's tongue cookies—which sound disgusting when you translate the name to English but are just long, crispy butter cookies— palmiers, and cinnamon stars. None of them are too difficult, need a lot of refrigeration, or are messy to eat as people walk around the festival. Also, they're popular and traditional. We're going to make the tarts in small, two-bite versions so they're easy to eat as people walk around.

"We should make macarons," Reine says when I run over the list. "Everyone loves a macaron."

"Have you ever made them?" I ask.

She shakes her head.

"They take a lot of time to learn the techniques. Since no one here is experienced in a pastry kitchen except for Remy and me, we need to keep it simple."

Max looks over the pile of ingredients I have on the counter. "No offense, Aurie, but this doesn't look simple."

"Just think of it as a song you're creating and once you've played it a couple of times, it becomes muscle memory."

"Max doesn't really know how to play, you know," Simon

says, which makes Remy laugh, and then everyone else laughs, too, while Max says something smart to Simon in Czech, but none of us know what. Simon and Remy are half seated on my mom's kitchen table, which would send her into a fit if she saw it, but they look like musicians with a lot of swagger and it's pretty cute. Our fans will love this. We always get a lot of engagement when Max and Simon banter.

"Okay, let's stay focused, because we have a good deal to go through today," I say.

We start with pâte sucrée because it's the base for three of the four tarts we'll sell.

"Maybe we should have people learn specific tasks, like an assembly line," Remy says amid the chaos of bowls and flour and butter cubes.

It probably would be best.

"Okay, who wants shells, who wants filling, and who wants cookies?" I ask.

"I want the chocolate part, whatever that is," Daniel says. He's a year younger than the rest of us, but he's not shy. He keeps talking to Max about guitars.

We all laugh. "Daniel is on Team Filling," I say.

We divvy up the rest of the jobs however people want. Remy leads Team Crust and I'm Team Filling. Everyone is on Team Cookie.

At first everyone is kind of reserved with each other, but by the time we've moved on to the shortbread, there's a lot of laughing and joking going on. My mom comes in and starts to help, mostly because she doesn't want too much of a mess in her kitchen. Armel has taken the TPs "on an adventure," which really just means the weekly shopping, but with the TPs it will become an adventure. I owe Armel a favor now.

Remy pulls me aside a few minutes later when our students are busy with their assigned tasks.

"I feel like you got the bigger burden of this deal. Maybe we should switch?" His eyebrows are creased.

"It's fine. I don't have to perform like you do, just plan and bake." Reine would be heartbroken if she suddenly found herself on Team Aurie.

"Aur, you've been running yourself ragged these past few weeks between Le Bac, school, our social media, and this festival. Have you even eaten today?"

It's well past lunch, which I only realize when Remy asks me. I've been so busy lately that I forget to eat except for family dinners or when I eat with Remy. I shake my head.

"I thought so." He goes to the refrigerator and peruses the choices. Then he makes me a sandwich while I help the troops. And not just any sandwich. He makes me a stacked jambon-beurre, but he adds his own version of a lemon-avocado paste with arugula and romaine.

"Eat," he commands when he brings it to me with some sliced apple and a large water with lemon.

"Aye aye, Captain. And merci."

"Well, we can't let our leader get sick," he says quietly. "Especially with Le Bac coming up."

My mom comes over. "Thank you, Remy, for making sure she eats."

"Of course."

She glances at Simon. "Why does that boy have tattoos all over his arms like that?" she whispers. "Is he American?"

"He just wishes he were," I say, and the three of us laugh. It's the first time my mom and Remy have ever laughed together, at least that I can remember. I wish this could have happened before. Before Remy and I were in entropy. Maybe it would somehow have made a difference.

I shove the last bite of sandwich into my mouth as Remy reminds me to eat the apple slices, so I take them with me as I explain how to make the fillings for the different tarts to my team of Kylian, Daniel, and Simon. Somehow, Reine and Olivia have landed on Team Remy with Max, as shocking as that is.

Then Remy and I teach them about cookies, which isn't that hard, especially as some of them have already baked cookies before.

"It's important to properly cream the butter and sugar," I say, "because that's what builds the airiness of the cookie."

Remy goes to pop a piece of chocolate praline tart in my mouth, but I'm not expecting it. I turn and he hits my cheek with it. We laugh it off, and it will be fine on the video, but we wouldn't normally have made a goof like that.

"So much for me making sure that Aurie is eating enough," Remy says to the camera.

He wipes the chocolate off my face with a wet paper towel and then he kisses my cheek where it was, just for show. I laugh, but my real boyfriend watching my fake boyfriend kiss me is more than a little weird. I touch my cheek and then glance at Kylian. He turns away and busies himself with washing up some bowls.

We finish cleaning up the kitchen just as the TPs come home. Daniel has to leave, but everyone else stays and my mom orders Thai food for us.

"Okay, so Remy and Aurie will split the green papaya salad and khao pad, but what should I order for everyone else?"

Even my mom knows that Remy and I have sharesies for anywhere we eat. I don't know how much longer I'll have Remy around to make sandwiches for me, or share our favorite dishes, but I'm glad entropy hasn't taken that from us yet. I just don't want Kylian to be hurt. He contemplates me when he hears my mom say this, so I send him a quick smile to try to tell him it doesn't mean anything.

The TPs are in their glory with so many big kids to get attention from, and of everyone, it's Simon who is the most patient with them, even listening to Delphine recite poems she learned in school. Thierry asks me why Simon draws on his arms like that, and I tell him to whisper because it's not polite to talk about someone's appearance. So then he whispers what feels like forty questions about Simon's tattoos to me. Thierry might grow up to be an investigative reporter.

After everyone has left and Armel takes the TPs upstairs for their baths, I help my mom clean up the last of the dishes. Kylian will video chat with me later, but these days Remy only texts me when he has something to tell me, or if I text him first. Some nights I hold out, stubbornly, because he could still text me if he wanted to, but other nights I break down and text him just for the satisfaction of seeing those jumping dots still in my life.

"Aurie," my mom says as she puts flatware into the dishwasher, "Remy is very thoughtful of you. I'm sorry I didn't see that before."

"Maman, just because he made me a sandwich, now you like him?" I laugh. "I've told you a million times that he looks out for me."

She shakes her head. "It's not just the sandwich. I've been watching him with you lately, since the two of you have been here more with all the tutoring and planning for this festival, and I've seen that he really cares about you. I was wrong about him."

I don't know how to answer her. There are so many things I wish I could tell her. I need her advice, but it's impossible to ask for it without telling her the truth. And that would get not just me in trouble, but Remy and Lille, and probably even Kylian. So I hug her instead. She looks at me with surprise, but then she hugs me back, hard. It's been a long time since we hugged like this. I guess when you're a teenager, you think you don't need your mom to hug you anymore. But sometimes I just want to be her little girl and have her tell me that everything will be all right. Remy used to do that for me when the world got to be too much.

"Kylian is a lovely boy, too," she says as she pulls away and rubs my arms. "I'm so glad he's tutoring you. You seem much more confident about your math."

"I am, although I can't promise that I've learned enough to make you and Dad happy."

"We just want you to try, that's all." I don't believe that, but it's nice to hear her spin it that way.

Before bed, Kylian calls me on video chat. We talk about all kinds of things, like plans for the festival and how many cookies Max ate and how his dad is taking Lille to the opera tomorrow night.

"Seriously? Lille is going to the opera?" I ask.

"She told him she loves it," Kylian replies.

I laugh-snort.

"So that's not true?"

"I mean, I can't envision Lille being able to sit still through an entire opera, can you?"

Kylian laughs.

"She must really like your dad."

"Argh, don't say that," he says, but he's kind of laughing. Lille never pretended to like soccer when she dated those Italian soccer players.

"Hey," he says, turning serious, "Remy told me today that you got into a couple of schools in the States."

"Not Harvard, like my dad wanted. I told him that wouldn't happen. But one is in Massachusetts and one is in New York, so he was at least happy about that. And I got into one in California, but he's not too happy about that one."

"Why didn't you tell me?"

"You knew I was applying to schools there," I say. "Just like I know you've applied to the University of Edinburgh and Oxford."

"I guess," he says. "But you told Remy."

I let out a breath. "Remy was with me when I found out about them. With the time difference, it was always during band practice."

"You're right, I get it."

It hits me that I've spent a lot more time thinking about what will happen to Remy and me when I go to college than what will happen to Kylian and me.

"I mean, just because we go to different schools, that doesn't mean anything has to change," I say.

"Is that what you want, for everything to stay the same?"

"Yes, sure, isn't that what you want?"

Kylian studies my face through the screen. "Truthfully," he says, "I want more."

I look down.

"I just mean," he says, "that I don't want to hide us forever."

I nod. Of course he doesn't. None of this is normal. What would we even be like together, as a couple, if we could date out in the open? What would it be like to spend a day together like we did today, but with everyone knowing that Kylian was my boyfriend instead of thinking it was Remy? What would it be like to kiss him without worrying that someone might see us? Under the stars? By the river? Instead of always sneaking kisses during my lessons as if it's wrong to kiss each other at all. What if he wants more than kisses? Would I want that?

"After the festival," I say, "I'll talk to Remy and Lille about getting an exit strategy."

"Really? Are you sure?"

I nod. "Remy and I can't pretend forever."

The clock is ticking on so many things. On Le Bac and high school. On my decision about college. On my friendship with Remy. On hanging out with the band. Maybe even on my career as a fashion influencer and my future with my family.

"You look tired," Kylian says. "I'll see you tomorrow."

"Okay."

We send each other kisses through the phone and hang up. Then I turn out the light and snuggle down in my bed. And I cry.

Twenty-Eight

June 15 is coming a lot faster than I hoped it would. The last couple of weeks have been packed with school, and festival meetings and details, and studying, and homework. You'd think our teachers could give us a bit of a slide out the door, but instead they seem to be ramping up as if they have to hit us with everything they have before we escape. But every time I feel panicked, Remy makes me do some deep breathing exercises.

Le Bac is only two days away when Remy stops band practice to get me some chamomile tea and make me breathe when he notices how stressed I am. The guys all sit with me and talk me down from the total conviction I'm having that everything is going to implode.

"You've done an amazing job with the festival, Aurie," Théo says, drumming on my knee for emphasis. "I mean it, it's going to be great."

"See?" Remy says. "She thinks I just say that because I love her."

I look up. We don't say things like that. Especially now. Remy's face flushes.

"We all love her," Max says, not picking up on the weirdness passing between Remy and me. I know Remy only means it as a friend, but it's still awkward. Until Max grabs me in a bear hug and they all pile on, chanting, "We love Aurie!"

"Okay, guys, I get it! I get it!" They pull away and stare at me until we're all laughing so hard that it reminds me of how I used to laugh this way with Remy all the time.

"So," Simon says, "are we good? Can we go back to practicing? Because we have a big gig in a couple of weeks and the festival organizer is a bit of a . . ." He trails off to let the joke be us supplying the euphemism for me being too hard on them.

I laugh. "Please do. You guys are taking up *all* my personal space. Not to mention you're my headliners, so you need to get it together."

They know I'm teasing, so it just makes them dogpile me again.

Remy's the last to leave. He tucks a lock of hair behind my ear and nods at me one last time to make sure I'm okay now. I nod back to let him know he can finish practice.

After they wrap up, he heads us out of Montmartre in the opposite direction of home. I don't ask where he's taking us, even though I don't know. He rides up to a spot above the Seine that we used to like to go to. It's been a long time since we were here. There are no crowds around, no one to recognize us. You have to pass through a rough bit of town and warehouses to get to it, but then it's this sweet little spot near some old, middle-class row houses that has been forgotten in a city teeming with people.

He pulls the bike up along the river and cuts the engine. Trees line the bank in little clusters. The breeze from the water is chilly. Remy shrugs his jacket off and turns just enough to put it around me. I lean my cheek against his back, and we just sit there, his legs outstretched to keep the bike steady, my feet resting on the foot pegs. We listen to the water lap the riverbank while the lights from the opposite shore dance and sparkle. We don't talk. There's the slightly off smell of the river, tinged with Remy's citrus cologne. I close my eyes and just breathe. I want to remember this so much that there's an ache in my chest.

"It's going to work out," he says eventually. "I believe in you. I always have."

My arms are still around him for support. I squeeze him so I don't cry.

He laughs. Just one very short laugh.

I don't know how I'm supposed to live without this. Without him. It's like the world is asking me to live without air.

Neither of us moves. Some clouds roll along and reveal a three-quarter moon with a spattering of stars, bright enough to fight with the lights of the outskirts of Paris. Jupiter pulses brightly, with Venus nearby but harder to see.

"We're supposed to be able to see Saturn tonight," Remy says, searching the sky. "But I don't know where to look."

"You're usually good with directions." At least the two of us can still be in sync over the night sky.

He doesn't answer. The warmth of him bleeds into me. He stares upward.

"This is Aurie, Mom," he says quietly. "She lets me be sad when I need to be. And then she makes me laugh. You'd love her."

At first, I think he's teasing me because a lot of the Korean rom-coms we watch have scenes where the boy or girl introduces the other to their dead parent at a cemetery. I'm trying to think of something funny to say when he sniffles.

My breath catches. I bury my face into his shoulders and hug him with my whole heart, my knees still wrapped around him.

He laughs. "Just thought I should do that while I still had the chance," he says. He clears his throat. "It never seemed important until it finally sank in that you're going off to college."

Before I can answer, he starts the Vespa. I move to pull off his jacket, but he tells me to keep it on for the ride. I hold on tightly all the way home. Neither of us says anything.

When we get to my place, I jump off and put my helmet in the top box and shake his jacket from me and hand it to him. He slips it on, and we look at each other.

I love you, Remy St. Julien rolls through my head like a catchy pop tune on repeat that you just can't escape.

I throw my arms around him and squeeze hard for a moment that I wish could last so long I'd forget why I even hugged him in the first place, and then I turn and run to the door before all these feelings spill out of me in words that I'll only regret.

I'm dreading Kylian's call. I never have before. I always look forward to them. But tonight, I see myself as I've been all along. Mamie told me once that the most dangerous liars are people who lie to themselves. I had no idea what she meant then, but now I do.

When I tap accept call, Kylian's sweet, honest face appears. He says "Hey," something he picked up from me and my American ways.

I try to smile. "Hey." I'm snuggled down in my bed, but it's hard to feel any comfort through the guilt.

"How was practice?"

"They did well, they're definitely ready." I don't mention the mini-meltdown I had, or that Remy and the guys deescalated me with their shenanigans. The festival has brought me closer to the boys, but beyond the festival feels like a cliff I'll be free-falling from. Without a hang glider or whatever people jump from cliffs with.

"Any hints on Remy's surprise guest?" Kylian asks.

I shake my head. "But he doesn't seem to have any clue about mine, so that's good. Max was needling me tonight about it, but I don't trust him to keep quiet, so none of them know."

Kylian laughs. "That's pretty cool that you got a-ha to come."

"I can't wait. He's going to love it."

Neither of us says anything for a moment. I need to screw my courage up and be honest with him. He deserves that from me.

"One more session before Le Bac," he says. "I know you're ready, so we'll just go over time management techniques tomorrow. You had a good grasp of the differential problems we went over today. And remember, it's okay to get some wrong. Just take your time and stay calm."

"Kylian," I say.

He lowers his head and raises his eyes at me.

"You don't have to tutor me tomorrow." I try to keep my eyes from tearing up. He's the one who is getting hurt here, not me.

"Why wouldn't I tutor you tomorrow? It's my favorite part of the day."

I'm such a horrible human.

"Kylian, I haven't been honest with myself lately, but tonight I finally realized that."

"Oh," he says after a moment. "I was wondering when it would hit you."

"Wait, what? You knew?"

He smiles ruefully. "I had a pretty good idea."

"I don't understand." I pick at a thread on my white comforter, but I can't completely keep the tears at bay.

"Aurie, I knew I was taking a chance when I suggested this. I knew you probably had feelings for Remy. I guess I hoped I could change that. But I've seen the way you two are with each other, and I don't think it's something either of you does on purpose. It's just who you are together."

I brush a tear from my cheek.

"I'm sorry I hurt you," I say.

Kylian shrugs. "It was worth the risk. Did Remy say something to you?"

I shake my head. "I just know that I can't really give you my heart because it's already filled with someone else."

He nods slowly.

"I never meant to use you, honestly. I'm so sorry I let you tutor me and waste your time."

"Hey," he says, "hold on a minute. You haven't wasted my time. I've loved tutoring you." He wobbles his head. "And even Remy, if I'm being honest. My life was a little boring before you guys came into it."

"Pardon?" I ask, not believing this.

"I'm serious. I mean, I had school, and school strike, but while I had a purpose, you showed me how to really be transformative with it."

"Being an influencer definitely gives you leverage."

"I don't mean just that. It's everything. How savvy you are with social media, how you reached out to all these corporations and other celebrities and got them excited about the festival. How you've led everyone to pitch in, and even go beyond. I may have taught you math, but you've taught me a lot, too."

He's serious. I look down and sniffle. "I can't believe how generous you are."

"Well, you weren't the only one lying to yourself. No one could see you and Remy together and not see it. No matter what, though, I hope we're still friends."

I look at his beautiful eyes, and he's so sincere. "I'd like that. You mean a lot to me. Honestly."

"Same."

"It takes someone special to teach you the language of the universe."

He laughs. "Turns out calculus isn't the only language the

universe speaks. It also speaks the language of love, even if it's just platonic love. You taught me that."

We don't say anything for a few moments, but neither of us moves to say good night. Somehow it's still comfortable.

"So, have you told Remy how you feel?"

I look up. "No way. Nothing's changed between us. In fact, tonight he told me goodbye, for when I leave for college. He doesn't think of me that way."

"I think he does."

I shake my head. "No, it's just that when Remy loves you, he's very protective, because of what happened with his parents."

"I can understand that. I still think you should tell him, though."

My head is like a pair of windshield wipers moving slowly. "No, it's better like this. I don't want things to be any more awkward between us than they already are. Especially once he finds out you and I split up. I don't want him to know that it's because of him. I couldn't take that."

Kylian gets up from his desk and goes to his bed and lies down. "You don't have to tell him, then."

"What do you mean?"

He presses his lips together before he answers. "I mean that if you want, we can go back to fake dating. That way nothing has to get weird for you. You can tell him whenever. No pressure."

"You'd do that for me?"

Kylian laughs. "It's not like it's a big sacrifice, Aur. No one even knew we were dating but Lille and Remy anyway."

"Just until the festival ends," I say. "Le Bac results will be in around then, so I'll have to decide what's next. And Remy and I needed to figure out how to break up for our fans anyway. So you won't have to do it for long."

"It's fine, honestly. It's not like it changes my life if Lille and Remy think we're dating."

"Thank you," I say. "For everything."

"Same," he answers. "Argh, why does that guy have to be so . . ." He pauses, looking for the right word as he rubs his hand through his auburn hair.

"Remy?" I supply.

Kylian laughs. "Yeah. So that. Even I kind of love him." He lets out a big puff of air. "So, tomorrow, we'll go over those time management techniques, yes?"

I smile. "Yes."

"And the day after, you crush Le Bac."

"And the day after, I crush Le Bac, with you and Remy and Reine and Olivia." Realistically, we'll just be crushing the first part of the test, because it's four days long, beginning with philosophy, then specialties, and then there's still the oral exam three days after the written part ends.

He smiles indulgently. "Good night, Aurie. Sleep tight."

"Good night, Kylian," I say, and hang up. I turn out the light and hug my pillow tightly. I may have a broken heart, but no girl in the world has ever had two better fake boyfriends than Aurélie McGinley, celebrity fashion influencer.

Twenty-Nine

The first day of Le Bac, my stomach is so twisted that it feels inside out. Remy texts me in the morning. *Deep breaths. Hwaiting.*

I laugh. That's what I need to remember if I get nervous. The Konglish for "You've got this." It will remind me of all those nights tucked away with Remy watching my Korean rom-coms. Those were the best days ever. Remy and I haven't done movie night since I started dating Kylian. I might not have them anymore, but just like my grandmother, they're in my heart when I need them.

Kylian texts me, too. *I'll see you on the other side. Don't forget you're a star.*

I mark his text with a heart and text him back.

Show them what a math genius looks like.

He marks my text with a thumbs-up emoji.

When I open the philosophy test, I can hardly believe my eyes. I don't even notice the scraping of chairs as people settle in or the way my school always smells like cheap French cologne. The test asks us if we can have absolutes in a universe that is dynamic and ever changing.

It's asking about the philosophy of calculus. Somewhere in a high school in Bercy, Kylian is opening his test and smiling. He's completely prepared me for this with his endless discussions about the interpretation of knowledge, truth, existence, and cognition through the lens of calculus. A subject I once hated.

I'm not saying I love calculus. I'll probably never love it. But I no longer fear it. At least, not with the kind of fear that leaves you clammy and hyperventilating into Diego Aubert's snack bag. I outline my answer and get started, trying to remember all the super-smart things Kylian threw at me in those discussions. Sometimes they made my head squeeze up, but he always helped me through it. It happens a couple of times as I write, where I suddenly feel like the ideas are all merging in a kaleidoscope way, but I take a breath and unravel them. Just like a knotted necklace chain, patiently, slowly, and with hyper-focus.

Later I meet up with Kylian, Remy, and Reine at Mamie's. We stuff ourselves sick with pastries and compare the answers we wrote.

"I'm so proud of you," Remy says when I explain how I answered the question.

"It's all thanks to Kylian," I say, sending him a look of gratitude as I gesture toward him with open palms up.

Remy glances at Kylian, and then at me. He looks like a

puppy who thinks he might be in trouble. And still, somehow, he manages to be incredibly, heart-achingly adorable. "Kylian, I'm sorry I didn't trust you when we first met," he says.

Kylian smiles. "It's okay. I get it. I've seen the way people try to cling onto you guys just because you're famous."

"It's hard to let people in," Remy says, "when they always want something from you. I was worried about what you wanted from Aurie."

"I know," Kylian says. "You always look out for her. Believe me, I'm glad for that."

For a moment they just look at each other, as if they both want to know what the other is really trying to say. I say a little prayer of gratitude that Remy still thinks Kylian and I are dating. Otherwise I would be dying right now.

"We need drinks," Remy says, switching the topic. "I'll get some waters."

Reine offers to help him, so they go into the kitchen together. Kylian raises his eyebrows at me.

"If you change your mind, you can always tell him the truth."

I shake my head. "No, it's better this way. Trust me. I know Remy better than I know myself."

"Okay," he says skeptically.

The rest of the week is a blur of tests and pastry-fueled recaps and last-minute cramming. I don't think most of the test is too hard, but the math section is really challenging. I fight to keep my head from shrinking up, reminding myself over and over that Kylian has taught me this. I even write myself little messages across my scratch paper to keep me focused on that and not on the panic I'm battling. I scribble things like "Whatever happens now, I've given it my all for the past three months," and "hwaiting," and "Remy believes in me."

And then it's over. The proctor calls time and tells us to put our pencils down. There are a few questions that I had to skip over because I just didn't have the slightest idea where to start, but I've at least checked over the ones I've finished. I feel like crying, as if all the stress of the past year is refusing to leave my body without some attention.

I meet the others at Mamie's. Remy says we should go for steak frites, his treat. We head to a restaurant down the block and have dinner together. We're a little subdued, as if we're all just learning to exhale for the first time in a long time.

"No more Le Bac talk," Reine declares when our meals come. "I don't want to ever think about it again!"

Kylian laughs. "Who wants to tell her?"

We all laugh, including Reine. It's pretty much the biggest day in every French kid's life when the results come in. You go to your school and your score is posted for you to find. Since they reformed the process, they also post them on your school's website, but it's kind of a rite of passage to go to your school to get the news. And cry happy or sad tears with your friends. And then call your parents.

"We should go together to see the scores," Kylian says.

"But only you and Reine and Olivia go to the same school," Remy says.

"Well, we could go to Aurie's and then ours, and then yours."

"Why do I have to be first?" I ask.

"When do you want to go?" Kylian asks.

"Last. That way, if it's bad, I can just go home and throw up and cry."

Remy leans over and puts his arm around my shoulder, but then he pulls away with a glance at Kylian.

"You aren't going to need to go home and throw up and cry," Kylian says.

"Yeah," Reine says, "it will be fine. You and Kylian have studied hard."

"Thanks," I say. That might be the first nice thing Reine's ever said to me.

The three of them make a pact that includes me, and then we switch to talking about the festival. Except for baking, we've reached that point of planning a party where you can't really do anything else until it's time to go full speed, although I've been sending reminder emails to the management company so often that they've started to send me a daily check-in to try to head me off. We start our baking the day after the grand oral exam in a few days.

This is probably the easiest part of Le Bac for me. I'm used to public speaking, and I know how to adjust my presentation to meet my audience. That's one thing I learned from Remy. Some nights when he takes the stage, the crowd is like frenzied hyenas who want to devour every note with him, and other nights they're more subdued. It's a lot easier to be a showman when the crowd is happily buying into it than when you have to make them believe it. Any musician will tell you they feed off the energy of the crowd, and public speaking is like that, too. You can usually tell how your audience is reacting to you, whether it's from heart emoji flying up your screen or the facial expression of someone in front of you. I've done thousands of vlogs and interviews, and even some charity and award presentations. And since the festival planning started, I've made a lot of presentations to corporate boards, while wearing their latest fashions, about how their sponsorships can benefit them. So facing a panel of teachers to present on my other specialty besides math, literature, doesn't seem that hard.

Kylian's helped me with my presentation because there are some nods to the mathematical order of calculus on the universe as I discuss the importance of the English system of enclosure to the deeply egalitarian messages of Jane Austen's novels. I'm not cocky, because as the world has shown me, no one likes girls who are cocky. Cocky only gets a pass when it's men, particularly musicians who look like they were sculpted by Michelangelo. But I'm confident, and the panel asks me questions I can answer.

Still, when I walk out of there and am finally done with France's Le Bac, it feels like an enormous weight has been lifted off my chest. Maman has organized a celebration dinner. She wanted me to invite my friends, and Remy, but instead I tell her that I'd like to spend some time with my family, just us. Tomorrow the weight of the festival will come crashing in, but tonight I want to spend with the TPs and my mom and Armel. My mom is thrilled. She doesn't say anything, but her smile is brighter than I've seen it in a long time.

I even video chat my dad.

"Boy, have I missed you, kiddo," he says. "But I know you've been under a lot of pressure."

"It's been intense. I think I'll improve my math scores over the SATs, but, Dad, I wouldn't get your hopes up too much."

"Well, you've already gotten into some pretty great schools," he says.

One of them has allowed me to defer my answer, but the other two made him put a deposit down to save my spot.

"I'm sorry about the deposit money," I say.

"Aurie, it's a big decision, and the French system is so far behind us that I understand."

He means chronologically. I think. While everyone in the States has made their decision and is getting welcome packets and roommate selections, kids in France haven't even found out yet where they'll be admitted. Everything depends on Le Bac.

I nod. I wonder if he'll be this understanding if I decide to stay in France.

We chat for a while longer about family and that two of my cousins are going to be in some of the big hockey showcases in Boston next month. He tells me that Granddad tried to pick up a guy for me at the restaurant they went to last night and the kid thought Granddad was hitting on him and told him off for being a creepy old perv. Dad and I laugh so hard that he can hardly get the story out and my eyes are tearing.

"And then, and then," he says, stopping to take a breath, "the manager comes over and wants us to leave because he thinks that I'm Dad's date, and he tells me that I'm too young for him, let alone the college kid serving the water!"

"Stop!" I say, laughing so hard that I grab my side. "Well, maybe this will teach him not to try to pick up dates for me!"

"Ahhhh," my dad says, wiping his eye. "I don't think it will, but it was so funny. All I could think of was how much you'd wish you could see it!"

"From another table where no one knew he was my grand-father!"

We laugh.

"I miss you, Dad."

"I miss you, too, sweetheart. More than you know."

After we hang up, I spend the rest of my night with my family. My mom has made one of my favorite meals, salmon with a beurre blanc sauce, roasted vegetables in a lemon crème sauce, and smashed potatoes. While the dinner is very French, the potatoes are a nod to my other half.

We eat and laugh. The TPs all tell me how they would do on Le Bac if it were their turn, even though they don't really understand what it is except that it's a big test you have to study a lot for. Thierry says he'd shoot it with his sword, which makes Armel crinkle his eyebrows at Maman.

"Well, if I fail and have to repeat it, I will definitely try that," I say.

"I'll help you," he says as he stuffs a cheesy puff pastry into his mouth with the seriousness of a professional chef judging a high-stakes cook-off.

Maman won't let me help clean up and Armel is on bath duty, so I go into the living room and sit down with a book. It's so weird not to have to study. I should be doing some socials, but we told our fans that we'd be taking a hiatus during Le Bac. "You wouldn't see us doing anything except studying, complaining, and eating pastries anyway," Remy told them. "And there might be some crying," I chimed in, but I said it playfully.

It's kind of glorious to just sit still for a moment. But it's been so long since I've read a book for pleasure that my mind wanders instead of reading. I'm just sitting there, daydreaming, when Armel comes into the living room. He smiles when he sees me there.

He comes over and sits down next to me. "That's a nice sight that I'm not used to."

"Me reading?"

"No. You taking a moment just to exist."

I smile at him. We don't seem to know what to say next.

"The kids have really liked having you, and your friends, around more. I guess I just wanted to say thank you."

There are suddenly tears in my eyes.

Armel smiles and pats my head. "I'm not trying to make you feel guilty. I understand you need to go out and find your way."

"How does someone know how to do that, though?"

"Hmm," he says thoughtfully. "From watching my students

every year, I would say it's by trying things to see what matters to you. You've really grown over the past few months. Not just academically, but personally. I see a big shift in you. You're more confident, more engaged, you take the lead more. I think finally accepting help with your disability has been really good for you."

Even when he's being a stepdad, Armel still sounds like a teacher.

"If I went to the States for school, you would take care of them all, right?" The words spill out of me in a panic.

"Hey," he says, and puts his arm around my shoulder to give me a squeeze. "Of course I would. You don't have to worry about that. We all want you to stay, but if you go, we'll be rooting for you like you're Les Bleus in the World Cup. And we'll come visit you so much that you'll wish you had stayed!"

I half laugh.

"But what if I make the wrong decision?" I blink back tears.

Armel purses his lips before he speaks. "Then I will instruct Thierry to pack his sword when we go to collect you, and we'll shoot all the bad decisions."

I laugh. And then I hug him. I hug my stepdad for the first time ever.

Thirty

By the next morning, the stress of Le Bac has been completely and fully replaced with the stress of the festival. This has to go off without a hitch. I owe it to Kylian, and it's a massive display of Remy's talent. We've garnered a lot of international attention, from US news outlets to the BBC and Australian media. Television stations from all over Europe have sent TV crews to get interviews with the stars. Most of the acts are from Europe, but we have a couple of bands from the States and Australia, too. We don't have any super-big names, but we have bands with a lot of street credit and solid fandoms. And, most importantly, a-ha is coming to sing with Remy.

Kylian and Lille know this, but no one else. There's been a lot of buzz around the surprise acts for the festival, but so far none of the news outlets have figured it out. The slots are saved for late Sunday afternoon, with Remy's guest artist and then my surprise as the last act.

Lille has set up a streaming contract with a European

distributor that will give a portion of the proceeds to the charity we've set up to fund the students. That was a major undertaking, as all the acts had to agree to it. Even the secret ones. But between Lille, my mom, and me, we got it done.

The baking begins in earnest the day after the grand orals. We're all still a bit dazed, but everyone shows up at four o'clock as planned. Mamie's too busy to have us here in the early morning or during the day. She does her prep work for the next day every evening between seven and nine. But the kitchen is ours from four to seven and again after nine. Remy and the boys had to change practice to earlier in the day, but now that school is out, it's not a problem for him. High school graduation here isn't the big deal it is in the States. One day you're still going to school and the next you aren't. There aren't elaborate ceremonies and parties. But considering we've all just been through a crucible test, we still feel a huge sense of accomplishment.

Remy's gotten us pizza from the place we like a couple of streets away, and we get going. Mamie has ordered the extra ingredients we'll need, and her shelves are bursting, but I remind everyone not to waste anything. "Be careful and get it right the first time," I say, which makes them salute me as if I'm running a sweatshop.

"Is she going to be like a Russian mob boss the whole time?" Max asks.

"Very funny," I say. "Mamie's pâtisserie is a well-oiled machine, and I don't want any of us messing that up."

Simon comes over and hugs me. "She's such a cute dictator, am I right?"

I push him off me with a laugh and we get to work, everyone lighthearted and goofy. I think we're all really excited about the festival, even if it's for different reasons. Olivia wants to see her favorite Italian band and Daniel is excited because Max has promised to introduce him to a guitarist Daniel idolizes. Reine and Kylian are excited for the charity, and I'm excited to surprise Remy one last time.

I was kind of dreading this group baking project when I planned it. The idea of watching Reine flirt nonstop with Remy made me a little sick. Especially when I started to worry that he liked her back. Not that he can't like anyone he wants. I just couldn't bear to have front-row seats for that show. But Reine's affection for Remy seems to have cooled, and I think she and I could possibly be called friends now. She even texted me a few times this week to talk about Le Bac. It was kind of nice.

Remy gets Team Crust started, but not before Max whips out T-shirts he's had made that say *Team Crust* and *Team Filling* on them, with little cartoons of pastries.

"Seriously?" Remy and I say at the same time.

Max shrugs happily and throws each of us a shirt.

Everyone makes fun of them and then puts them on. Daniel gets Max and Remy and Simon to sign his, and Olivia gets Remy to sign hers. While Remy has Team Crust making crusts, I get started with Team Cookie. We're going to make dough and freeze it until the festival.

"When is Team Filling getting our chance?" Simon asks. "Everyone is Team Cookie."

"When there are crusts existing to fill," I say, while Max swats him in the stomach as if that was a super-dumb question.

Everything is moving along better than I expected. In fact, it's great. Everyone is having fun, we aren't destroying Mamie's kitchen—although I spend a lot of time following them around cleaning up—and we're making on-target progress for the spreadsheet I've made of how many of each item we need and when.

And then Lille shows up. With Pierre Naillon in tow.

Remy and I exchange a glance and shake our heads to tell each other we had no idea.

"Lille, what the hell is going on?" Remy says while I echo him before I realize he said it, too.

Lille turns to Naillon and says something too quietly for me to hear.

Remy and I march over to her. I wish I were a Russian mob boss right now. I twist my face into a smile at Naillon. "Would you excuse us, please?"

Remy points at him. "Don't take a single photo in here." Then he turns to the group. "No one talk to this guy. We'll be right back."

We yank Lille into the shop.

"What are you thinking?" I ask.

"We need the publicity, Aurie." She's wearing a bright blue pantsuit that makes her look like a flattened robin's egg with a head. Or maybe it just seems that way because I'm so mad at her.

"No, Lille," Remy says, "we don't need publicity. Aurie has this thing sold out."

"Well, *I* don't have it sold out, you and the other acts do," I say.

Lille looks at the ceiling like she's asking for divine intervention to stop us always putting the other first.

"What we need," Lille says, "is to have the tabloids happy with us. They don't like that you undercut them. And Naillon particularly has a vendetta with you two after the way you embarrassed him when you started vlogging yourselves all-access."

Remy shakes his head. "Too bad. It's worked. They haven't followed us around for two months."

"But with the festival, they want more, and if we don't give them some structured access, then there's no telling what they might print. It's only for today."

"You think that, in bargaining with the devil, he's going to keep promises to you? Come on, Lille, you know better," Remy says. He shakes his head at her.

"Remy's right, Lille. We have too many secrets to let that viper into our den."

"I understand, Aurie, but there's a reason for the saying 'Keep your friends close and your enemies closer.' I don't think he's interested in scooping you two."

"Well, he's interested in scooping someone, Lille," Remy says. "Even if it's not us, all the acts will be here because we asked them to, because they trusted us."

Lille seems unmoved.

"Oh my God, are you dating him?" I ask. He is exactly her type. I should have warned Kylian's dad.

"No," she whispers ferociously. "I've just flirted with him a little to get him to let his guard down."

"Ever think that's why he's been flirting with you?" Remy asks.

Lille pouts.

"Seriously, Lille. We can't have him here," I say.

"He's agreed to show me every photo he takes before he leaves. He just wants to have some inside views of the event."

"That he'll spin into some fantastical story," I say.

"Well, if you kick him out now, he's going to really be gunning for you two. And neither of you can afford that right now."

I look at Remy. She's right. She's put us in a terrible position.

"Lille, I swear, if this guy blows us apart, I'm finding a new manager," Remy says. I've never seen him this angry. Not even when he tried to beat up Kylian.

"Understood," Lille says. "But not giving him access was just as risky at this point. You can't expect to pull off a festival of this size and not have a media frenzy."

"You should have talked to us first, Lille," I say. "And if you hurt Kylian's dad, I swear I'll fire you."

She narrows her eyes at me. "I like Kylian's dad way too much to seriously look at Naillon. You just keep your real boyfriend in check and everything will be fine."

Right. My real boyfriend. The one who isn't my real boyfriend, but who Lille and Remy think is my real boyfriend while I pretend to be Remy's real girlfriend and wish I were. Easy peasy, nothing to worry about.

"Whatever," I say, and push past her to the kitchen.

I walk up to Naillon. "You can take photos of me, Remy, and the guys in the band if it's okay with them. Everyone else is off-limits. Got it?"

Naillon nods in a smart-aleck way, his lips pressed together.

"These guys are all under eighteen and they aren't celebrities," I add, pointing to the others.

Remy's been recording. "One word about any of them, Naillon, and we're turning this in to the authorities, got it?"

Nailon throws up his hands. "I just want some shots of the event preparation. That's all." He sounds very believable, which makes me distrust him more.

I gesture for him join us. The mood has changed, though. All the lightheartedness has flown. Max and Simon are suddenly treating this like a job they're getting paid for, heads down and productivity up. Kylian, Reine, Olivia, and Daniel seem a little awestruck, like they're not sure what's just happened.

Lille stands in the corner and watches, arms crossed. Remy and I try to smile and act like lovebirds, but we're both so mad at Lille it's harder than usual.

"How's Team Filling doing?" Remy asks.

"Waiting for crusts," I answer, and he laughs. But both of us are a bit subdued.

"Everything okay with you two?" Naillon asks.

"Of course," we say in unison.

"We just don't like having someone here who'd be happy to hurt us," I add.

Naillon smiles. "Why? Do you have secrets you're keeping?"

Remy nudges me, I think to tell me to laugh it off.

"Yes," I answer.

Naillon's eyebrows arch eagerly.

"Mamie's recipes," I say. I turn and help Team Filling make the chocolate praline custard. I glance over at Remy. He's looking down and biting back a smile.

When we pack up to give the kitchen to Mamie for the night shift, Naillon and Lille go into the shop. He shows her the photos he's taken. Remy and I watch from the doorway. Lille looks through his camera roll and nods and they say good night.

Remy exhales hard. "This is going to end badly. I can feel it."

I lean my head against his arm. "I have the exact same feeling."

Thirty-One

The rest of the week before the festival passes quickly. Naillon shadows us way more than I'd like, but except for the occasional weirdness where Remy catches Kylian and me talking together and tries to give us space without it seeming like that's what he's doing, I think it's going okay. Naillon hasn't sold anything salacious to the tabloid outfits he works for, just cute pictures of us getting ready for the festival. Still, if he found out the truth, he'd gladly scoop it without a second thought. I think he'd see hurting us as a fortunate bonus.

I contemplate telling Remy the truth. It would be one less thing for him to worry about this week. But then he'd be worried instead that his best friend is in love with him and that he'll break her heart. That seems worse for him than trying to be thoughtful of Kylian and me without giving anything away. Once the festival is over, everything will start to change anyway. It's probably best just to ride this out.

When we aren't at the bakery, Remy and I are either

checking the venue or welcoming acts as they arrive. Remy, Simon, and Théo show them the stage setup, which is mostly finalized by the middle of the week.

On Tuesday, the results for Le Bac are posted. We check each school's time. Kylian, Reine, and Olivia's school is supposed to be posted by ten a.m. Remy's says between ten and noon, and my school promises the results will be posted by two o'clock. I wonder if it's a bad omen that my school is so much later than the rest of them.

We meet in Bercy at lycée Paul-Valéry at nine-forty-five. Kylian's school looks like a prison, with a long flat roof and small windows. The scores are posted near the entrance, and there's a lot of jostling as people try to get close enough to see. Remy and I hang back and let the others go meet their fates. The morning is warm and sunny, with the scent of too much perfume in the air. Of course Kylian's smashed the test with a solid 19 out of 20. He gets the highest honors, the Mention Très Bien, which means "with distinction." He's even gotten Félicitations du Jury, which is an unofficial extra congratulations the panel can give to someone who has scored at least an 18, if they think the student's work is exceptional.

We all hug him. Reine has done well, too, getting Mention Assez Bien. In English, it translates to "good enough," which is a jerky way to say honors, but that's France. Even when they're giving compliments, they make it sound bad. Olivia looks next. She's also gotten Mention Assez Bien, just barely, and she starts crying and rushes off to call her mom because she thought she would get Sans Mention, which is the French education system's way of saying without honors.

We lose Olivia in the crowd and she's not answering texts, so the rest of us decide to head to Remy's school without her. We take the subway. Remy's got his *Hunting High and Low* T-shirt on. I lean into him. We're in public, so it's expected, although he sends Kylian a glance. But right now, I need him close, even if it's only as my best friend. Kylian stares discreetly at the glass window. I'm happy for my friends, but I can't help but be scared that my results won't be as good. I'd be thrilled with Assez Bien. Remy picks up on my nervousness. "It's going to be okay," he whispers. I nod like I believe him, and he squeezes my hand a little tighter.

When we get to his school, the results have been posted for a while. People are on their phones or jumping up and down or crying. Some of the crying is happy, but not all of it. My Stateside cousins don't understand how much worse it is here. You choose your life path by the time you're sixteen, and most of your high school record depends on Le Bac, which means your whole future is riding on these results.

Remy tows me through the crowd to the wall where the scores are posted, and we search. He's gotten Mention Bien, or high honors, with a solid 15.7 score. I hug him and start laughing.

"Why is this funny to you?" he asks.

"Mamie's going to ask why you couldn't get a sixteen so you could have had Mention Très Bien with that high of a score!"

His face turns serious. "Maybe I could just say I got a fifteen. That wouldn't be a lie, right?"

He mulls this over a moment until Kylian and Reine come to jump him with hugs. A reporter pops up in his face to ask him how he feels about his score and then announces it to the world. So much for keeping it from Mamie.

When the interview is over, Kylian turns to me. "That just leaves you," he says. "But your scores aren't ready," he adds, checking the time on his phone.

"Let's grab lunch," Remy says. "It's on me."

"Sounds good," Kylian answers.

"I'm starved," Reine says, linking her arm through mine.

We go to a little bistro, but I can't really do much but pick at my croque monsieur while the rest of them dig in. I nudge Remy under the table.

"What?" he asks.

"Look outside," I say. Naillon is skulking around the sidewalk.

"Ignore him," Remy says. "He isn't going to find anything on us." He laughs for show and kisses my temple.

Remy holds my hand as we leave the restaurant and Naillon takes his shots. We head to the pâtisserie, and we all hop in the Peugeot. The midday Paris traffic slows us down. I wonder if this, too, might be a bad omen. Remy nods his confidence at me so much that it becomes almost comical. Somehow, though, he gets us to my school, Collège-Lycée Jean-Baptiste-Say, before two o'clock.

"Let's get ice cream while we wait," Reine says, but some kids are already leaving when Remy finds a parking spot out front.

"They must have posted early," I say as we get out and head to the central pavilion at the heart of the historic buildings which make up my school. It already feels weird to come back here, as if I don't belong anymore. A couple of kids I know stop to tell me their scores. Both have gotten Sans Mention. Passing sounds good right now, with or without honors. I need to be happy if I just pass. Even if it disappoints my parents, at least I really tried. By the time we get to the postings, I'm trembling.

Remy pulls me aside and drapes his arm over my shoulder. "Hey, it's all right. You already got into three good schools in the States." He doesn't mind me leaving. I take a breath and nod.

When I finally find my score, I have to put my finger against the line and make sure I've read the right one.

"Does that say what I think it says?" I ask Remy. Kylian is right behind us, and he yells, "Yes!"

I've gotten Mention Bien. Just barely, with a flat 14. But it doesn't matter. It's still high honors. Before I realize it, I'm sobbing and shaking and Remy is petting my head and Kylian's on my other side, laughing. I hug Kylian with all my might and thank him over and over again.

"It's good," he says in English. He wipes away my tears. "It's all good. I told you that you could do it!"

Even Reine is jumping up and down for me.

"I have to call Maman," I say, tears still streaming down my face. Around me, kids from school congratulate me, and some ask Remy for autographs.

I step away from the others and call. "Maman," I say when she answers, "I got Mention Bien!"

"Oh, Aurie, that's wonderful!" she says. "I knew you could do well! Aren't you glad I made you take math as a specialty?"

I'm really not. I don't think she has any idea what she's put me through. But I let her have her little victory, because it wouldn't change anything to take it away from her.

"We'll have a celebration dinner. Bring Remy and your friends," she says.

Kylian and Reine are going to celebrate with their families, but Remy nods when I tell him that Maman wants him to come for dinner. Not without glancing at Kylian first, though. I wish he'd stop doing that. He acts like he needs permission from Kylian to even touch me, as if I belong to Kylian or something. Having them be friends is almost worse than when they were enemies.

We walk to an ice cream place nearby and treat ourselves. Remy and I post a video of our dessert celebration, and we're laughing like we haven't laughed since our last movie night.

For the first time in what feels like forever, the first time since my mother put me on this path to conquer my disability, I can fully exhale. Thanks to Kylian, I'm no longer terrified of math. Afraid, yes. But not terrified.

I'm still disabled, and that's never going to change. It's still ridiculously painful for me to do math, and I will always have to use my strategies to compensate and to keep my anxiety under control. It will always take me longer than it takes normal people. But I can learn it with enough time and care. I doubt I'll ever find anyone willing to help me the way Kylian has, but that's okay. It's up to me now to figure out how to carry forward everything he's taught me.

"Aurie, why are you crying?" Remy says.

I shake my head and brush the tears off my cheeks with my fingers. "It's just really good to have friends," I say, and the three of them hug me until I can't even believe how lucky I am, fake-boyfriend-broken-heart and all.

Thirty-Two

I wake up the first morning of the festival feeling like I've spent all night on a train. No, I feel worse. I barely slept at all worrying about the festival. At least on a night train, I always got some rest snuggled up against Remy. Still, I hop out of bed and go shower because it's showtime. I know this feeling because I've been to so many of Remy's gigs with him, but it hits a little differently now that I'm the one who needs to perform. Not onstage, but still. I have to make sure this goes well. Before I leave the house, I vlog my outfit, a Dani Meadows halter dress, and my makeup, which is my nighttime dramatic look complete with eyeliner because it's going to be a long day with a lot of photos.

My mom has volunteered to help run Mamie's stall at the festival. She even took the day off work, so she drives us to the pâtisserie to pick up today's inventory.

"I'm really impressed with everything you've accomplished in the past few months," she says to me on the way. Then she smiles. "You look supercute, too, by the way." My mother never comments on my looks. She doesn't want me to value myself on something so immaterial and fleeting. It feels nice, though, to have her say it, as if it's a blessing on my influencer status. Well, not a blessing, but maybe an admission that she doesn't absolutely, one hundred percent hate my career now that I've shown I can also succeed at school.

"Merci, Maman." We're stopped at a light, and she reaches over and strokes my cheek.

"You don't seem happy, though," she says.

The light changes and she turns her attention back to the traffic, so she doesn't see how wet my eyes get.

"I'm happy," I say. "It's just a little bittersweet."

She nods.

"I used to worry about you going away, but I don't anymore. I know now you'll always come back to us, even if it's just for visits. I know we aren't going to lose you."

I have the feeling she wants to cry, too. I wish I could tell her how my heart feels like someone ran it through a mandoline and then a blender just for good measure. But she thinks Remy St. Julien is my boyfriend. And I need her to keep thinking that until Remy and I find a way to fake break up, because if she knew the truth, she'd fire Lille and probably never speak to Remy again. Not that I imagine I'll see much of him after I leave for college, but the idea of her hating someone I love so much hurts my heart.

When we get to the venue, there are a million things for me to check on, so I show her the stall and leave her with Reine to get it all set up. People are queued outside the fenced areas waiting to get in, and in the VIP area bands are getting ready, with the first acts doing sound checks. The day is warm but slightly overcast. Lille finds me backstage as I make sure everyone from paramedics to security have shown up as promised.

"You look perfect," she says. Unlike my mom, Lille always critiques my outfits. I'm about to ask her if she's heard from a-ha when Pierre Naillon suddenly appears, taking shots of us as if it's Remy and me.

"Good morning, Pierre," Lille says. The pastry I grabbed at Mamie's for breakfast turns in my stomach. I smile anyway. If I let my face show how annoyed I feel, the photo would be used to concoct some story about my manager and me fighting at the festival.

Naillon makes small talk with us. I don't really have time for this, but I smile through it as best I can. I don't need to give him more reasons to target me.

Remy and Kylian come over.

"Give us a shot?" Naillon says.

Remy and I nod. He slips his arm around my waist, and we pose. The citrus scent of his cologne washes over me and it's kind of like realizing you're finally home after a long trip. I feel this way every time I settle in at my dad's house for summer visits, and every time I come back to France. Although I guess I never realized it until now. I guess they are both home.

Naillon starts shooting, but he and Remy are watching Kylian. Panic seizes me. *Could he know?* Naillon smiles and lowers his camera and tells us thank you as if everything is normal. I'm being paranoid.

The music starts at noon. I barely see Remy or Kylian the rest of the day. At four o'clock, Kylian switches with Reine, and she and I go back to the pâtisserie to bake more cookies and fill more crusts. Daniel stays at the festival to help Kylian, but Olivia meets us at the pâtisserie after her summer job as a waitress at a bistro. We help Mamie with her night prep and have dinner. Then we get to work again.

It's past eleven o'clock when Remy arrives.

"It went so well," he tells us, smiling like he's just won a Grammy. "I can't believe how smooth everything went today. The bands were smashing it, and the crowds were killing it."

"It sounds like a riot," Mamie says. "You should have called the police!"

She's just teasing, and we all laugh. It's especially funny because she's such a tiny, serious person most of the time.

"Drive the girls home, Remy. You've all done enough for one day," she adds.

We take the Peugeot. Remy drops me off last. I wonder if I've taken my last ride on the back of his Vespa.

"Why are you so sad?" he asks as he pulls up to my house.

I shake my head. "Exhaustion."

He nods. "You've done an incredible job."

I think about mentioning Naillon, and how he was watching Kylian while Remy and I posed this morning, but then I don't.

My grandma McGinley used to say that you shouldn't borrow trouble. As I say good night to Remy and get out of the car, I definitely have more than my fair share of trouble. I don't need to borrow any more.

Thirty-Three

I wake up and there's no trouble on my social feeds, no frantic texts from Lille, no remorseful messages from Remy. My suspicions seem silly now, like when you're a preteen home alone at night and you're sure there's suddenly a horde of zombies outside your house just waiting to break in and make you one of their undead. Then, when your parents get home, you make fun of yourself for how ridiculous you were.

Remy texts me while I'm getting ready.

I'll come and get you. The crowds are too big for you to take the Metro.

I think about telling him not to worry, but he's probably right. Even if it were perfectly safe, I'd likely get so slowed down with people stopping me that I'd be super-late.

When he shows up on his Vespa, I smile. At least one last time, I'll get to hold on to him as we zip through the streets of Paris. I slip my arms around him the way I used to. Or maybe I cling a little tighter, I don't know. What I do know is that I savor every moment. And not just Remy. I savor the sights and sounds of Paris, beautiful, chaotic, quaint, and colossal, and all of it in dizzying disproportion and grace. To stay or to go doesn't really matter. This city will always have a piece of my heart, just like Boston does.

At the festival, Kylian, Reine, and Daniel are setting up Mamie's stall. We help them and then I have to go check in with the bands. Remy comes with me because this is his favorite part, walking around backstage before a concert. Most musicians don't know what to do with themselves in this space, but for Remy it has the same effect as going to church has for some people. It's where he communes best with his parents.

It's almost noon and the first concert of the day is about to start. La Place de l'Hôtel de Ville, the city hall square, is jammed with people of all ages eagerly waiting for the concert to begin. The July sun beats down and people stroll through the vendor areas grabbing lunch and, I hope, pastries. I'm peeking out at this amazing scene from the edge of the backstage area when Remy comes up behind me and rests his chin on the top of my head, his arms around my waist.

"You did all this," he says.

I lean my head back gently. "We did all this. With a lot of help."

He laughs.

"Have you seen Naillon?" I ask.

Remy pulls away. He's wearing Converses, jeans, and an old Foo Fighters T-shirt with his hair loose. My heart puddles like melted chocolate. "Why would you want him?"

"I don't. But I think it's odd that I haven't seen him here today. He's been shadowing us like a detective."

Remy frowns and scans the area. "You're right."

The first concert starts and the crowd cheers. The whole place seems like it's running on an electrical charge of human emotion. And the conduit is the band playing.

It's late in the afternoon when we finally discover why Naillon hasn't been around. Remy and I have been vlogging behind-the-scenes videos throughout the day, but like someone turning out the light, our feeds change from enthusiastic love pouring down to something I can only describe as hate for me and pity for Remy.

How could she cheat on Remy St. Julien?

She's a psychopath.

I always hated her.

Poor Remy, I'd console him in a heartbeat.

Remy and I look up at the same time. "Naillon," we say.

We frantically pull up tabloids. It's in one of the worst ones. *Aurélie McGinley Secretly Dating Her Math Tutor, Shatters St. Julien's Heart.*

The pictures are horrible. The first ones are of me hugging Kylian with all my might and crying happily when I got my Le Bac results. There's also one of Kylian holding my hand in the Parc de Bercy, when he was consoling me for my disability. A series of photos show me smiling alongside Kylian with Remy looking away or unhappy. The final shots are of Remy alone and looking dejected. The actual moments Kylian and I spent as a couple couldn't look more convincing.

"I'm so sorry," I say as I try not to cry.

"That bastard knew this whole time and was waiting until he could inflict maximum damage."

Lille comes running up just as my phone starts buzzing. It's my mom. On video chat. I'm in so much trouble.

As soon as I answer, my mom launches in, wanting to know what the hell is going on, with Lille asking the same questions beside me like surround sound. Remy shepherds us to a small empty area that's used as a greenroom. It's not exactly private, as it's made from curtains, but at least no one can see us.

I tell them everything, leaving out the part about being hopelessly in love with my best friend.

"Wait," Remy says, "you broke up with him and you didn't even tell me?"

I open my mouth, but nothing comes out. What am I supposed to say?

His jaw hardens. He's definitely mad at me. This is the second time I should have told him something and didn't. Although the first time shouldn't count, since I had just made up the thing I was telling him. I've messed up more times than even best friend status can overcome.

"Well," my mom says, "I'm more disappointed in you than I can say, but right now we need to get you home. You aren't safe there."

"I'm safe, we have security," I say.

"Aurie, have you seen the comments?" Lille asks without any of her usual bossiness. She's genuinely worried about me. Remy is texting someone.

"Aurie, I want you to come home," my mom says. "I'll come get you."

"Wait, Madame Derise," Remy says. "My security guys are coming. They'll bring her home."

"Why can't I stay? It's not like anyone is going to rush backstage to attack me."

Remy turns to me with such a look of pain on his face that it's like being punched. "Aur, these comments are bad. And crowds are dangerous. We can't take any chances. Can't you just trust me?"

I've hurt him. Maybe more than our friendship can handle. Maybe he just really doesn't want me here. "Fine. I'll go."

"Merci, Remy," my mom says. Lille pats my arm. She's the one who gave Naillon the access to do this. But it's my fault, not hers. I hang up with my mom.

"I'm going to find Kylian," Remy says as soon as the security team arrives. "Make sure he's okay."

I nod.

He stops and looks back before he leaves. "It's not your fault, Aurie. We're both to blame."

"Don't tell anyone that," I say, shaking my head. "Let me take the fall. It doesn't matter if I lose my platform. But you can't."

"Do you understand what you're saying?" Remy asks.

"I can take the heat." Especially if I lie low for college. "I'll be fine. Your fans can't hate you." I guess the decision to go back to the States has just been made. "Let them think I'm the bad guy here, Remy. You have to promise me."

"I can't promise that," Remy says.

"She's right," Lille says. Quietly.

Remy exhales. "Let's talk about it later. We can gauge the fallout and figure out what to do. But, Aur, you can't be here tomorrow. It's too dangerous."

"People say stuff online all the time that they don't mean—"

"Aur," he says, and it stops me. Lille shows me her phone so I can see the comments. People want to do everything from beat me to a pulp in a dark alley to firebomb my house. There's no way my mom's going to let me come, protection or not.

I turn away crying and walk out surrounded by Remy's three security guys.

Thirty-Four

My mom and Armel are waiting when I get home. Remy's security have all walked me to the door. Paparazzi are on the sidewalk, along with former fans—or maybe always-haters, because no one is an influencer without some of those—who are booing and cursing me. A rock lands in our yard from who knows where.

"Thank you for bringing my daughter home," my mom says as she wraps her arm around my shoulders. She starts to close the door, but one of them, Stephan, puts his arm out to stop her.

"Ma'am, we're under strict orders from Mr. St. Julien not to leave Ms. McGinley's side. We'll be taking shifts, and I'm first." He's in his thirties and looks like he watches too many FBI shows.

My mom scans the crowd; then her glance takes in the rock. She nods for him to come in.

When the door closes, I collapse into my mom and sob.

She doesn't yell at me, which surprises me.

"Aurie," she says after a few moments, "there's something you haven't told me yet, isn't there?"

I nod because I can't speak through the tears.

She leads me to the sofa. Thierry crawls into my lap and pets me. Camille sits beside me, and Delphine stands in front of me, her hand on my knee. Armel sits opposite us, bent forward, hands on his knees.

"Delphine, sweetheart, go and get your sister some tissues, please," my mom says.

"I'll make some tea," Armel says. He goes into the kitchen and putters around while Delphine brings me tissues and I wipe my tears and blow my nose. Stephan stands by the window and squints through the shutters.

When Armel comes in with the tea, I tell them the rest. Stephan pretends he's not listening, but I can tell by the way his face changes that he hears me admit I'm in love with Remy and that I dated Kylian to convince myself otherwise, until I couldn't lie to myself anymore.

Sometimes one of the TPs will try to ask a question, but my mother shushes them.

"Does Remy know this?" Maman asks, her hazel eyes fixed on me.

"No, and I don't want him to. He'll just feel sorry for me, and it will make everything worse. It's better if he thinks Kylian and I didn't work out for other reasons."

My mom purses her lips.

"What?" I ask.

"It seems to me that lying in the first place got you into all this mess. So maybe continuing to lie isn't the best idea."

"It's just not the whole truth. Remy doesn't need to know that I love him that way."

My mom takes a big breath and she and Armel exchange glances.

"Remy loves you, too," Thierry says.

I pat his head. "Not like that, darling. He only loves me as a friend. It's kind of how you love me as a sister."

He doesn't nod because he doesn't fully understand. Which is okay because I don't understand anything about my life anymore.

"What are we going to do?" Maman says, but she's looking at Armel.

"We'll have to weather it. It will die down soon, I'm sure," he says.

"I'm sorry. I never meant for any of this to happen."

My mom pulls me over to her and I cry on her some more.

"Lille will figure something out," I say.

My mom scoffs. "She's done enough. She's finished managing you."

"Don't say that, Maman. Lille is a better person than you think." She's just like me. She misses the mark more than she hits it.

I'll be eighteen in a couple of months. My mom knows she

can't stop me from contracting with Lille on my own then. But I want to have her blessing. If future me even needs a manager.

Reine is also mad at me. Apparently she's been in love with Kylian all along, and her whole chasing of Remy was to get Kylian to notice her, and she didn't like me because she knew that Kylian liked me, but then, when we all got closer, she decided she was being ridiculous and she should just wait for Kylian's crush on me to end, and she thought I was her friend, but I lied to her so now I'm not, all of which I learn because she texts and unloads this on me like a machine gun. Not that I blame her.

Later my mom, Armel, and I have a video chat with Lille and Remy. Kylian hasn't spilled my tea and I'm grateful. Everyone but me decides it's too dangerous for me to be at the festival tomorrow. Lille has spent most of her time since the news broke having different platforms take down threats against me.

"I can't miss tomorrow. It's Sunday. It's the surprise acts."

"You're going to have to watch the live stream, Aurie," Remy says. "The last thing we need is to have you in a riled-up crowd. I still think we should tell everyone the truth."

I shake my head emphatically. "No, there's no reason for both of us to go down for this."

"If it took some of the hatred off of you," Armel says, "it would be worth it."

"No," I say. "No one is really going to hurt me over this. It's just online chatter. It's not worth Remy losing everything he's worked so hard for."

"What about everything you've worked hard for?" Remy says.

"I don't even know if I want any of this anymore. Maybe I'm ready to just walk down the street in jeans and a T-shirt and not have anyone recognize me."

We go back and forth like this for a while. My mom would love it if I gave up influencing, but she tries not to be too obvious about it. In the end, I'm being forced to stay home, and everyone agrees to let the world think that I cheated on Remy. I guess that will have to be the win.

Thirty-Five

I try to stay home. I really do. But by lunchtime, I know there's no way I can miss seeing Remy onstage with a-ha. Besides, everyone is already so upset with me, what's one more mess-up now?

After lunch, Armel takes the TPs for some fresh air. He drives them to a park in another neighborhood because if they walked to ours, the TPs would be exposed to the fallout happening on our doorstep. They're already confused enough about why people are being mean to their sister. They're all paying for my choices.

But I have one more bad choice in me, and it's to see Remy onstage with a-ha.

That leaves my mom and another of Remy's security guys, Hugo, for me to get through. And everyone in Paris under the age of twenty-five.

As if the universe is sending me a sign that I should disobey everyone, my mom realizes she needs to go to the grocery store because we're out of several things the TPs consider essential to their survival, like milk and these little Italian frog-shaped cheese crackers.

I tell Hugo I'll be up in my room live streaming the festival. "Okay," he says.

I go to my room. I put the live stream on loud enough to be heard through the door, then pull on Remy's old sweatpants, a graphic T-shirt of my dad's favorite group, the Electric Light Orchestra, and an ancient bucket hat of Granddad's with fishing lures on it. I don't wear makeup. I grab my cheapest sunglasses, the no-name ones I let Camille play with, and go.

I tiptoe down the back stairs and slink out the kitchen door. There'll be a few paparazzi behind the house, but the yard is fenced along the alleyway. I slip through my neighbors' yards and emerge several houses down. I don't check to see if they spot me. I just walk toward the bus stop as if I have no reason to arouse suspicion. With any luck, they won't realize it's me.

When I get on the Metro, I exhale. So far, no one has recognized me, and my mom hasn't discovered I'm gone. If she had, she'd be calling me nonstop until I answered. When I look at myself in the subway car glass, I almost don't recognize myself. Is this who I would be if I weren't Aurie McGinley the influencer? Or is this just another side of me that I never get to explore?

I'm at the festival within the hour. I flash my security badge to get in backstage. I just need to avoid Remy. He'd recognize me no matter how I was dressed. Lille, I'm not so sure. It seems like she'd never recognize me outside of my influencer uniform, but sometimes she surprises me.

I slink past the greenroom area where a-ha is supposed to be. They're all there, so I leave before anyone recognizes me. Then I slip out front to the crowd. It's too dangerous to be backstage. Remy could run into me at any moment.

It feels like five o'clock is never going to come as I stand with the crowd, but then it does, and Remy takes the stage to introduce his surprise act. He looks tired, like he didn't sleep at all last night. It's weird to be in the audience and not watching him from backstage. At least at a big event like this one.

"So, this next artist is a little surprise I put together for Aurie," he says. The crowd erupts immediately into a giant booing chorus. I glance around. I'm the only one not booing. I join in so I don't look out of place.

Remy puts his hands up and shakes his head until everyone settles down. "I don't want anyone blaming Aurie McGinley," he says. There's a collective groan and scattered wisecracks, but Remy holds out until they stop. "There are lots of things you don't know about Aurie and me. So whatever you guys are thinking, trust me, you're wrong."

Everywhere in the crowd, people turn to each other and ask what he means. Remy waits until it gets quiet.

"This is a song I wrote for Aurie, with the help of our next artist, and I just want her to know that I mean every single word."

Remy's written me a goodbye song, something about how

we'll always be friends. I should be touched, but I want to cry. Then the music starts, and Yoon Seon-Ho walks onstage. The crowd erupts. Remy's written me a K-pop song! With Yoon Seon-Ho!

It's an upbeat tempo. A lot of it is in Korean, but some is in English.

내가 당신을 알고 지낸 지 얼마나 됐나요?
진실을 말하는 것만으로는 충분하지 않습니다.
나는 당신을 얼마나 많은 밤 동안 사랑했습니까?
이 청춘은 너무 무서워

그리고 우리는 함께 자랐고,
한걸음 한걸음 손잡고
단 하루도 없었어요
넌 내 계획에 없던 곳이었어

All I need is your happiness
All I need is your smile
My whole world is you
Even walking separate miles

We'll be under the stars
Just you and me
Dancing in the dark
Three thousand miles apart
Girl, you still own my heart
You still own my heart

우리는 별빛 아래 있을 거예요
오직 너와 나
어둠 속에서 춤을
삼천 마일 떨어져 있는
당신은 여전히 내 마음을 소유하고 있어요

당신은 여전히 내 마음을 소유하고 있습니다
사랑한다고 말했어야 했는데
사자였어야 했는데
양고기 말고
널 내 것으로 만들었어야 했는데
네가 아직 붙잡고 있는 동안
내 손

If it's not too late
Fall in love with me
Fall in love with me
If it's not too late

You'll always own my heart
Tell me I'm not dreaming
It can't be too late
Fall in love with me

I may not have any idea what the Korean parts mean, but the refrain can't be for real. I look around. Everyone seems to be either into the music or talking about the meaning of the song. I look back at Remy like I'm seeing him for the first time in months. All those times I thought he couldn't stand the idea of me liking him, I was completely wrong. I touch my cheek. It's wet with tears.

"Hey, that's Aurie McGinley!" someone near me says.

I turn toward the sound instinctively and then realize my mistake, because all I've done is confirm it for any nonbelievers. Before I know what's happening, I'm lifted into the crowd and being bodysurfed as people shout "Throw her out" until it becomes a chant. I'm bounced up and down as people pass me from one person to the next, their hands all over me.

"Put me down!" I scream, but the hands keep sending me on. I turn my head to the stage, which is getting farther and farther away as I'm jostled toward the back. Remy turns in our direction. I try to raise my arm to wave at him for help, but that just makes someone lose hold of me, and I'm dipped down, banging my head into some guy's shoulder.

"Ouch!" we yell at the same time. For a moment, my ears ring.

The music stops. Remy puts his hand over his eyes to shield them from the lights. "What's going on? Is someone hurt?" he calls out. There's a sea of screaming people separating us.

"Remy!" I yell, but there's no way he can hear me over the noise of the crowd. I'm not even sure he can see me with the lights in his eyes. But the people below have stopped surfing me. They lower me down. A guy shoves me and I bounce off several kids behind me, who then push me away from them. I turn and try to get to the fences, which I think are to my right, pressing against people to get there. People push back.

"Aurie? Aurie, is that you?" Remy calls out from the stage. I jump and wave, but I'm so much shorter than most of the crowd there's probably no way he can see me.

Some girl trips me and I get knocked down from behind. The knee of Remy's sweatpants tears, but I spring up and keep moving toward where I think the fence is. I need to get to the backstage area. The whole square is bursting with noise and I'm disoriented.

In front of me, the crowd parts. Stephan and his second

partner, Jacques, in their black T-shirts stamped *Sécurité* and marked by reflective bands on the sleeves, push people aside as they rush toward me. My bucket hat is long gone, and my hair is disheveled. The heel of my right palm is bleeding, along with my knee.

Jacques wraps his arm around me and leads me toward the stage area.

"Can you walk? Are you hurt?" he asks. I can barely hear him over the crowd noise.

"I'm okay," I say, but I'm shaking all over. He relays a message into his headset. He's covering my head so no one can hurt me as Stephan makes a path for us to follow. We're almost to the stage when Remy comes bursting through the crowd to reach us.

"Aur, Aur, are you okay?" he says, frantically scanning me.

"I'm all right, really." I hug him, but then I start sobbing and can't stop. This was worse than Oslo. In Oslo, it was accidental.

"It's okay, it's okay, we've got you," he says, and guides me backstage.

There's an announcement that the festival is temporarily suspended while a security incident is addressed. It's Lille's voice. Remy calls the paramedics over to check me out. I'm not hurt that much, mostly just scared. Remy stays by me, with Yoon Seon-Ho, and Lille, and all the guys from Remy's band, while security stands watch.

The paramedics address the cuts and convince Remy that

I don't need to go to the hospital once they clear me for concussion.

"You guys need to get back onstage," I say.

"Why are you here?" Remy says. He kneels in front of me. "I told you to stay home."

"I couldn't miss your surprise."

He pulls me into him. "God, you scared the life out of me!"

"Me too," I say.

He pulls back. "I wrote you a K-pop song."

I laugh. "I know. I love it."

"Really?"

I touch his cheek and nod. "I love it. And you. Now go finish this festival."

He looks around like he's not sure I really just said that and laughs as he stands. Simon hugs me, and then Max and Théo hug me, too, before they head onstage.

I can see the stage from where I'm sitting.

Remy takes the mic. "I can't believe what just happened here. People bodysurfed Aurie McGinley, and hurt her, because they think she cheated on me. But Aurie was protecting me. She and I were never dating. Not for real."

There's a collective exclamation from the crowd. Then they explode in sound as people ask questions and yell stuff I can't even make out. Remy waits until they quiet.

"That's one secret that Pierre Naillon didn't ferret out. We were pretending. Because you all wanted us so much to be a couple. Because you didn't believe us when we said we were just friends.

"And you know what? On that one you were right. Because I've been in love with Aurie practically since the first day I met her. But I never had the courage to tell her."

The crowd is completely silent, except for some "aws" that reverberate through the square.

"Am I hearing right?" I ask Lille, wondering if maybe I do have a concussion.

Lille nods.

"In fact, Aurie didn't even want to do the whole fake dating thing. That was our manager's and my idea. And then Pierre Naillon completely manufactured a story about why she was at the pharmacy the day she met Kylian. Aurie didn't know him. He was just trying to help her out. And instead, Pierre Naillon, and all of you who believe these celebrity tabloids, turned it into something it wasn't. Not then, anyway.

"So if you want to be mad at someone, be mad at the paparazzi. Be mad at our manager. At me. Be mad at yourselves. But don't be mad at Aurie or Kylian. And anyway, they broke up. So leave the guy alone. He's my friend. And to those of you who hurt Aurie tonight . . ." Remy stops. He shakes his head as if he's telling himself not to say it. And then he hands the mic to Seon-Ho and walks offstage.

He comes and kneels in front of me. "Now we can be public enemy number one together."

I shake my head. "You shouldn't have told them. I thought you only wanted to be my friend. I thought you were stressed out, thinking that I liked you."

He laugh-scoffs. "I thought the same about you. And then

you started to date Kylian. I wanted you to be happy, even if it wasn't with me, but I was so jealous I could hardly stand it. I should have been honest."

"Me too. I was so scared of losing what we had."

He nods. "And then we lost it anyway."

I hug him, tears running down my cheeks. "But we found it again, right?"

He stares at me, studying me. "Why'd you break up with Kylian?"

I search Remy's beautiful green eyes. They may not remind me of a Grecian isle, but there's something so much more there. Something that feels like home.

"Because he wasn't you," I say, and when he kisses me, I'm back on the street outside Lille's office the first time Remy St. Julien took my breath away.

Thirty-Six

At the end of his set, Seon-Ho tells the crowd that he wants to bring Remy back onstage. Something Remy said must have struck them because instead of boos, the crowd starts whistling. Slowly at first, and then the whistles and cheers get louder and louder.

We're watching from the side, Remy's arms wrapped around me. "Go," I tell him.

He squeezes me and runs onstage and Seon-Ho asks him to sing with him again, this time one of Remy's songs that Seon-Ho learned.

Afterward the crowd is deafening. People start chanting for them to play "Aurie's song" again.

"Will you let us finish it this time?" Seon-Ho asks the crowd.

"Yes!" they roar. Seon-Ho and Remy start the song again. Remy comes and pulls me out. I'm scared everyone will boo, but this time they cheer. Remy and Seon-Ho sing a full English version with the mixed Korean-English one. The whole square is jumping up and down, hands waving in the air. To the love song that Remy wrote for me.

How many days have I known you
Not enough to tell you the truth
How many nights have I loved you
Too scared in all this youth

And we grew up together
Step by step and hand in hand
There's never been a day
where you weren't all my plans

All I need is your happiness
All I need is your smile
My whole world is you
Even walking separate miles

We'll be under the stars
Just you and me
Dancing in the dark
Three thousand miles apart
Girl, you still own my heart
You still own my heart

Should have told you I love you
Should have been the lion
Not the lamb
Should have made you mine
While you still held
My hand

If it's not too late
Fall in love with me
Fall in love with me
If it's not too late

You'll always own my heart
Tell me I'm not dreaming
It can't be too late
Fall in love with me

When the song ends, Seon-Ho and Remy bow and we run offstage. Remy picks me up and swings me around.

There are tears all over my face, but I catch a glimpse of a-ha coming. "That was the best present anyone ever gave me, but you should get ready to go back out there."

"What do you mean? Do you know how hard I worked on this with Seon-Ho? You have to gush over it!" Then he looks past me, and his eyes widen. "No way!" He says it two more times as he sets me down. My heart squeals at how surprised he is.

The guys from a-ha come over and hug him and talk to him about his parents, whom they knew a little. But it's time to go onstage, so they invite him to sing "Take On Me" with them.

Remy looks at me. "Is this for real?" He's got his *Hunting High and Low* T-shirt on, and I didn't even have to ask Mamie to keep it unlaundered until today to make sure he wore it. Of course he'd save his favorite tee for the last day.

I laugh and push him toward the stage. Kylian and Reine run up as I watch from the side.

"Are you okay?" Kylian asks, draping an arm around me.

I nod. "I'm really sorry, Reine. I never meant to lie to you."

"It's okay. I shouldn't have gotten so mad. What I did, flirting with Remy to get Kylian's attention, wasn't any better." She takes Kylian's hand. I guess she and Kylian have sorted out their love problems, too. That just leaves Lille and Kylian's dad, but I kind of think that Lille was serious when she said she liked him enough not to mess it up.

"I really want us to be friends."

"Same," she says, and hugs me.

I've never seen Remy have more fun onstage. He comes off after the song and the four of us watch the rest of the show huddled together. Remy introduces me to Seon-Ho, and I fangirl over him while he says he watches all my vlogs. We promise to take him to the Eiffel Tower and dinner tomorrow.

The last performance is a-ha, and the crowd is deafening as they close the festival. We celebrate backstage as we wait for the crowd to clear out. Lille has the preliminary numbers of what we've raised and it's more than enough to meet Kylian's goals. She seems a little nervous around Remy and me, but I doubt she believes either of us is going to fire her. Once we know the management company has the cleanup underway and the bands are all packed, Remy takes me home. We have a lot of explaining ahead of us with my family, which my mom let me know she's expecting after she saw the end of the live stream.

Remy drives us past the Eiffel Tower. It's beautiful, all lit up against a deep, bright sky.

He pulls the Vespa over to a parking space. We walk to a

bench and watch the twinkling lights. People mill around taking photos. But none of them are interested in us.

"So now what?" Remy asks.

"I don't know. I don't know what to do. I don't want to leave you and my family here, but I don't want to disappoint my dad and his family, either. Or give up on my American side."

Remy squeezes my hand. "Do you know who Martin Josephson is?"

"The American music producer?"

Remy nods. "He asked me to come to New York and work on an album. Next January, for six to eight months."

"That's incredible!"

"It's a big opportunity."

"So you think I should go to school in the States?"

Remy shakes his head. "I think you should go to school wherever you want to go. But, if it is here, maybe you could do a semester overseas at the school in Boston you got into. That's not far from New York."

We smile.

"Not at all. But then what?"

Remy kisses me. Just a quick little kiss, but it rolls through my body like a wave. "And then we can figure out what comes next. We don't have to decide everything from the start, Aur. If you want to vlog, then do it. If you want to quit, that's cool. If you want to live here, we will. If you want to live in the States, we can do that, too. Or stay bicoastal. We'll figure it out together."

I think of the poem that used to be in my grandmother's

foyer. The heart can make all the plans it wants, but life will make sure it always has to reimagine those plans.

Remy kisses my nose.

"My mom said she's not scared of me leaving now, because she knows my ties here have grown enough to withstand the separation."

Remy looks around, smiling. "Something tells me that, no matter where we go or what we do, our paths will always lead us back to Paris."

I take a deep breath beneath the sparkling lights of the Eiffel Tower. I'm not worried about the future anymore.

I look at him and smile. I'm pretty sure Remy St. Julien, my very real boyfriend, is about to give me one of his gold-medal-worthy kisses. I close my eyes, and for the first time in what feels like forever, I let my heart take the lead.

Acknowledgments

There are always so many people to thank when you get to the last page. Thank you to my wonderful writing group, who keeps me straight while apologizing for quibbling over details. Your quibbling always makes my writing stronger: Amanda Hooper, Sally Alexander, Heidi Brayer, Jane (Shoshana) Ackerman, Linda Casey Kustra, Dave Crawley, and Alan Irvine.

Thanks to my cheerleaders, Cristina Rouvalis and Lisa Slage Robinson; my wonderful agent, Michelle Hauck; and everyone at Storm Literary Agency. Special thanks to my amazing editor, Wendy Loggia. Two books in and I'm still thinking, "Wendy Loggia is going to see my stuff?" And thanks to all the wonderful people at Penguin Random House, Delacorte Press, and Underlined who do so much for me. I am truly awed and grateful.

Thank you to my beautiful bluebird for keeping it real, and to her lifelong friends for dreaming big with me, especially

Rachel Silverman, Claudia Brelsford, and Hannah Brelsford. I love you girls. Thank you to *all* the McCloreys for the years of love and support, especially when I needed it most.

And thank you to Wyatt for keeping me company, no matter how long I spend on my computer.

매우 감사합니다

Merci beaucoup, tout le monde!

IT'S A FAIRY-TALE ROMANCE IN THE ETERNAL CITY. WILL IT HAVE A FAIRY-TALE ENDING?

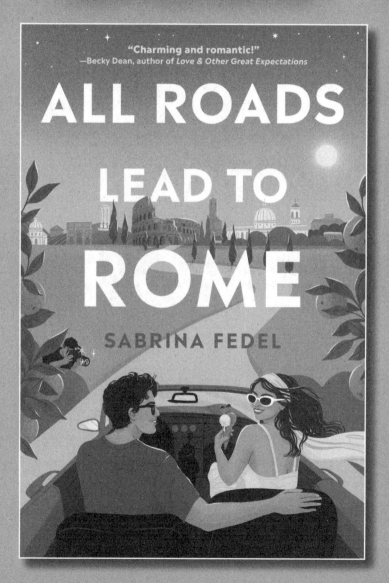

"Charming and romantic!"
—Becky Dean, author of *Love & Other Great Expectations*

ALL ROADS LEAD TO ROME

SABRINA FEDEL

One

Rome is sweltering as it waits patiently for the sun to set over the Spanish Steps. It's the kind of vapid heat that makes me wonder how the lions had the energy to leave their cages, let alone maul anyone.

I'm in John Keats's bedroom, the room he died in, overlooking the sprawling steps below. Horses sweat in the middle of Piazza di Spagna as they wait to give carriage rides, immovable in the small throng of late-May tourists. Most of the passersby don't even know this was Keats's house, despite the enormous crimson plaque on the side of it. They come here for selfies on the famous steps and never give John's shrine more than a careless glance. For me, the Keats-Shelley House is the best part of the neighborhood. I wonder if he stood exactly here, watching the people outside the way I do.

Anna Maria comes and stands beside me. "It's closing time, Story," she says in Italian. "No more people-watching today."

"Mmmm."

She follows my gaze to a cluster of kids my age, dressed like conspicuous American teenagers. They've stopped at the bottom of the steps. A group of tourists in matching red T-shirts flows around them like a school of minnows sliced apart.

"Wait," she says, "is that the infamous Dip Squad?"

I purse my lips and nod. They're all there: Kelsey, Guin, Alicia, and the twins, Patrick and Jack. We're the kids of the American diplomatic corps stationed in Rome, but I've called them the Dip Squad since last fall when they welcomed me with one prank after another to show me how things work here. They thought I was stuck-up because I keep to myself so much. The worst was when they convinced me a stray cat near the embassy belonged to a cute Marine assigned to guard duty. They told me the cat had been lost for days, so I brought it to him. He thinks I made the whole thing up to hit on him. He still smirks every time I visit my mom at work.

"Which one is the dark-haired boy?"

"That's Jack."

"But Patrick is the mean one, sì?"

"Sì."

"Jack is pretty cute." She elbows me.

I scrunch my nose, and she laughs.

"You should stand up to them. They don't seem worth being miserable over."

"They're not. But I'll be out of here soon. Jack is the only one I'll ever have to see again."

"He's the one going to Princeton with you?"

"Sì."

"Story, don't let other people keep you from living the life you want," she says, poking my arm. "Come on, I have to get home. I have an exam tomorrow." Anna Maria is in her second year at Università di Roma. She works two afternoons a week at the Keats-Shelley House, where I spend more time than is normal for a seventeen-year-old girl, even one as nerdy as me.

We say ciao as she locks the door, and she heads to the metro. The Dip Squad has, blessedly, disappeared. I've promised my mom I'd go to the Gucci store on Via Condotti to buy a ridiculously overpriced necklace the ambassador wants to give to a visiting dignitary. I don't understand why people flock to designer stores to buy ugly things for thousands of dollars when they could find vintage treasures on the Via del Governo Vecchio for a few euros, but I don't get most things about people.

When we moved here last August, I found my way around by using a copy of Fodor's *Italy in 1951* that I bought in a used bookstore. "Never out of date" it says on the cover, which makes me laugh, but the Eternal City is pretty eternal. There's something obscenely unromantic about a smartphone map.

As I reach the edge of the piazza, I spot Patrick's blond buzz cut leading the Dips back in my direction. I duck into a gelateria.

"Buonasera," says the middle-aged man behind the counter.

"Buonasera."

He looks at me expectantly, because most people come into an ice cream shop to actually get ice cream. My mom will have takeout waiting at home, but I might as well have dessert now, since I need to give the Dips time to go past. I look over my choices.

"Un gelato alla stracciatella vegana, per favore."

People burst through the door, and I turn my head, thinking it must be the Dips coming to harass me. But it's a guy and girl about my age, both of them looking like wealthy tourists. The girl looks a lot like the American singer Jasmine. But celebrities and celebrity look-alikes are as common as good pizza in this part of Rome. She has her dark hair in a ponytail like me, and we both have on yellow, though I'm wearing a vintage summer dress that Audrey Hepburn might have worn, and she's wearing a romper some stylist probably thought was retro chic.

The man behind the counter asks me in Italian what size gelato and whether I want a cone or cup, but he's watching her.

"Una piccola coppetta, per favore."

"Sì, signorina."

The girl's voice is almost hysterical. "Do you think they saw us?"

Maybe they're hiding out from the Dip Squad, too. The bad part about being a loner is there's no one to share your jokes with.

"I'm sure they didn't." The boy has a Scottish accent. He cranes his neck to look over her head without getting too close to the window.

"They can't see me with you."

"They won't, keep the heid," he replies, but then he changes course. "Ah no, I think they're coming."

I'm paying the man while they make this exchange, and he's listening intently.

"You are Jasmine, no?" he asks her in heavily accented English.

"Yes! Is there a back way I could go out?"

The man nods, and Jasmine slips behind the counter. He ushers her to the back as if he suddenly thinks he's working for the CIA. "I'll meet you back at the hotel," she calls to the boy while she slips the gelateria guy a fistful of euros.

I walk past the Scot and step outside. A quick scan for the Dips only shows me a group of people with cameras rushing toward the shop, ready to run me over. My gelato is already sweating, so I take a bite. The boy comes out of the gelateria, and they snap his photo.

"Where's Jasmine?" they all yell at him as if he isn't close enough to hear them. The flashes are so bright, I squint even though their lenses aren't pointed at me.

"Who?" the boy says.

"We all saw you go in with her!" one shouts as the rest clamor about where Jasmine is and click their cameras.

"Where is she, Luca? Where's Jasmine?"

"You're mistaken," this Luca kid says as the whir of cameras almost drowns him out. He steps toward me and grabs my elbow as if it's a beer mug. Melting gelato flies off my spoon. "This is the girl you saw."

And that's the moment I envision going down in history with the Dip Squad if they ever saw these photos: my mouth open, filled with stracciatella, surrounded by paparazzi blinding me with flashes as I'm held up like a prize marlin by some guy named Luca while he covers for the reigning Queen of Pop, whose music I don't even like.

The paparazzi seem to be thrown. Several of them lower their cameras to examine me.

"I could have sworn it was Jasmine!"

"She has a ponytail! And she's wearing yellow."

"You said it was Jasmine," one says in Italian. The rest are using English but with accents from all over Europe.

"Damn, I thought it was!"

"Who's this girl?"

"Nobody!"

While I'm perfectly aware of my nobody status, this seems pretty harsh, and the Scot hasn't even given me so much as a "please play along" look. It's like he just assumes I'd be thrilled to have these people insult me just so I could be in a photo with him.

"Well, this nobody is going to head out now." I say it in the language of Rome, because there's something about Italian that makes it sound a lot more serious than saying it in English.

"Who are you?"

"Who is she, Luca?"

"Is this your latest, Luca?"

"Where'd you find her? She doesn't seem like your type."

I stare at this Luca kid to let go of my arm, but he doesn't. He's looking between them and me, clearly calculating how much risk to benefit there is in throwing me to the lions. I shake my head at him.

"She's a tour guide," he says. "Obviously."

I just look at him. I don't think I look like a tour guide. I also don't think my Italian is fooling anyone that I'm a native, including him. Maybe it's the quickest way to get these people away from me, though. Luca is clearly somebody they consider worth taking pictures of. If I'm nothing more than a tour guide, then there's no chance those open-mouthed-bass pictures of me are getting published in any of the celebrity magazines Guin and Kelsey love.

"Sì, sì," I say, and stop speaking Italian before they realize I'm not actually a local. I do my best to impersonate Anna Maria's accent when she speaks English. "I was hired for the day, that is all." This is nothing like *Roman Holiday*.

"You lot need to back off," Luca says. "She isn't used to this kind of attention. She's just a local girl my butler hired to show me the sights."

His butler? Hoo boy, as my grandfather from Maine says. I nod at them, and I don't even need to pretend I'm annoyed. But it's still better than getting into any of these online magazines.

"See, nobody!" I say in my Italian-accented English. "Now, please let us alone, as I want to bring my client to Fontana di Trevi before the after-dinner crowds! Vieni!"

The paparazzi lower their cameras and mumble to each

other. I turn toward the street that will take us to the fountain and pull Luca along by the rolled-up sleeve of his expensive button-down. I'm practically on Gucci's doorstep, and now I need to take a thirty-minute detour, but it was the first monument I could think of that would be pretty close but still lead us out of their circle.

"That was pure dead brilliant," Luca says as we leave them behind, looking back at the paparazzi, who seem unsure of whether they should follow us. One or two do.

"You're welcome." I drop my wilted stracciatella in a trash bin along the bricked pedestrian street.

"Oh, right, of course, my manners. Thank you, Miss—?" He looks at me expectantly.

"Herriot. Astoria Herriot. But most people call me Story."

"Charming," he says, and I can't tell if he's being sarcastic.

"Look, I need to go to Gucci for my mom. So I'll take you to the Trevi, we'll pretend we're talking about it for a few minutes in case they're watching, and then we'll separate, okay? That should be enough to get rid of your entourage. And if they ask, you can tell them my clock ran out."

He pulls his head back as if he's a little shocked by my brusqueness, so I add, "No offense or anything." Sometimes I feel like introverts should wear T-shirts that warn people we don't know how to interact.

"None taken." He strides along beside me, a little more slowly than I'd like. "So, where did you learn to speak Italian like that? Do you live here?"

"Just for the past year. I'm a Dip kid."

He looks at me like maybe I'm a little unhinged.

"My mom's in the diplomatic corps," I add.

"Ah!" he says. "So that's why you knew exactly where to go for the Trevi."

I shrug. "Roma is classic."

He laughs. "Well, yes, the ancient Romans and all."

"No, like Audrey Hepburn classic. Rome is one of a kind."

He puts his lips together like he might whistle, I guess to keep from laughing at me. "I stand corrected," he says. "It must be right barry to live here for a wee bit."

"Barry?"

"You know, great, fantastic."

"Oh, yes. It is."

"Where else have you lived?"

"Well, home is technically Washington, DC, but we're hardly ever there. Let's see, Tokyo, Rio, Lisbon, Zagreb, and now here." We've reached the fountain. People scatter along the perimeter, trying to get selfies with it, but it's not so thick with tourists that you can't see well.

"So, tour guide, tell me about the Trevi."

My mouth twitches into an automatic frown, and he laughs. "Seriously, I bet you know all about it. Please?"

A paparazzo who followed us stands across the street casually keeping watch. "Well, you could spend hours talking about the Trevi, but I'll give you some highlights. The Trevi, named for the tre vie, or three streets here, is one of the oldest water sources in Rome, dating originally to about 19 BC. Then, in 1730, I think, Pope Clemens of some number, because I can never remember the numbers, held a contest to rebuild it."

Luca smiles at my loose grasp of the facts, and I sweep a strand of hair behind my ear.

"A relative of Galileo was awarded the commission, but he was from Firenze, and the locals pitched a fit, so they gave it to a Roman architect named Salvi. The fountain wasn't completed until after Salvi's death, about forty years later, but most of it's his vision."

"I knew you'd make an excellent guide," he says. His smile is dangerous, or maybe it's the way his grayish-blue eyes look at you.

"I'm not a tour guide."

I look around, afraid someone has heard how ridiculously defensive I sound of my nerd expertise.

"Of course. And who is around Neptune?" He points to the center statue.

"That's Oceanus, not Neptune. You can tell because he's supported by seahorses and tritons, who are half men and half mermen. Neptune would have a trifork and dolphins. Didn't you ever watch *The Little Mermaid*?" I point to the left of Oceanus, making a big show of it for the paparazzo. "See, the triton on the left is struggling with his horse, representing rough seas, while the one on the right represents calm seas." I glance behind us. The guy seems to believe I'm giving a tour. He's started to scan the crowd, probably for other celebrities. Rome is littered with them.

"I have seen *The Little Mermaid*, and wasn't the trifork called a triton in it?"

"No, Ariel's father is King Triton, that's what you're thinking of."

"Oh, I should have studied my Disney classics more," he says, so deadpan that I smile in spite of myself.

In front of us, a little boy throws a coin into the fountain, over his shoulder.

"And is that for love?" Luca asks. "He seems a bit young."

I laugh. "No, one coin over your shoulder ensures a return trip to Rome. Two will bring you love. Three and you're getting married."

"Got it, don't throw three."

"Definitely not. I should get going."

He drops his smile. "Aye, and I should get back to my hotel. Can you point me in the right direction? It's on the Via dei Condotti."

Of course it is. All the hotels there are for the uber wealthy. "So is the Gucci store. Come on." The paparazzo has disappeared. "I think we've lost your friends."

Luca looks around and seems to relax. I take him north toward Condotti by a different route in case there are still paparazzi waiting for him the way we came.

"So, why are you so popular?" I ask. "Are you a musician, like Jasmine?"

Luca looks at me with raised eyebrows and a bit of a smirk. "No, I'm not. I just hang around people like Jasmine."

"And why can't she be seen with you?"

He glances around as if making sure no one is listening. "Her EP with Rowdy Funkmaster is about to drop. The label has her under strict orders not to do anything that might give it bad publicity." He puts his finger to his lips and whispers, "Shhhh!" even though I haven't said anything. Rowdy is Jasmine's longtime boyfriend—everyone knows that, including me.

I want to tell him that maybe she shouldn't be cheating on the guy, then, but it's not my business.

"You won't say anything, right?"

I just look at him, because who would I have to tell and why would I brag about being this guy's cover?

"I'll pay you."

I shake my head. "I'd rather you didn't and we just forget this whole episode ever happened." Although, I'm still mad about my stracciatella.

He seems almost offended. But he's got the confidence of someone who is used to girls fawning all over him.

"So, what else should I see while I'm here?" he asks. "I mean besides the Colosseum?"

"So much. There's a street going up to the Villa Borghese if you walk to it from Piazza di Spagna that will give you a breathtaking view of the whole city, about halfway up. And the villa is a pretty cool place on a rainy day. No tourists, and it feels like you're in some golden-age-of-Hollywood movie. My absolute favorite places, though, are just little side streets and back stairways where you feel like you could be in any century you choose."

He's staring at me, and I feel the burn rush up my face. Honestly, I sound like a twelve-year-old who only leaves her house for cosplay. I need to not get carried away over talking history to strangers. As if I ever talk to strangers.

"How long are you here for? There are lots of day trips from the city that are pretty cool," I add to cover my awkwardness. I don't know why I bother, though. It's not like you can explain the essence of Rome to someone breezing through with a pop star.

"For the summer, I think. Although my plans aren't totally fixed. Friends, you know." He ticks his head to let me know he's really here for Jasmine.

I nod, like, yeah, of course, whose plans don't depend on friends? But I've never lived anyplace long enough to have real friends. A few pen pals and an occasional local friend like Anna Maria, but I'm not like the other Dips. They all clique together and become lifelong besties, splashing social accounts with photos of them looking amazing with comments like *omggg* and *ur unreal* and *stunning.*

We've reached the Condotti, and I point out the direction of his hotel.

"Well, thank you, Miss Astoria Herriot," he says in full Scottish gallantry. "Are you sure I can't do something for you? I could go with you to Gucci and buy you something. You could pick out whatever you like."

"That's okay," I tell him with a smile. "There's nothing at Gucci I want. But thanks, anyway." I almost wish my mom had said to buy something at Tiffany's. I've always wanted something in one of their robin's-egg-blue boxes. Not that I'd actually take a gift from him.

He hesitates, and I knit my face into a question mark. I'm pretty sure we've successfully covered up his clandestine shenanigans.

"Well, right. Thanks again. You were brilliant. Pure dead brilliant with that Italian accent." He smiles.

"Anytime," I say, and he steps back to let me cross in front of him in the opposite direction toward Gucci. I get an awkward feeling when he's behind me, as if he's watching me walk away. Suddenly all I can think about is how I'm walking, as if it matters, and I could swear I'm not walking normally. But at least I have enough self-respect not to look back. The bigger problem is that I almost want to.

About the Author

Sabrina Fedel is the author of *All Roads Lead to Rome.* She has worked as a litigator and is a civilian environmental compliance attorney. She earned her MFA in creative writing from Lesley University and has taught in the English department at Robert Morris University as an adjunct professor. Her fiction and poetry have appeared in various journals. Sabrina loves Italy and the Cape Hatteras National Seashore, animals, chocolate in any form, Oxford commas, and, most of all, her kids.

sabrinafedel.com

Delacorte Romance

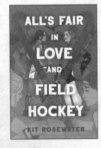

IT'S A LOVE STORY.